a
miki starr
collection

also by miki starr martin

Well Runs Dry

Broken Promises

Blueprints

Zella Dora

poetry

Resplendent Thoughts: Muzik for the Soul

The Miki Starr Storybook:

"How to Write a Love Story"

A classic collection of short "love" stories

by Miki Starr Martin

A REIGNSTORM PUBLISHING

PUBLISHED BY REIGNSTORM
A division of Starr Eclectic Concepts

Saint Paul, Minnesota

ISBN: 0-9721246-5-9

Printed in the United States of America

Book design by Starr Eclectic Concepts

www.mikistarr.com

For me ☺

Book 1:
Mikaela's Story

All's Well That Doesn't End

"Rayvon, your girlfriend is a lesbian."

"No she's not, she's just a little confused."

"She came on to me."

"She told you that you're pretty."

"She kissed me."

"You kissed her back."

"I was drunk, besides it was my first ever experience. I'm sure she's no stranger to eatin' the oochie coo."

"If you say so."

Rayvon took a large bowl of grapes from the refrigerator and walked over to the sofa with me following behind him. We sat side-by-side facing one another.

I popped a grape in my mouth and carried on with our conversation. "Accept it, it's a fact bro'."

"So, does this mean that you're a lesbian now?"

"Nope. She's a good kisser though."

"No bullshit." Rayvon and I slapped palms and snapped our fingers away. "But you kissed a woman and sooo…"

"So I had a once in a lifetime drunken gay kiss, that's all. Don't change nothin'. I'm still strictly dickly."

"Is that riiight?"

2

"Yes, that's riiight."

I turned my attention to the movie that was beginning on Rayvon's big screen television. I curled up in the corner and yawned and ran my fingers through my hair. Hell, I was tired. I'd been working too hard lately. Actually I'd been busting my behind for years and all that energy I was putting into not having to go back to work for anyone other than the Lord and myself was taking a toll on me. I needed a vacation like nobody's business.

The problem wasn't that I couldn't afford it, these days money was the least of my concerns. I just didn't know how to vacation. Six months ago I made arrangements for a week's vacation in Jamaica. After two days of doing nothing I felt useless and spent the next five days in paradise on my laptop working my butt off.

You don't know me so let me back up and give you a little history on myself. Ms. Mikaela Johnson a.k.a That Pretty Bitch or PRTYBCH as the license plate on my Navigator says (that could be mistaken as Party Bitch but either way it suits me). Yea, I'm a little vain, what the hell. I look good, so what would be the point of being insecure? Almost tall, golden skin, bright brown eyes and long beautiful thick brown hair, what is there to be ashamed of?

But besides beauty I do have intelligence. I double majored in Business and English, combined that expensive education with my own creativity and self published my first novel when I was twenty-three, a year after I graduated from college. Long story short, I'm working on my eighth best seller and making a mint. Who the hell needs publishing agencies?

Life has been good to me. It hadn't always been but I really don't like to speak on my past. I'd just purchased a five-bedroom, six-bathroom home on the waterfront in Miami Beach. I'm sure my neighbors are going to be pissed when they see my black ass step out on the deck. And I finally had a relationship that was going somewhere. I'd met the love of my life Jibari Owens at *Club Goddess* almost four months ago and we were very happy. Jibari is in the music industry and works tightly with a couple high demand artists and so he travels quite often.

But I wasn't too lonely in my oversized home. My baby sister Janelle was going through a bitter divorce and she and my two nieces, three-year-old Kya and one-year-old Brianne, were staying with me until things settled down some. And then there were my own babies Farrah (my cat), Mischka (my kitten), and Langston my "vicious" Terrier.

But a house full of stinky diapers and litter boxes was no substitute for the company of a warm, stiff dick. My lack of sex was contributing to my tension and exhaustion. I don't know about anybody else but I slept much better at night after my pussy got pleasure, that's real. And with my Jibari on business in London, I was spending many a nights with Big Booty Hoes in the DVD player and my fingers on my G-spot. That's why I kissed Rayvon's girlfriend. Dammit I was drunk and horny as hell. Normally if she would've looked like she wanted try something with me I would have popped her upside her head. But under the circumstances it didn't bother me when Lena wrapped her arms around me, pinned me to the bar and slipped her tongue in my mouth. Damn, I really gotta stop drinking…really.

Despite the fact that I pretty much cheated with his girlfriend, Rayvon is my heart, I love him dearly. He was the first person I met when I settled down in Florida. I'd roomed with him in this very condo for nearly two and a half years back when we first met. He'd been a wonderful friend from the beginning but he wasn't my only close friend. Since high school I kept in close contact with my childhood friends Anne and Richard. Annie has been like a sister to me, my Italian sister. We've been tight since Freshman year back in my hometown of

Chicago. I've tried my best to convince her to settle down here after she dropped out of UIC but she got a job working for her lawyer uncle Carlisle and is very happy with her life as it is.

And then there was Richard, "Ricky" Lear. Oh my damn, lemme tell ya about him! Twelve years I've known fine ass Ricky and quiet as kept wanted him. What kept me from getting with him? A pact Annie and I made back in the day was that neither of us would get involved with him in the interest of maintaining our friendship. But I must admit it's impossible not to be attracted to his tall pretty brown skinned self! Hmpf, now he's in Minnesota and in a so-called engagement to some chic he went to UIC with named Jewel Nihalani. I've never met her but I'm sure Rick and Jewel are not going to go through with it. They've planned a wedding every year since they've been together and he's been trying to get with me just as long.

A key turned in the lock and Menisa walked through the front door with a large black bag on her shoulder. Her beautiful curly auburn hair was pulled back into a raggedy ponytail and she appeared to be out of breath. She was wearing no makeup and one of her earrings was missing. She looked like a broke-down Cuban Angelina Jolie. She leaned against the door jamb and stared at the ceiling leaving Rayvon and me wondering what the hell was wrong with her. She was such the drama queen.

"Menisa," I spoke.

"Huh?"

"What the hell happened to you?"

"Oh, just a rough night at work. Just glad to be home."

"Hmpf." I rolled my eyes and returned my attention to the movie. Menisa was my girl. I was the reason that she and Rayvon were roommates, I'd introduced them. I loved her dearly but she was too over dramatic and too damned stubborn. I was doing very well for myself and offered her a job as my personal assistant but she refused to accept it. Something about me being too difficult to work with. Hmpf. She would rather continue answering other people's phones and waitressing part-time on weekends to put herself through law school apparently than assist me. Whatever.

My Motorola sang the tune of the Mexican Hat Dance. I snapped it open and read the message from Jibari saying that he'd come home early. My nipples were instantly hard and my coochie throbbed. I licked my lips as I read the message requesting a private meeting in my bedroom in an hour. I jumped from the sofa and grabbed my sneakers from against the wall. I snatched my purse from the coffee table and ran to the door with my hair flying in the wind.

"Jibari?" Rayvon asked paying me no mind.

"You know. Love ya," I called back and I was out!

*

Janelle rolled her eyes at me as she passed me in the hallway when she saw me letting Jibari into the house during booty call hours. I shrugged it off and welcomed him with a big hug and wet kiss. My coochie muscles contracted as his tongue did a soft sensual dance around the inside of my mouth and his hands gently trailed downward to settle on my round and firm backside. I rubbed his shiny baldhead and felt chills as his stiffening penis pressed against me.

"I missed you baby," he whispered when he finally came up for air.

"I missed you," I told him.

I stepped aside and locked my door before taking his hand in mine and leading him up the stairs and to my master bedroom. I was naked and oiled beneath my soft pink silk robe. No sooner did my door close behind us did Jibari slipped my robe open and begin to nibble my shoulders. I gasped as his tongue traced the side of my neck while his large hands massaged my C-cup breasts and his thumbs swept across my erect nipples. Jibari pushed the robe completely to the floor and stepped back to admire my nakedness. He licked his full lips as he looked me over. I relished in his appreciation of my body. I worked hard on it and was thrilled to know that he enjoyed it.

"Lay down," he whispered. I obliged. Jibari leaned over my body and softly pressed his lips against mine. He wrapped his mouth around my breast and took turns teasing each one. I moaned and exhaled as his warm breath enveloped my flesh. I tensed in anticipation as that powerful tongue made its way down my stomach and to the center of my love. I gripped the sheets at first touch and moaned and called to the heavens as he caressed it and sucked it, tickled it and shoved his tongue inside and out. My lower body gyrated when he finally hit my spot while simultaneously stroking my hard throbbing nipples.

"Oh sh…! Oh-oh! Oh my God!" I called out. The more intensity I felt the more effort he put into it. My body jerked violently as the reward for his actions consumed me. I begged for him to stop but he refused to comply, he continued until fluid broke forward and leaked from my body and I collapsed flat onto my back.

I sensed his pride and expressed vanity as he stood from his position between my shaky thighs. My eyes were closed tight as my legs jerked. I didn't see Jibari remove his clothes but I felt him when he slowly stuffed his stiff latex-covered penis inside my sensitive "virginia". I clawed his back as he thrust in and out. He shoved himself deep inside of me, as though he were searching for something.

"Oh shit gurl you feel so good," he mumbled as he worked himself to orgasm. "Ooh shit, I'm about to cum! Oh...oh! Oh shit baby, damn!"

He collapsed his hot, sweaty body on top of me. I rubbed his back softly, until he rolled away and pulled his baby filled condom off. He lay on his back with his eyes closed. I turned on my side and watched him lie peacefully.

Over the past couple years a lot of guys had come in and out of my world. Used to be a time that I was open to most any type of man that interested me but then I began to realize that what I was really doing was settling. I had made my mark on the world and there wasn't anything any guy could buy me that I couldn't myself afford. I needed to narrow the margin some kind of way.

So I decided to only date men that had something to offer me. If I dated a lawyer I'd get free legal advice. If I dated an athlete, free tickets to see the Heat or the Dolphins play. And if I dated an A&R like Jibari, I'd get to meet and mingle with some of the big names in the music industry. Hell I'd already sent autographed books to Jay Z, Eric Sermon, Erykah Badu, and Andre 3000, per their request, just to drop a few names. This was why there was no way that I could get with Corey but unfortunately Janelle couldn't seem to comprehend that.

So now the question that is forming inside your mind is "Who the hell is Corey?" The first year and a half that I lived in Florida I worked part time answering phones for a large credit card company to supplement my then meager income from writing, which by the way is where I met Menisa and Corey amongst others. I will admit, Corey is a very handsome man and back in the day I was attracted to him buuut he had a woman at home so I got over it.

Fashion designer Amori Allen is a mutual friend of ours and Janelle and Corey met for the first time at one of her runway parties. Well J got this mistaken notion that he and I were meant to be. Yes, I was crushin' big time back in the day but these days Corey and I do not get along. Yet Janelle finds every possible excuse to have his crabby tail up in my crib. Besides that, since I left the company the highest he's climbed up the corporate ladder was as a team leader, wow. What could he do for me but tell me my balance and have one of his subordinates dispute a charge for me?

Janelle had some crazy idea that I have a fear of commitment. I wasn't really afraid to commit. I just didn't want to commit to Corey and I really doubted that these days Corey gave a second thought to committing to me. And besides, whether she approved or not, it was my belief that Jibari was the man for me.

*

I caressed the side of Jibari's face and whispered his name, "Jibari, baby can we talk...about something?"

"Yea, Kae wassup?"

"I was umm, thinking about us. And uh, well, I know you're spending all that money renting that house out here aaand...well, it's kinda a waste of money when you could stay here. I mean, even with my family here I have a lot of space. You could even turn the spare bedroom into a studio and we could share the office."

"Whoa." Jibari huffed and breathed a number of ways making me regret opening my big mouth. He was quiet and though we were still laying side by side he suddenly felt distant.

"Y'know, I'm jumping the gun here. I'm sorry JB, never mind. I was just...I uh..."

"Naw, naw, it's cool. I'll think about it."

"You sure?" I asked trying to hide the excitement in my voice.

"Why not?" he answered with much less enthusiasm than I'd had. I leaned in to kiss him but he turned and slid from the bed before my lips could land. "I'm about to take a shower, alright?"

"Yea, okay."

I laid naked and sticky in my king-sized bed feeling like just as big an idiot. I wasn't even sure why I'd allowed myself to make such a fool of myself like that. Now Jibari was intimidated. He'd think that I was rushing things...trying to put pressure on him.

Jibari stopped naked in the bathroom doorway. He turned to face me. "Ay baby, you wanna jump in here with me?"

"Yea," I spoke in my innocent girl voice. I slipped from the bed with a sly sexy smile on my face and walked up to my man. He wrapped his arm around my waist and pulled me against his body. We kissed before disappearing behind the bathroom door to make sweet love in the shower.

Mikaela's Story
Reality Check

I'd been gone from Florida for a week. I had a couple of book signings scheduled in San Diego area bookstores. Touring was nice but it oft times got pretty lonely. Surrounded by all these strange people who love you because you somehow told their life story. But if you'd never had your full-color headshot on the back of a book, would they even notice that you existed? Would they care? I realize that I am getting all philosophical but it all boils down to one fact - I was missing Jibari. I'd been home for two days and had yet to see him. I finally caught up to him on his cell and was looking forward to spending this evening with his sexy ass.

I climbed out of my bed bright and early, awakened by tummy grumblings. I was always so hungry when I came home from tour. It wasn't that I couldn't eat much or that I couldn't eat well for that matter. The deal was that no one could cook like Janelle, bottom-line. I could smell the turkey bacon, scallops and eggs and biscuits as soon as I opened my bedroom door.

My stomach became louder as the scent became stronger. In short shorts that could have easily passed for panties and a wife beater with no bra, sweat socks on my feet, I jogged down the stairs and to the large eat in kitchen, not surprised to find

Corey's big ass sitting in front of a plate just as big as his body.

"I left a robe on the chair over there," Janelle spoke not taking her eyes off the fresh orange juice she was squeezing. I rolled my eyes at the subtle double take that Corey took before stuffing his mouth full of cheese eggs and gluing his eyes back to the television. I wrapped the thin robe around my body and returned to the kitchen. I grabbed the plate of food Janelle had fixed for me off the counter and took a seat at the table with Corey.

"What are you doing here so early?" I sneered at him. His response was pointing at his plate as though the answer were obvious. I pursed my lips and ate.

"He's here to finish building the bureau for the girls clothes, if that's alright with you Ms. Johnson."

"I don't care, just wondering why so early."

"Cause contrary to your beliefs, I got other things to do with my life, that's why," Corey answered irritated.

"Whatever." I giggled under my breath.

Corey set his fork down and glared at me. I suppose I should have been intimidated but screw that; I turned and looked back at him as I shoveled a fork full of scallops in my mouth.

"Janelle I'mma gone ahead and finish up aiight, let you and your *lovely* sista bond." He stuffed the final piece of biscuit into his mouth and washed it down with the glass of juice Janelle handed to him.

"Aw Corey, you don't sound like you mean that." I felt the burning tension of Corey and Janelle glaring at the back of my head but do you think I gave a damn? Hmpf. I heard Corey walk out onto the patio where Langston was soaking up some sun and the half-built bureau awaited him.

"I don't understand why you display so much negativity toward C. He's a damn good man and you need to chill that attitude. You would do good to get with him instead of that sneaky ass Jibari."

"Janelle, he's rude. He's ignorant. If you think he's so damn good you give him some."

"Well I ain't seen Jibari around here since you been back. What's up with that? Don't he fly his ass over here with his dick whipped out as soon as he cross the Florida state line?" Janelle carried her plate to the table and sat in the seat which Corey had previously occupied.

"He's been busy. He does real work unlike your new best friend out there."

"Do you think he's faithful to you?" Janelle asked, "I mean really, while he's out there running the streets–"

I was getting agitated. "He's not running the streets J, he's working."

"Whatever he's doing, while he's doing it do you think that he's being faithful?"

I shifted in my seat and rubbed the middle of my forehead with my index finger. I didn't like the line of questioning and didn't want to have to think about conveying an honest answer to such a ridiculous question. Fortunately I wouldn't have to.

"Mommy," Kya's groggy voice filled the air putting an end to Janelle's desire to defend the man of her dreams for me.

"Good morning baby girl, you hungry?" Janelle asked her daughter putting on her innocent mother voice. Kya nodded and Janelle jumped into action.

I kissed my niece on the forehead and helped her into her seat. Full, I dumped my plate and let my Langston indoors, he was always so happy to see me. I turned and let him chase me out of the kitchen and up the stairs to my bedroom.

I took the robe and threw it across the bed on top of a sleeping Farrah. She was too cranky; she would do well to loosen up some. She reminded me of Corey. She squirmed from beneath the robe and jumped from the bed. I could swear she glared at me as she strutted out the bedroom door with her tail high flaunting her ass at me. I grabbed my PDA off the nightstand and typed in a message, then sent it to Jibari. I had to get dressed. Amori wanted me to come by early and be fitted for some of her designs before I had to leave for my dates in Houston and Seattle. I always wore her designs on tour. It kept me looking good for free and gave her free promotion; it was a nice trade off.

I wanted to be comfortable for the day. I stood in the doorway of my huge walk-in closet looking at hundreds of pieces of clothes yet having nothing to wear. I really need to go shopping. I settled on a pair or low rise, frayed Baby Phat jeans and a very low-cut matching shirt. I checked my phone, no message.

I waved it off and jumped in the shower. I washed my body down and jumped out quickly when I heard my phone chime. I ran naked and wet across my bedroom to check it. It was Amori saying that she wanted me over as soon as possible because she had an important show to prep for. I grabbed my house phone and dialed Jibari's cell phone number. It rang a couple times but there was no answer. Hmpf.

I dressed and put my hair into two braids, which were reminiscent of my part Native American culture. I slipped my feet into a pair of crisp white K-Swiss and jogged down the steps and to the kitchen. Janelle sat at the table supervising Kya and Brianne as they ate their breakfast. I leaned over each girl and kissed her on the forehead.

"You leaving?" Janelle asked.

"Yea, you know how Amori is. All about business, business, business."

"That's why Amori stays in business."

"You know. I'll be home later this evening and please don't have unwanted guests here when I get home."

"Yes, well, I'm going to ignore that comment and I'll see you when you get home."

*

I called Jibari from my cell phone as I drove to Amori's large Miami Beach home which was but ten minutes from mine. She was the reason that I'd bought my house in the first place. Hers was so big and beautiful I just had to have one of my own. The view of the river was so breathtaking, especially at night. I was just so thrilled to have that view to call my own.

There was still no answer. I huffed and tossed my phone back into my Coach as I pulled up to Amori's house. I climbed out my car and walked up to the door, which was answered by her maid Belle. I could hear Amori yapping at high speed as her footsteps neared the door.

"I got it Belle, go on, thank you. Mikaela hurry up and get out of those clothes so we can do this. I have a crap load of things to do before this show tonight."

"Why didn't you tell me about this show before? Me and Jibari could have made plans to attend."

"No, no, it's not a big deal. Anyway, come on."

I followed behind her as she power-walked to the studio in the back of her house returning her conversation to the person on the phone. It was so hard to believe that Amori was from the Bahamas because she moved like a native New Yorker. I laughed to myself but that quickly faded when I hit the corner and came face to face with Jill Lauren.

"Amori, why didn't you tell me that you had company?" I asked as Jill and I eyeballed one another.

"Mike, hold on. Kaela, Jill, you know the rules up in my home. I don't give a damn about whatever issues you have just keep it up out of here. Now, not that I need to explain anything to you but today is Brenda's daughter's birthday so Jill stepped in to help. Now strip down to your draws and put that two-piece on. Okay Mike, I'm back."

Jill Lauren was a gonna-be supermodel and was Corey's best friend. She didn't like me and I could not stand the super diva bitch. We never got along, not from the day we met. Over the years she and I had gotten into so many altercations it was hard to keep them straight. The only reason that we'd never actually come to blows was the fact that there was always someone else around to intervene. I got the feeling that if we saw each other alone on the streets we would make it physical. And now I was going to have to spend a morning/afternoon with her. She pursed her lips and went back to the stitching that she was doing and I pulled out of my clothes and put on the burgundy two piece jacket and mini skirt that was laid out for me.

Three hours later I was still posing for Amori and was tired of it. I was hungry and ready to go. I wanted to go shopping. I needed to pick up something for my evening date with Jibari. I was relieved when she announced that she was done and Belle brought us sandwiches and drinks. I could hear my cell phone ringing inside of my purse. "Finally," I spoke out loud as I dug it out. I frowned when I saw Menisa's name in the screen.

"Hey, Nisa."

"Wassup Mami, what's going on?"

"Nothin', I'm having sandwiches at Amori's."

"Really? That's nice. Doing another fitting?"

"Yea girl. Gotta go back on tour in a couple days."

"We need to hook up before you bounce again. That's why I was calling, to say I finally get a whole day and night off and me and Rayvon and Lena are going to Levels tonight. You think you can make it?"

"Aww girl I would love to but me and Jibari are supposed to hook up. I haven't seen him yet since I been back from Cali."

"Well alright then, I can understand that. If you and Jibari wanna meet us there let me know."

"Okay." I hung up the phone and held it staring out into space. I couldn't understand why Jibari hadn't gotten back to me yet. It was so unlike him. I began to feel a little suspect but I tried to brush those feelings aside. I wanted to call him back but not from my phone. As usual Amori was on her cellular phone trying to sound busy. I glanced over at Jill and the available phone sitting beside her. I took a deep breath and weighed my options. I could take my chances and call from my phone or wait for Amori to finish with hers. There was a house phone that was specified for business and business only and you knew better than to ask Amori to use it. Or I could...

"Jill,k may I please use your phone?"

She looked around as though she was trying to figure out if there were someone else that I could have been speaking to, then looked at me like she'd misunderstood the question. "No," she answered plainly and returned to eating her salad.

"Bitch," I mumbled under my breath.

"Excuse me but I know you just did not call me a bitch."

"And so what if I did?" I asked standing up in response to her standing like she wanted to do something.

"Felicia, hold on," Amori spoke into the phone. "Hold on, don't make me get ugly up in here. You all had better calm that mess down up in my house, you know the routine. Now Jill sit on back down and Kaela, use the phone in Brenda's office. And make it brief."

I brushed past a glaring Jill and went into Brenda's office and called Jibari, this time he answered. "Jibari what is going on? Why aren't you returning any of my calls?"

"I'm sorry, I was just a little busy."

"Whatever, what time are you picking me up tonight?"

"Uh, Kaela I can't make it tonight. I have to fly out to L.A."

"L.A? Since when? Why didn't you tell me?"

"It was sudden. I'm sorry, I'll make it up to you," he answered trying to sound sincere but something didn't feel quite right. I had no reason to accuse him of lying so I quickly backed down and let it go. I reminded him that I was only home for a couple more days before I was off to Houston. He promised we'd get together before I left, so I hung up.

"Amori, we done?" I asked stepping outside of Brenda's office.

She nodded. "Take those and come back and pick this one up tomorrow."

She went back to talking on the phone. I gathered the clothes and kissed Amori on the cheek. I laid the clothes out on my backseat neatly then pulled out my cell phone and called Menisa. I told her there was a sudden change of plans and I'd be joining them.

*

The club was packed when we stepped inside. The DJ was rocking, playing all the old skool cutz. I was looking fine as ever and the fishies were already biting, I just hoped that Lena wouldn't become one of them again. She hadn't made any advances toward me but then we hadn't had anything to drink yet. It was feeling pretty good to be out again. Menisa and I headed to our favorite first stop-off - the bar.

"Two Blue Long Islands," I told the bartender after fighting for his attention. I drummed my fingers along the counter top and bobbed my head to the beat as we waited. "Oh my goodness Menisa, look who's coming our way."

"Oh not them ho's," Menisa grumbled.

'Synergy' and Natasha were headed right for us. We did not like these chics and they damn sure couldn't stand us. It was a club thang however, not personal like my beef with Jill Lauren. Every time, every club we showed up at there were 'Syn' and Natasha trying to take our spotlight.

"Look who is here. Long time no see. Wha make ya come ta dis club eh? 'Cause ya figure we be 'ere right?" Natasha asked, calling over the music in her thick Jamaican accent. I had to admit to myself and myself only that there was something hypnotic about Natasha with her bright green eyes and long dark hair but I still didn't like her or her little Indian friend.

"I see you still trying to be like us huh?" I stated reaching for my drink. 'Syn' laughed as if I'd meant to be funny.

"That's real cute girl. Just stay out of our way tonight okay?" Not taking her eyes off of me, 'Syn' tossed back her drink and sat her glass on the counter. She looked to Natasha and then back at me, looking Menisa and me up and down before breaking out into uncontrollable drunken laughter.

I shook my head as they walked away. "One day, Nisa I swear I'm going to wear that girl out."

"Girl don't even think about them. I'm about to get my party on, y'heard me?"

With drink in hand I headed for the dance floor. I grabbed a fine, tall dark-skinned brother with a baldhead by his waist pretending not to see him dancing with 'Syn'. The competition had officially begun.

*

Sweat beads popped up on my forehead. I was sure the club had been filled beyond its capacity. I fought my way through and toward the bar to get a cold bottle of water.

"Excuse me," I said to a tall guy who was blocking me from my destination. "Jibari?" My heart stopped and everything around me froze. My breathing became rapid.

"Mikaela. Uh-huh, whassup? What are you - what are you doing here?"

"Excuse you. You're supposed to be in L.A., what the hell are you doing here?" I asked becoming more and more angered.

"Yea, well it got cancelled."

"Then why didn't you call me? It's too loud, can we step out and talk?"

"Kae, I have to go. I'm sorry, I'll call you tomorrow okay?"

"Jibari?" I stood pissed and feeling like a fool as I watched his back disappear out the door.

"Was that Jibari?" Menisa asked coming up behind me.

"Huh? Oh, uh-uhn. Naw girl. I told you, Jibari's in L.A."

"Mm, it sure looked like him. Anyway while you standing there order me a beer."

I took a deep breath and vowed not to let it ruin my evening. I ordered her beer and another Long Island for me and went back to partying.

*

I was half through my engagement at Borders in Miami. I was tired and the cheap asshole that ran the store kept the thermostat on HELL. I was trying to look appealing while sweating my behind off. I was getting ready to catch some serious writer's cramp and still had twenty more minutes to ride out. Another of my books was slipped before me. I smiled at the young heavyset sista with the braids holding a small brown big-head child on her hip. My jaw dropped when she said -

"Make it out to Tamika and Jibari Owens Jr." I knew my shock was obvious when she continued to speak, "Mmhm, you heard right. Jibari is my husband. Don't worry, I ain't gone make a scene or whip yo' ass or nuthin' 'cause I know my dog of a husband ain't tell you about us. I'a still buy yo' books and even tell my friends about 'em 'cause I like how you write. But bitch if I find out you still screwin' my man after today, I *will* cut you."

My body began to shake with anger. I wanted to jump over that table and grab that tramp by her phony hair and whip her ghetto-fab ass. Not over Jibari but for having the audacity to try and punk me at my got-damn work! But I had to remain professional and besides that she had a toddler on her hip.

"Are you going to sign or what?" she asked, freeing me of the fantasy tail-whipping I was giving.

"Huh? Oh." I scribbled some words on the first page and watched her walk away without giving me a second thought.

*

Janelle was pissed when I told her about what had happened.

"What I tell you Kae? I guess you think because you're older than me I can't tell you anything."

I dialed Jibari's cell phone number for the fifth time that afternoon but still no answer. "I'm going over there."

"What? Kae you can't just go showing up at a man's house unannounced by yourself like that."

"Forget that Janelle, the punk ain't answering the phone and we about to deal with this. I don't appreciate his so-called wife frontin' me when I'm working, that's some nonsense."

"I didn't tell you not to confront him. I just said you can't go by yourself."

"How are you going to go? What about the girls?"

"Rayvon. I just got off the phone with him before you came home and he said he ain't going anywhere. Let me just make sure he's still at home."

Janelle and I dropped my nieces off at Rayvon's house and took a chance at going to the studio where Jibari was supposed to be but he wasn't there. I put on my baddest-bitch façade and drove directly to his home not knowing if he'd be there or not. I pulled up in front of his house behind his car. Janelle and I jumped out and charged to his front door. I banged on it until he finally opened the door trying to be discreet.

"Kaela, w-w-what are you doing here?" he asked.

"Jibari, what the hell is going on? Why some chic come to my signing with a baby and say she was your wife? And why are you not returning any of my calls? And why are we standing outside like I'm the damn mailman or something?"

"Kaela baby, I don't know what you're talking about. I don't know who came there claiming to be my wife but I'm in the middle of something so you have to go, I'll call you later okay."

I stood back for a moment contemplating what he'd said, but more importantly how he said it. "Why are you whispering, J?

Is someone here?"

"Kaela – "

"Naw bump that we gone deal with this now," I said pushing past him in time to see the fat braided chic coming toward us. "You don't know who I'm talking about huh?"

"Bitch, I warned you now I'm gone have to mess you up! Jibari, what is she doing here?" Tamika threatened as she tried to get to me while Jibari held her back. "Why she know where you live?"

"Baby, baby," Jibari pleaded. "Tamika, I told you I ain't messin' wit' her. She's crazy. We went out once or twice but that's it and it was purely innocent. Now she stalking me. Listen baby, I'll get rid of her. Now calm down, it's not good for the baby," Jibari said rubbing her stomach.

Heat radiated from my cheeks as I listened to him make me out to be some sort of desperate psycho. I reached back and with all my might slapped his ass open palm across his face. "Son of a bitch! I'm crazy? That's what you trying to say, I'm crazy? Nigga, let me show you crazy!"

Janelle grabbed me and pulled me back from him while Jibari did his best to keep Tamika from me. We screamed threats and profanities back and forth as I was dragged kicking and screaming to my car. I snatched away from my sister and climbed in the passenger seat of my truck and let her drive me away. Neither of those bastards was worth the effort. *F'k Jibari*, was my new mantra that I repeated over and over as Janelle drove me back to my neck of the woods.

Mikaela's Story
I Keep On Falling

I think "Bitch" may have been the word used to describe me. I couldn't say I disagreed, these days in particular. Ever since Jibari's secret ghetto fab fam surfaced, my attitude worsened, even I can profess to that. It was just so unexpected; I'd never imagined that Jibari or any man for that matter would pull something like that on me. Not at this point in my life.

I'd been played before, I'd be flat out lying if I claimed to never have been, but back then I was just Kae Johnson, *That Girl.* Now I am Ms. Mikaela Johnson, *Somebody.* People know my name throughout the U.S. My words have stretched beyond country borders. Pardon me while I reference my hood roots and say *nigga's ain't shit!* With my status I am not supposed to be subjected to their y-chromosome induced bullshit!

*

Grandma Daisy invited Janelle and me over for dinner. It had been such a long while since I'd had the opportunity to see her and my grandfather Pop-Pop. So Janelle and I packed up the girls and invited Menisa and Rayvon to join us. I love my Pop-Pop dearly. I have him to thank for my successes. He and Grandma Daisy raised Janelle and I after we lost our parents.

But sometimes he said things that were inappropriate. Now was one of those times.

"Ayy, ya legs must be tired 'cause ya run tru me mine all evening, heh heh, " he said in inappropriate jest to Menisa in an accent that reminded us that Daddy was part Jamaican.

"Pop-Pop!" Janelle spoke up, her eyes big.

I dropped my head into my palms and shook it back and forth. Fortunately Menisa was used to it so she was able to laugh it off without being offended.

"Pop-Pop how many times do I have to tell you about the way you speak to young ladies?" I scolded.

"Chile when ya grow as ol' as me, ya do wha ya gotta do ta keep young an vibrant. Ya soon enough know what I mean."

"Yea, I guess," I mumbled.

"You guess. Lawd have mercy pon Miss Percy, ya hear dis gal Daisy, she say she guess. Ya not keep ya yout forever gal. Enjoy it while it last."

I wasn't going to argue, that was Pop-Pop for you. Janelle and I didn't know our mother's parents. All we knew is that they lived somewhere on a Minnesota Reservation, if they were still alive. Pop-Pop migrated here from Jamaica when he was a young man and met and married our American Grandma Daisy. No wonder our family was so screwed up but I'd rather not go into details of that.

*

Rayvon had to pick up Lena from the airport and Menisa had class in the morning, so we called it an early night. I needed to finish writing the last couple of chapters of my current novel *Sister Geneva* anyway, so I didn't object. I'd been invited to speak at Black Sistahs United Book Club in South Carolina and had to fly out in two days so I wanted to get as much work done as possible while I was home.

After I'd showered I tied a scarf around my head to hold my

hair away from my face, threw on a pair of sweats and a sport bra, and settled in front of the computer in my office. I picked up the remote that was beside me and hit play. Jill Scott's soulful voice relaxed me and allowed me to feel the story that I was trying to express. Partway through my moment the house phone rang. I tried to tune it out but the persistent ringing was too much of a distraction.

"Hello?" I answered annoyed, as though the person on the other end could have known I was busy but called anyway.

"Wassup Kae, you busy?" It was Annie; I was never too busy for her.

"Nah, not really. What's going on? How are you?"

"Good, good and you big timer? I saw you on the morning show, you look like you lost weight."

"Yea, I didn't mean to though. I work out the same as always but with all this running around the country and refusing to eat anyone's cooking but Janelle and Grandma Daisy's what do you expect? I'm trying to gain some of it back though, I am too old to be skinny!"

"Girl you crazy. Hey I wanted to tell you something though. Girl guess what. Ricky is finally getting married."

"How is that news? Ricky's been getting married for years."

"No, no, no. I mean he set a date. Girl, he mailed invitations and everything. I wanted to warn you before you suddenly got yours in the mail. I don't even know if I'm happy or not so I know you trippin' over there."

Annie kept talking but I didn't hear anything else she said. It felt like someone slapped me hard in my face and kicked me twice in my gut. First I find out Jibari has a wife, now Rick is about to make someone his? Could this be real? Maybe…maybe Annie was exaggerating. Yea, I'm sure they spoke about it and she's just taking the whole thing and blowing it out of proportion. I made the decision to take Annie's revelation with a grain of salt, though it still tugged at me a little, irritated me some. Annie went on but I couldn't focus on what she was saying.

"Annie listen, I appreciate the heads up but I have a lot of work to do alright? I'll call you later this week."

"Okay girl, try not to let it get to you too much."

"Please, I am not thinking about Ricky Lear. I'm happy for them, that's all I gotta say. Anyway I love you."

"Love you too, bye."

I pushed the TALK button on the cordless and held it in my hand contemplating what I'd do or say if Annie was right. I dialed the 651 area code followed by Rick's home phone number, Jewel answered and pleasantly advised me he wasn't home but she'd give him the message that I called. I held the phone to my breast and stared across the room deep in thought.

I inhaled deeply and reached for my remote. I toggled through the CD's until disc five took its place at the head of the pack. Portisheads' *Nobody Loves Me* wafted from the speakers. I sat the phone in its cradle and attempted to put all my energy into my work so that I wouldn't think about Rick and Jewel tying the knot.

*

"What's with your attitude today?" Janelle asked me in an exasperated tone.

"I don't have an attitude baby sis, I just don't feel like being bothered."

"Please. You've been pitchin' a bitch about everything anybody says."

"Whatever," why couldn't people respect other peoples desires to be left alone? I slammed my empty glass on the kitchen counter and stepped off the stool. I turned quickly, my hair whipping behind me and with my cellular phone in my hand walked to my living room. I collapsed on the sofa and pointed the remote at the television. A specialized tune sang from my phone. After spying the caller ID, I answered.

"Hey sweetheart, " Ricky said from the other end.

"Don't sweetheart me, Annie called me and told me you and Jewel set a date," I said with as much of a tone as I could muster.

"Yea we did, on the 26th. You get the invitation yet?"

I took the phone from my ear and looked at it with my mouth dropped open, "Just like that you're getting married on the 26th. What's that like three weeks from now?"

"Just like that? Kae, I've been engaged for over two years now."

"You couldn't tell me personally?" The pitch of my voice was beginning to rise. "I thought…why…Ricky what about us?"

"What about us Kaela? I've tried to get with you since we were what, like sixteen? You and Annie made that dumb ass pact, that's what about us. I moved on with my life Kae, I can't sit on my hands forever waiting for you to want me. Man, look I got a lot to do so I'll holla at you later. Think about it and R.S.V.P."

Ricky hung up before I could say anything in my defense. My breath became heavy and ragged. Aaarrgh! I slammed the phone against the wall; it shattered into tiny pieces that crashed to the floor. Janelle came running to see what had happened with Kya and Brianne staggering behind.

"What the hell is wrong with you?" she yelled at me.

I glared at her, heaving and chewing the inside of my mouth. "Just leave me alone Janelle," I mumbled.

"Kaela-"

"Don't talk to me, just leave me alone!"

My yelling upset Kya and Brianne but I was in selfish mode and couldn't stop to care. I rushed past and ran upstairs to my bedroom slamming the door behind me. I walked into my large bathroom and stood looking at my reflection in the mirror. I could pin point every flaw on my face. My dark hair hung past my shoulders. My eyes were bloodshot. I opened a drawer and pulled out a pair of scissors. I lifted my hair and held the scissors to the long, thick piece in my hand but hesitated. My mind drifted to Jibari and his pregnant spouse and child. I pictured Ricky saying, "I do" and making Jewel forever his. I took a deep breath and closed the scissors on my hair. I set them on the counter and through blurry brown eyes, stared at the hair in my hand.

"Maybe I should consider being a lesbian," I mumbled. I set the hair on the counter, picked up the scissors and cut until I could cut no longer.

Janelle was busy mopping the floor when I came jogging down the steps. She paused and rested her weight against the mop when she spotted me. I paused and sucked my teeth before continuing forward.

"Mikaela, why did you cut off all of your hair? What's going on with you?"

"Janelle, it's nothing I want to talk about okay, so just please leave it alone," I spoke rationally.

"My God, you're such a friggin" drama queen! You're slamming phones into walls, frightening my girls and you just cut off about six inches of beautiful hair, you're damn right I want to know what's going on."

I looked at Janelle…my sister. She was right of course; she did have every right to know what was going on in my head and my heart. I stood at the bottom of the steps and ran my fingers through my straight ear-length mane. I twisted my lips and decided to keep my mouth closed. Without saying another word, I walked out the front door intent on a destination that was for the moment unknown.

*

It was twelve hours later when I finally came home with a more even, short, feathered hair cut and a tiny piece of mind. I realized that Janelle would be angry with me in the morning and would have much to say but I had to get away in order to try to clear my head.

I gently closed the door behind me and walked up the steps to my bedroom. I stripped down to my underclothes and sat on my bed to flip through the mail that Janelle had left for me. Bills as usual, car payment, insurance, cable bill and, sigh, a wedding invitation. I stared at the postcard, which was inviting me to watch another woman walk away with the man for me, and fought back tears. Why had I never given this thing a shot? Was it my pact with Annie? What about the fear of ruining a life long friendship? Whatever it was, was it even worth it?

I ripped the invitation into tiny pieces and threw them as far as the wind allowed them to travel. In nothing but a pair of panties, disturbing Farrah's slumber, I gently grabbed her from the center of my bed and curled up with her. I was expressionless as the tears rolled down the side of my face and onto my arms as I stroked my baby and was relaxed by her soft purr.

Gotta Get Away

My world had spun out of control, I was coming apart at the seams and I knew of no way to weave it back together. I was uncertain of how things could have possibly gotten this way. I was becoming one of the characters that I'd written about. My life could have been a book, a series of episodes that late at night when there was nothing left to do people sat up and read about anxiously awaiting the drama that was to unfold next. And they'd call it *Mikaela's Story* or better yet, *Mikaela's Drama*. It probably could have made a good book if I had the energy to delve into all of the emotions involved and write it out.

I dipped my finger into my cooling cappuccino and sucked the flavor off. I stared out the window of the Houston Starbucks that was in the lobby of the hotel I was staying in waiting for Jones Grey, the co-coordinator of the Freedom Readers Annual Benefit Dinner. I was invited to participate as a speaker, which was a great honor especially since I'd be amongst some of the greats, Terry McMillan, Iyanla Vanzant, E Lynn Harris, Susan L Taylor. The keynote speaker was Maya Angelou. I'd reached a great level of success in my career as an author but I didn't feel I'd yet achieved the level of these authors and was amazed to find my name amongst theirs. But that was Jones, we'd only been connected for a year and a half but he had my back like that of a life long friend.

I looked up from the ink stained notepad before me just in time to see Jones step through the door. He was still sexy for a light brown brother. Not very tall but has a body to rob, cheat and steal for! The sexiest pair of lips that God created he blessed Jones with. I'd never tasted those lips before nor felt that body, smelled the scent he left behind the morning after sex.

To my despair there was a Mrs. Jones (or Angela) Grey and Jones was very much committed to his "Angel" and their three children. In his clearly expensive Gray Armani suit, Jones took a seat across from me and smiled a ridiculous over-sized grin. He was the silliest man I knew matched only by his wife Angela.

"You're a fool," I said unable to contain my giggles.

"You waiting on me or trying to pick up a date?" he asked in jest.

"Depends if you're yet available," I flirted and he had the nerve to blush.

"Girl you an idiot!"

He and I laughed and made small talk for a short while before we climbed into his big black SUV and headed for the amphitheater. Beautiful black educated people networked at the black tie charity event. So many big names I was rubbing elbows with. I had to contain any desire to get groupie ghetto singing out praises and asking for autographs to take back to my Grandmamma nem. In my long black spaghetti strap Amori Allen gown I glided through the crowd schmoozing with everyone from "Joe Blow" the corporate exec to avid reader and actor Lawrence Fishburne.

At the close of the evening when Jones returned me to my hotel to prep for my flight home the next day I felt at ease. At ease for the first time in a long while. I knew that feeling wouldn't last past my drive to the airport to board flight 1150 to Chicago on my way to that wedding. I hung my dress and lay across the bed. I stroked the definition lines on my belly with plans in my mind to get up and take a shower. My eyelids became heavy and I drifted away to sleep.

*

Back to life, back to reality. The dress that Amori was finishing for me was beautiful but that didn't matter. As far as I was concerned it represented loss to me and that got me hot. My nerves were shot and my mood was worse. I sat on the cushy curved sofa picking at my nails when Jill walked into the studio. I rolled my eyes aggravated at her presence. I looked around. Brenda sat behind a desk shuffling through papers, a tiny portable radio at her side. Amori was busy fixing the hem on the gown while yapping away on her cell phone.

I heaved and huffed and puffed a couple times ready to get out of the house. Amori looked up and waved Jill over to her side. I couldn't tell you why Jill's presence annoyed me so much. She and I had never gotten along so we just ignored each other when in one another's presence but I was feeling bitchy and childish and I really didn't care.

"Amori are you almost done?" I asked as Jill began to remove her short denim jacket.

"I'll be done in about 15 more minutes."

I huffed and shifted in my seat. "Jill what's up? You here to help out again?"

"Yes, as a matter of fact I am," she answered plainly.

"What, you don't think Brenda is capable of handling things by herself?" I picked.

"I can handle it but I don't mind if Jill helps," Brenda volunteered.

I rolled my eyes again and ignored her.

"Don't start with me Mikaela." Jill grabbed a bag of material from the corner and began to sift through it.

"Amori how much longer?" I whined.

"Mikaela, 10, 12 minutes alright?" she answered impatiently.

"Mikaela don't worry it won't be much longer, Amori is good at what she does, you know that."

"Brenda, seriously, was I talking to you?" I asked in an exasperated voice. "Why don't you mind your own business sometimes?"

"Let me call you back," Amori told the person she was talking to. She spoke up to me cutting off Brenda before she had a chance to respond, "Mikaela what's the problem? Why are you taking your little attitude out on Brenda and since when do you think you can rush me?"

"I'm just ready to get out of here that's all."

"You have a problem and you need to deal with that crap another way," Jill jumped in.

"Dayum, was I talking to you? What's up with people answering to other peoples questions?"

"I don't give a good got-damn who you were talking to you need to get your shit together. You phony bitch, I can see right through you. You've been so unreal since I first met you. Stupid drama queen, you take your damn life from those lame ass books you write. Don't take your so-called problems out on Brenda, she didn't do a thing to you."

"Excuse you but I don't know who the hell you think I am but you got me so terribly twisted."

By this point Jill and I were nose to nose with Amori and Brenda off to the side watching and listening.

"So what you think, you gone do something? You feeling froggy bitch just jump."

"No, no, you two need to stop this right now. Jill, Kae doesn't want to fight you - " Brenda intervened trying to be the Good Samaritan she was known for being.

"I'll tell you what Brenda, you nosey ass heifer, why don't you sit back down and take a phone call and mind your own business for a change," I spoke thoughtlessly knowing how wrong I was once the words slipped through my lips yet not willing to take responsibility for it.

And then it happened. Before I knew it was coming I had stumbled backwards and lost my balance landing flat on my behind on Amori's marble floor. My cheek throbbed and my blood pressure had risen. I heard shouts of threats and profanity as I struggled to get back to my feet.

I can't believe she'd hit me. Jill Lauren with full fist hit me in my face. I finally made it to my feet and charged for her but Amori stopped me and held me back while Brenda held Jill away from me.

"Bitch I will whip your ass! Let me go Amori!"

"No, you are not about to disrespect my house any more than you already have!"

"What? She hit me and you expect that I ain't gone hit her back? Bump that Amori!"

"Mikaela I think its time for you to leave."

"This is a joke right? She hit me in my face and you're putting me out?"

"You deserved it! I don't know what's gotten into you lately but you've been coming in here with this stank attitude and now you're taking it out on Brenda and that mess ain't fair and it ain't right. So yes, I am telling you to leave and Jill will stay and you may return when you get your head right."

I was in awe. Flabbergasted. Amazed that for as much business as we'd done together she expected that she could let Jill hit me and put me out and I was supposed to simply go along with it.

"Forget that Amori. You're not right but that's cool. Keep that dress. I'll advertise Helmut Lang or Chanel."

"What? You can't possibly be – whatever, you do that then, I don't give a damn just get the hell out."

"Don't let me catch you on the street," I yelled back as I

headed for the front door.

"Damn that Brenda let me go. We can handle this right outside."

"Jill, uh-uhn. Not in front of my house you ain't. These White folks don't hardly want us Negro's in their neighborhoods as it is. You are *not* about to bring down my property value. Kaela, good-bye," Amori stated.

I stormed out of her house and climbed into my car. I peeled out of the cul-de-sac and sped home.

*

I had a day left before I had to catch my flight. My bags were packed and I'd bought a John Galliano gown and Dolce Gabana shoes to wear to the wedding. It wasn't nearly as nice as what Amori had created for me but I hadn't spoken to her. I was working my best at controlling my temper and containing my negative attitude but I was anxious to have a run in with Jill Lauren.

Rayvon was throwing a party and Menisa and I were out shopping for something to wear to it. Sure it was only a house party but who knows, I could meet the next man of my dreams there. I had to look good for it. We dipped in and out of stores naying outfit after outfit until we finally found something that was slightly interesting in the first store that we'd initially gone to.

We had a nice lunch at a restaurant before together going back to she and Rayvon's place. I decided to just change there since I'd be coming there anyway. I stretched out on the sofa in front of the television and held the remote in my hand as Menisa and Rayvon straightened up and fixed food.

"Uuh, Mikaela I know you're a big celebrity and all but you think you could get off your butt and help us straighten up?" Rayvon called from the kitchen as he mopped the floor.

"Why? I don't live here."

"Ray, you forget miss Queen Bee got maid service now that Janelle moved in," Menisa volunteered.

"Forget both of y'all," I laughed. "I know how to clean."

I rolled off of the sofa and turned the television off. I grabbed the vacuum cleaner from the hall closet and began to clean the carpet. The three of us got the house spic and span and prepared and laid out the food before we started to dress.

Rayvon was in the shower when Lena arrived. Menisa disappeared to the guest bathroom to get ready leaving me alone to entertain her. I began to feel mischievous. Lena sat on the big recliner chair as though she was exhausted. She ran her fingers through her blonde hair and held it on top of her head as she stretched out her legs and placed her feet on the coffee table.

"So how have you been Miki?"

"Why do you insist on calling me Miki when no one else does? My name is Mikaela. That too many syllables for you, then you can call me Kae," I stated.

"It's just different and I like to be different."

"Yea, well we know that don't we."

"And what's that supposed to mean?"

"Why did you kiss me that night Lena?"

"What? Oh, girl that was so long ago I'm not even thinking about that anymore."

"But I am. Lena, are you a lesbian?" I asked. I knew it wasn't any of my business and there was no point to my question but I had to take my aggravation out on someone and she was as good as anyone.

"Excuse me? Why are you asking me this? Because I kissed you while we were pissy drunk?"

"Well, that could be a reason."

"If I'm not mistaken you didn't stop me but if you really want to know then fine, I've been attracted to women and yes I find you attractive but I'm not a lesbian. I'd never meant to act on my attraction for you but, well things happen."

I sucked my teeth as the wheels of my mind turned. I wanted to mess with her, mess with her the way I felt everyone had been messing with me. I needed to feel as though I'd gotten even, gotten back at Jibari and Rick and Jill and everyone else that had wronged me, Ms. Mikaela Johnson.

So I screwed with her. I licked my lips and ran my French manicured fingernails through my short mane and slid closer to her not taking my eyes off of her. She looked back at me and I recognized the lust in her eyes, the same lust that resided there the night that she pinned me to that bar. This was too easy.

"Things happen huh? So how do we make things happen again?" I asked seductively.

"What? Are you serious? Don't play with my emotions girl."

"What you got on your mind Lena?"

Lena paused, eyeing me with suspicion. She laughed, "You're full of it, *Kae*. Rayvon is in the next room. "

"In the shower."

"Mikaela…"

I leaned closer. "Lena…"

"I guess if you're serious then come over here and let me show you," she said pouting her bright red lips.

I stood as she stood and I walked to her. As she reached for me I leaned back and with all my might connected my palm with the side of her face. In shock she fell back into the chair and held her hand to her cheek.

"Chic don't you ever think about putting your lips on me again or I will kick your ass!" I looked down and saw Jill and Jibari and Jibari's wife and anyone else who'd messed over me sitting in that chair and I felt liberated, powerful, vindicated.

"What the hell is going on here?" Rayvon bellowed as he entered the scene from his bedroom with nothing but a towel wrapped around his waist, his big belly flopping over.

I said nothing. I sat back on the couch and took the remote control in my hand and flipped through the channels. Lena began blubbering out how I'd come on to her and hit her. I hadn't thought about how I'd explain it, I hadn't really thought about it at all. I needed to vent, I hadn't planned for it to be Lena but then I didn't really care at the particular moment that it was. I didn't deny it when Rayvon asked me if it was true. I laughed.

"Kae, leave. I don't know what your problem is but you - you just need to leave my house now. I don't hit women but if you stay much longer I just might make an exception."

"Yea whatever Rayvon, your girlfriend kissed me and was willing to do it again but you put me out. Hmm, interesting. That's cool though, I'm getting kinda used to people putting me out for dumb ass reasons." I took my bags and left.

*

I wasn't sure as to how I would make this right with Rayvon though for the time being it was unimportant to me. I felt better about some things. I was ready to take on the world and this new challenge which was ahead of me. Sure I was behaving unlike myself but I was tired of being the person that I used to be. Maybe it was time for change; time to let people know that they couldn't run over me. I was not going to stand for it.

I actually felt good driving home, that feeling of elation had returned to me after all. I was finally excited about going to this wedding because little did Rick and Annie know, I was no longer going there to be supportive. Little did Jewel know, I was going to take what rightfully should have been mine. I was going to take her man.

Mikaela's Story
Actions Speak Louder Part I

I was relieved when our plane finally touched Northern earth. Ever since September 11th I was subject to this queasy discomforting feeling whenever flying the so-called friendly skies. After two planes in two days I was feeling quite jetlagged and anxious to stretch my black behind out in someone's bed. I would much rather it be my own king sized pillow top but beggars cannot be choosers and I was begging worse than a drunk man on a date.

My infinite trip began two days prior. I'd flown into Chicago to meet with Annie so that she and I could take the trip into Minnesota together. It was probably a bit of a waste but we wanted to have the opportunity to spend some time solo. And so she and I enjoyed stuffed spinach pizza from Giordano's and talked well into the night while sitting on her living room floor sipping slightly better than cheap wine.

Needless to say we hadn't gotten much sleep before having to hop onto flight 856 to Minneapolis/St. Paul. My stomach growled as we walked the stretch of the terminal to the baggage claim area. The extra (tiny) bag of Rold Gold and can of ginger-ale that I had to force that uptight flight attendant to spare me hadn't done my tummy a damn bit of justice.

Annie touched the top of my hand and pointed to the carousel for ATA where our bags would soon be sliding down. I scanned the area looking for Ricky's handsome face. I unconsciously adjusted my clothes. I didn't want to look as though I'd just gotten off an hour and a half flight even if it were true. I shifted the large cracked leather belt that I wore around my worn-look Express jeans that were cuffed high to resemble capri's. My dark tan Linea Paolo mules were the perfect compliment to the thin linen top that hung loosely off of my perfectly tanned shoulders. The floppy brown hat and large hoop earrings set the look off perfectly.

I'd spent two days prior to leaving Florida on the beach lying beneath the afternoon sun tanning as much skin as I could without offending anyone. Not that my body should ever incite such a reaction but as Jose put it so eloquently, jealous. ones. still. envy. It held true as young fourteen-year-old girls cut their eyes and sucked their teeth at my adult brilliance.

A small black woman with startling red hair and freckles tapped my arm interfering with my thoughts. Irritated I turned my attention to her. I didn't acknowledge her verbally but the look in my eyes and expression on my face should have warned her that I wasn't in the mood to be messed with.

"I'm sorry to bother you Miss, you just look real familiar. You're not Mikaela Johnson - are you?" She asked. She looked in my face as though there was a small sign or symbol that would give her the truth even if I lied. My expression softened as I'd never want to deter a fan.

"Yes I am. I take it you've read my work?" I asked with my rehearsed smile and enthusiasm.

"Girl yes! *Preaching to the Choir* is my favorite book! It's like you're telling my whole life in that story. It's deep! I read it two times already, gurl. It's da bomb!"

I nodded and smiled as she went on and on briefing me on my characters and their crazy antics as if I didn't know. My mind wandered to Rick as she rambled. I hoped he would appreciate my beauty and remember what separated me from the average chic, as I was so sure his woman was.

"So can I?"

"Huh? Oh sure, you have a pen?" I asked realizing she'd asked for my autograph. I scribbled a quick *"Never Stop Reading! With Love Mikaela"* on the back of her airline ticket. She parted while squealing about how she couldn't wait to show her sister. Annie shook her head from side to side as she handed me my large suitcase.

"Girl you and yo' damn fans. You see the type of mofo's that read your shit?" Annie laughed. I just pursed my lips and rolled my eyes at my best girlfriend. "Umm, Kae. I think our ride is here."

Annie slyly pointed across the aisle at a shapely young woman looking around awkwardly. She was quite attractive with smooth ebony colored skin and strikingly bright hazel eyes. She had thick, silky, dark hair that was swept over to the side of her head in a ponytail. Her style was comparative to my own. She wore a short denim mini, revealing beautifully tanned and toned legs. Her muted green top hung off one shoulder.

She held a sign in front of her that read 'Annie & Mikayla'. I cringed at the sight of my misspelled name. She obviously did not realize who I was. Hmpf, the non-spelling bee bitch might turn out to be comp after all. I took a deep breath and slipped on my huge Versace bug eye sunglasses as Annie and I began in her direction.

"Jewel?" Annie asked as we approached the video-ho type chic.

"Annie? Ah, oh my goodness, it's such a pleasure to meet you!" she said as she pulled Annie into a tight embrace. "Oh look at you. Rick didn't tell me you were this beautiful!"

I thought she was laying it on a little thick. Yes, Annie was beautiful but she didn't have to fawn over her the way she was.

Ricky wasn't around so just who in the hell was she trying to impress? After she finished playing in Annie's blond hair and pouring on so much sugar my teeth began to ache she finally noticed me.

"Mikaela Johnson. This is so unbelievable. I can't believe I'm going to have a real celebrity in my home. I enjoyed your last book a great deal. You're going to have to sign it for me before you leave."

"Definitely, definitely. So where is Ricky? Why'd he make you deal with us?" I asked smiling my trademark picture perfect smile.

"Oh, I just had a few errands I needed him to run." She looked me directly in the eyes when answered but I wouldn't flinch. Her smile was as rehearsed as mine. I wasn't sure if she was genuinely sweet or up to something herself but I was pretty certain it was the latter. I was always suspicious of new broads as they were always suspicious of me.

"Besides," she continued finally breaking her stare, "you ladies are family and I wanted to meet you and have the opportunity to get to know you. You'll see Rick soon enough." With that, she looked at me again. "Let me help you with your luggage."

"No thanks, I got it," I said suddenly not trusting her and being glad that I'd soon break up her relationship. She turned and took Annie's suitcase and rolled it behind her as the two made small talk. I was annoyed that the heifer didn't have the decency to acknowledge just how beautiful I am. Jealous ones still envy.

*

It was very trusting of Jewel to allow Annie and me to stay in their home as opposed to a hotel. Trusting or maybe smart. Truth is the skank thought she was being slick. What she was really trying to do was keep her comp close. She could care less if Annie slept on her sofa as opposed to some semen-stained bed at the local Motel 6; it was me she wanted to keep tabs on. Fine by me, I was always up for a challenge. And the race began as soon as Rick stepped his perfectly shined Ferragamo's through the front door!

It had been quite sometime since we'd seen Rick though we kept in constant verbal contact. The Negro was so much sexier than I could ever recall! It was as though he slipped into the crib in slo-mo. His beautiful brown skin was clean and clear and those bushy eyebrows gave him a rough animal-like quality, which I found to be absolutely irresistible though I had no choice but to resist. I could feel Jewel's eyes burning holes in my back as I pulled Rick into a warm embrace.

"Damn boy look at you! Steppin' out in suits and shit now!" Annie exclaimed as she took him over.

"Well y'know, what can I say? Brotha's livin' kinda good now," he bragged. "Look at y'all. I never knew my girls were so fine!"

His smile was killer! Sly and crooked flashing even white teeth. Full lips which I recall being soft to the touch from the one and only time we stole a private moment, before my friendship with Annie intervened. I shifted as all too familiar moisture built up in between my thighs.

"So how was your flight?" he asked as he jerked his tie loose while walking toward his fiancée. He kissed her lips before mumbling some secret words that made Jewel smile. She took his leather duffle and slipped from sight.

"Long!" I sighed as I plopped down onto the sofa and landed across from my girl. With my freshly manicured hand I pat the space between us. Rick slid in between and rested his slender yet masculine arms around our shoulders. "Damn, I can't believe you're actually doing this. I feel so incredibly old now, what with having friends who get married!"

"Woman, don't say that. I ain't old and don't plan on even acknowledging it when it happen."

"I know that's right," Annie chimed in. "But why - why now? I mean don't get me wrong, your girl is straight y'know. But damn y'all so young. You sure you ready for this? Don't forget I know you playa, playa. You really think you can give all that up?"

Rick laughed a hearty laugh and shook his head. "Damn chic kinda bold to bringing up a brother past with his lady in the next room. You might make her start asking questions and thinkin' thangs."

Annie fidgeted slightly and rolled her eyes. I knew my girl was thinking what I was thinking, *F'k that hoe.*

"But nah man seriously, those days are over," Rick continued. "My baby trust me and I'm not about to mess that up."

On cue his "baby" made her grand reappearance announcing that dinner was ready to be served. The three of us stood in unison. My hand sort of "accidentally" slid down Rick's back lightly grazing his firm rear. Rick turned to face me, our eyes locking letting me know that there was still hope - that is if I could get him alone!

Mikaela's Story
Actions Speak Louder Part II

Three days in the same house as my old high-school infatuation Ricky Lear and not a damn thing had gone down between us. It began to matter less and less to me as the time ticked by. All I'd really wanted when I began this mission was to take my pain and frustration out on someone else, make someone feel as low as I had been. I mean, yes I maintained some feelings for Rick but I was certain it was remnants of a schoolgirl crush, left over love as it were.

As far as Jewel, I guess home-girl was aiight. I decided to forego my vengeful plan, as the wedding was already less than two days away. After it was done I could just pack my emotional baggage and take it all home where it belonged.

We'd spent days running around with and for Jewel in an effort to get her prepared for her big day. It wasn't anything that I was thrilled to do but I had to wear my mask and play the part. Besides somehow Annie and Jewel managed to click so I couldn't be the odd man out. And hey, shopping was my thing anyway no matter what circumstances I was dealing with and so it wasn't so bad.

What was awkward was seeing Rick and Jewel interact with one another. To see them kiss and snuggle and flirt and fondle made my stomach churn and my eyes roll back.

*

Near six in the evening and the house was packed. It was the Friday before the wedding. A couple guys we'd gone to school with, Amir and Daniel, as well as one of Jewel's girlfriends were gathered in celebration. Laughter and cigar smoke filled the air as stories of our crazy high-school antics were shared. Aaliyah's freshman joint BACK AND FORTH was pouring through the speakers.

"Oh snap! That's my joint!" Annie jumped from her seat on Rick and Jewel's love seat and ran to the stereo to pump up the volume.

"It's crazy y'all but do you realize that these are our dusties!" I stated briefly feeling aged. Annie, Jewel, and her girl Tiff and I formed an impromptu dance show imitating the moves we recalled from a then 15 year-old Aaliyah's video.

"Y'all need to just sit down. Leave the dancing to the pros," Amir said while refilling his glass with Remy Red.

"Shut up boy, let's see what you can do," I challenged.

Amir took a final gulp of his drink and set the glass on the coffee table. He stood and rubbed his hands together as he sauntered over to where us women were still gently swaying our hips to the beat. He slipped between us and did a funky two-step, which seemed to be a cross between the electric slide and the wop. We doubled over in laughter as the men cheered and woofed him on.

"You a fool dog!" Daniel shouted holding a half empty glass in the air as maybe a salute to their manhood.

"Ok, ok, enough of all that. It is time for y'all fools to get out of here," Tiff said while pushing Amir toward the front door.

"Damn ma wassup?" Amir asked grinning, showing off his sexy dimples.

"Ya gotta go son, ya gotta go. My girls are going to be

through here any minute. Bachelorette time baby! "

"Strip tease!" Daniel called out as the guys gathered their belongings. It was time to part ways so that us women could celebrate Jewel's final hours as a single sister and they could do the same brotherhood tradition for Rick. My heart dropped slightly at the thought but I kept up appearances. We'd started our evening off right and the alcohol had us feeling quite nice. I pressed my body a tad too close as I hugged Rick good-bye but fortunately no one but us noticed.

*

"Don't stop, pop that coochie, let me see you doo-doo brown!" blasted from the speakers as a bunch of horny, crazed females stuffed dollar bills down the g-strings of the two buffed strippers. There was Antonio the Cubano copper and Mauricio the Black Mandingo. I was sure that those two would find themselves wrapped in each other's arms after the set while us women took turns in the bathroom secretly massaging our coochie's.

I will confess to having behaved like a sex-starved teenager. Too many Jell-O and tequila shots had me in my mid thigh length skirt with my leg wrapped around the waist of the sexy Latin lover. Ay papi! Mi amor! Whew damn, I'm too drunk to go on…

*

I couldn't sleep through the night. Normally I was a pro at holding my liquor. This time I'd mixed too many varieties of alcohol and it wasn't sitting quite right. I rolled out of the full sized bed in the guest bedroom and sat upright on its edge. I glanced at the digital clock through blurry eyes; it read 4:36 am. I stretched, yawned and stood up damn near loosing my balance and falling back onto my behind. Tiff had thrown one hellified party from which I was feeling the effects and I was not completely disappointed.

After stopping off in the bathroom I stumbled to the kitchen and cracked open the refrigerator, the light shocking my sensitive system. I closed my eyes tight and felt around for the carton of orange juice. I opened my eyes just enough to confirm that what my hand was grasping was in fact the juice that I was seeking and nothing else. I'd just poured half a glass and sat down at the table to enjoy it when I heard the soft click of the front door. Moments later Rick staggered into the kitchen. He jumped slightly when he noticed me in the darkness.

"Damn girl, you scared the mess outta me. Couldn't sleep huh? Too wired?" he asked. He stumbled a bit as he walked over to join me at his table, clearly inebriated.

I shook my head no. "Too much liquid in my system as is apparently in yours."

"Yea, yea I know about that," he laughed. He took the carton of juice and put it to his sweet lips. I was way too tired and much too tipsy to get too turned on. "Ay, c'mon. Let's go sit out back and get some fresh air."

I stood and walked with him to the back porch. We sat in the large lawn chairs that occupied space in the backyard. We were silent for awhile, just enjoying the warm night air which was a far stretch from the dense blanket of humidity which was ever present on most Florida nights. The sounds of the North danced in my head. They relaxed me.

"So how's the book writing business going?" he asked.

"Good actually. *Preaching to the Choir* is a best seller, so I'm happy. I've been doing a lot more book signings lately. It's so crazy because now that I have been doing this on my own for so many years the big publishing houses keep throwing wild amounts of money in my face."

"So why don't you accept one of those offers? Y'know, relax for a change and let someone else do all the leg work, you just focus on the craft."

I looked at Rick like he'd surely lost his damn mind.

"Brotha puh-lease. This is my livelihood…it's what keeps me going. I'm about ready for the next phase of this business and start taking submissions myself. I make plenty money and have mad connections. I don't need their recognition and attention now. Where were they when I thought I needed them to get put on? "

"Calm down, my goodness chic it was just a thought. If what you're doing makes you happy then do the damn thing."

Silence returned. I had become more alert and my body was beginning to acknowledge Rick's presence. I looked at the side of his face maybe longer than I should have. He turned and met my gaze. I didn't look away.

"What?" he asked chuckling.

"Nothing. I…nothing." I turned away. I felt Rick's fingers on my chin; he turned me to face him again. The pace of my heart quickened as he leaned forward, pressing his full lips against mine. They were soft, reminiscent of down pillows, just as I'd recalled. His tongue eased its way into my mouth. I tasted the stale alcohol as his tongue danced a tango with my own. I was drunk though not on the Tequila or Rum that I'd had hours earlier, I was drunk on love and lust.

His hands stroked my exposed flesh. Instinct took over and I found myself on his lap, my arms wrapped around his neck. Rick pulled me closer and held me tight, his true desires becoming ever present by the stiffening bulge in his jeans. The kiss was more than I'd expected it to be. Underlying feelings of which I was blind to began to consume me.

My mind raced, filled with thoughts that should not have been entertained. Thoughts that proved once and for all that Mikaela Johnson was in fact not without a conscious. One thought stood out in my mind and like a news flash it said *I'm in love with Ricky Lear!*

I pulled myself from his grasp and jumped from his lap. My breathing was heavy and ragged. I looked in Rick's eyes. I was truly in love with him but he was marrying her. Thousands of words on my tongue yet I said nothing. I rushed back into the house and curled up in bed. I lay there awake, listening. A piece of me hoping that he would come after me, take me in his arms and tell me that it was me he wanted.

There was what felt like an eternal silence. I heard the soft click of the backdoor and gentle footsteps in my direction. They ended abruptly followed by contemplative quiet. Moments later I listened to the sound of Rick's shoes fading in the distance as he headed toward his bedroom to join his future bride.

*

I was up and fully clothed by 7:15 the next morning. I'd tried to get some sleep but it wasn't happening. Every time I closed my eyes I was kissing Rick. I'd always loved him but the reaction I was experiencing as a result of our actions said my feelings were much deeper than I'd realized.

There was no time to attempt to break up a relationship; the wedding was less than twenty-four hours away. I was bad and I knew it but damn, I am realistic. Besides that, Rick loved Jewel. He was drunk and horny, the kiss was great but it didn't mean that he loved me. Rick loved Jewel and there was no way that I could sit in a church and watch him give his promise of life, love and dedication to her. I'd already contacted the airline and had my ticket changed, I'd fly out in a couple of hours.

I sipped on a hot mug of black coffee. Rick entered the kitchen dressed for the day as well.

"We need to talk," were the first words out of his mouth. He appeared more handsome and sexy than he had anytime previously. My tummy began to flutter.

"Listen Rick, there's nothing to talk about. It was late, you'd just come from getting drunk and getting lap dances so you were horny. I understand."

"Nah, I don't think you do. Can we please step outside?"

I sighed but obliged. I followed Rick to the large shed in the back of the house which doubled as a laundry room. I defensively folded my arms across my breasts awaiting an easy yet unnecessary letdown.

"Kae, about last night-"

"Rick I told you, I'm cool. You don't have to explain yourself to me. But just so you know I'm leaving today so I won't be at the wedding. I think that may be best."

"What? Kae, baby listen, that kiss was not a mistake. I mean, yea I was drunk, yea I was pretty horny but I knew what I was doing. Otherwise I could've easily taken ten paces to my bedroom and tapped Jewel on the shoulder."

"Rick, that kiss meant something to me."

"That's what I'm telling you. It meant something to me, too. I kissed you because I wanted to kiss you. I've wanted to ever since you and Annie got here."

A soft thud in the distance caught my attention. "Did you hear something?"

"Hear what? Look Mikaela, don't leave. Amir is waiting for me so I gotta go right now but I want you to keep your phone on."

"Rick please don't do this. I've already called the airline."

"Call them back. I'll pay for it, just promise me that you won't leave, not without talking to me first. You can leave the house, get a room but Kae – don't leave Minnesota." Rick put a finger beneath my chin raising my face so that our eyes met. "Promise me."

"I promise."

Rick, leaned forward and kissed my lips softly and my soul melted. He looked deep into my eyes before turning to leave the shed. I maintained my position fighting back tears until I heard him pull out of the driveway.

*

Jewel was awake and preparing a fresh pot of coffee when I re-entered the house. Our eyes met, our silent stare broken when a hung over Annie stumbled in.

"Good morning y'all," she said through a yawn. "Whew goodness! Kae why are you dressed so early? Where you going?"

"Uhh, home. Back to Florida. Something came up and well, I need to leave."

"Whatever. I know you are not about to miss Rick's wedding for some nonsense back at home."

"Yea I know. I feel terrible but I have to get back to work."

Annie rolled her eyes at me. "Kae, you work for yourself. If there's anything wrong it's nothing that can't be resolved via cell phone, fax machine or internet access and you have all three at your fingertips. "

"Annie trust me, it's a little more serious than that. I need to be present to resolve this particular issue and no it cannot wait."

"But Kae-"

"Annie," Jewel intervened. "She's right, it is much more serious than that. Just let the bitch go."

Annie turned to face Jewel, blind fury brewing inside. I wasn't mad; it only confirmed my suspicions that everything was already out on the table.

"So you know," I calmly stated.

"Yes I know. Next time choose a better hiding spot than my freaking shed. You did the right thing by adjusting your flight arrangements but now you'd better get the f'k out my kitchen while I have this pot of hot coffee in my hand."

Annie looked back and forth confused. "What are you two talking about and Kae why are you letting her talk to you like that?"

"It's nothing, I just need to leave," I stated more firmly.

"Bull, nothing my ass. She's standing there threatening you, talking to you like you ain't nothin' and you backing down and now you wanna tell me it ain't about nothing?"

"Tell her," Jewel demanded, her voice rising slightly. "Tell her what a sorry and trifling slut you really are!"

I rolled my eyes and tried hard to control my breathing. My chest heaved in and out and my cheeks were warm. She was right to be angry but this heifer was definitely pushing it. I closed my eyes briefly and took a deep breath then stood from the table heading toward the living room and front door but Annie jumped up blocking my path. I was trying to be noble but these chics were really trying me.

"Mikaela."

I sighed. "If you must know, I kissed Rick last night. Jewel overheard us talking about it in the shed."

"You did what?" Annie backed away as though I'd just told her I had the plague. I sensed anger from my girl. Not anger caused by a betrayal to Jewel but more of a jealous rage ignited by what she viewed as my betrayal to our friendship.

"She kissed my man. Kissed him right in my home," Jewel spoke calmly as though she were talking to some invisible person that was standing near to her. "How dare you! How dare you, you trifling bitch!" she screamed, flinging the pot of coffee across the kitchen in my direction.

Annie and I quickly dove out of its path though I could not avoid being burned by small droplets that hurled through the air and settled on my flesh. The time for being noble and patient had passed, I was about to whip this heifer's ass.

The commotion caught the attention of the couple of female stragglers from the prior night's festivities. Profane threats and promises of pain and suffering were flung across the kitchen as Tiff and a friend held Jewel back and Annie pushed me toward the door.

"No Annie, let that bitch go!" Jewel screamed shoving a chair to the side to clear a path.

"Jewel, calm down. I will get her out of here but don't you make me choose sides."

"Damn that Annie, let me go!" I screamed. Annie was a thick white sista but my strength outmatched hers. I could have broken free but I allowed her to remove me from the premises. I wasn't afraid of Jewel but I wasn't up for a battle royale between her and her homegirls.

Annie grabbed my suitcase from by the door and guided me out. We walked a few houses down before she spoke.

"How could you do that Kae?" Annie asked stopping abruptly.

"Come off it, Annie. You may be speaking all these niceties to Jewel but you don't give a damn about her, this is about you."

"Come on, she's marrying the man tomorrow."

"So. What do I care, I don't owe that broad nothing. She ain't my friend."

"I am, at least I thought I was. We made a pact that we wouldn't let him come between us."

"A silly ass pact made by two silly ass teenage girls. Who cares? This doesn't have to come between us. He's not marrying you for crissakes." Our gazes locked. She was my best friend and I loved her so I backed down. "Look girl, I have a flight to catch. I'll call you when I get home."

"You know what Kae, don't even bother." Annie turned and headed back to Jewel and Rick's house.

"Whatever," I mumbled. I flipped my cell open and called information to get the phone number for Yellow Cab.

Mikaela's Story
Matters of the Broken Heart

"Meow...meow...meow..."

Farrah's cries were circling inside my mind as I wavered in the land between slumber and reality. I scratched my scalp as I rolled over on my bed.

"Meow...meow...meow..."

The cries became louder as Farrah crept closer. She jumped onto the bed and stalked toward my ear. Her persistent cries were simply her way of telling me that she was hungry, that and she was in heat. Hell she wasn't the only one. But either way I needed to get my lazy tail up and feed her. I wished that she would go plead her case to Janelle instead but I knew that wish would go unanswered.

I stretched my arms above my head and wiggled my toes. I exhaled and dropped my arms to my side. I blinked rapidly attempting to adjust my eyes to the sunlight streaming through my window.

This made day four since I'd returned from Minnesota. I'd been feeling down, depressed as it were. Monday morning I'd called and cancelled all of my appearances for the upcoming weeks. I didn't want to force myself to be happy and courteous when that wasn't what I really felt inside.

Rick had been blowing up my cell ever since he caught wind that I'd caught that flight out despite my so-called promise. I hadn't yet spoken to him. I rather let all of his calls go to voicemail, something I hadn't checked since I left either.

The one call that I was anticipating was Annie's. I expected that she would call me on this day. With the wedding on Sunday she would have flown home Monday. She would have wanted to settle back into her life on Tuesday and so it wasn't too farfetched to expect a Wednesday phone call.

I took Farrah into my arms and carried her down the stairs. The sound of happy young children rang out greeting me before their small honey sweet faces could. The pink robe laid across the seat of the old wood chair in the foyer told me there was company. I took a guess as to who it was, I was never wrong. A hearty laugh traveling from the kitchen confirmed my suspicions. I sighed but proceeded.

"Good morning y'all," I grumbled more than greeted.

"Morning?" Janelle asked, sitting the scissors she was using to cut coupons on the table. "Check the clock sweetheart."

The kitchen clock read 2:17 pm. I hadn't realized I'd slept so late. Okay, so a sista slept in, I shrugged my shoulders and took a carton of OJ out the fridge. It wasn't as though I had a job to rush to.

"Sorry, good afternoon."

Corey and one of Janelle's girlfriends nodded. Janelle eyed me sternly. I suddenly felt tension between my sister and myself. She was judging me as if I was her child and I hated that.

"What? What did I do now?" I asked sharply.

"May I speak with you in private?"

I felt like one of Janelle's children under her familiar motherly gaze. Like a teenager preparing to throw a temper tantrum I turned and sashayed to the foyer putting a tad too much force in my step. I plopped down on the chair and slumped down. I picked at my nails and waited to be chastised about something. Janelle calmly leaned her back against the banister and folded her arms defensively across her breasts.

"What J, what? I can't stand when you do this to me. Your kids are inside that room over there."

"I know that."

"So then why are you always making it your business to try and mother me?"

"Maybe because you're always in need of mothering."

"In case you've forgotten, I'm grown not to mention older than you."

"Then why don't you damn act like it?" she asked her voice heightening.

I sat upright in the chair becoming more pissed by the second. "What is this all about, Janelle?"

"I know what you did and frankly it unnerves me."

"It unnerves you? Pulling out dictionary.com words on me, you must be pissed. What are you talking about?"

"You should watch that little condescending mouth of yours before I slap you in it. Now I know you took your selfish ass up to Minnesota and broke up that wedding. I know you Kae, you did that crap on purpose. Couldn't get your way, couldn't make Ricky do what you wanted him to so you pulled a trifling stunt and messed up that poor girls whole world."

Now I was curious. I'd let that idle threat slide, I needed to know exactly what my sister was referring to. "You don't even know what the hell you're talking about. I didn't break up that got-damned wedding. I doubt that I could have even if I tried."

Janelle was agitated. Her cream colored cheeks had turned rouge. She pounded her fist into her hand as she spoke in a semi-hushed tone. "Don't damn lie to me, Mikaela. I already talked to Annie and she told me what you did. How you threw yourself at Rick and kissed him in that girl's house. "

"When did you talk to Annie? And why didn't she talk to me? She don't even know the whole story."

I was hurt. How could Annie run to my little sister behind my back? And what exactly did Janelle mean when she said I broke up a wedding. I knew there was no way Jewel was foolish enough to leave him over a little kiss. If only she'd known all the other more sexual things he'd done with other women while they were courting, she wouldn't hardly trip about a lip locking.

"Did you or did you not kiss Ricky?"

I stalled momentarily and tried to place my words properly. I wasn't looking good but it wasn't as bad as Janelle was making it out to be. I nodded. "But there's more to the story than just that. Why do you think I left? I didn't even stay for the wedding 'cause I knew it wouldn't be right. Hell he initiated it, not me. I know good and well Jewel did not break up with Rick over that."

"I don't give a good got-damned who initiated it. You shoulda slapped his butt and walked your fast ass away. And by the way, no Jewel did not leave him, he left her. So I suppose you're happy now."

"He what? Oh hecky naw, you're trippin'." I was stunned. Thoughts whirred through my brain a hundred miles an hour. Janelle continued to lay into me but I heard none of it.

I turned and headed toward the steps without another word.

"Uh uh, hell naw. You are not about to just walk away from me. You couldn't find it in you to back away from Ricky but you can walk your selfish ass away from me while I am speaking to you."

I stopped and turned. I looked past her and toward the small room under the stairs. "You may want to watch what you say."

Janelle turned to see the faces of Kya and Brianne standing focused in the doorway. While she went off to try to erase the incident from the girl's young minds, I ran to my bedroom taking two steps at a time.

Safely inside my room I locked the door behind me and dove across my bed. I grabbed my cell phone off of the nightstand and dialed into my voicemail box. I listened, smiling, to back-to-back messages from Rick saying how he needed to speak to me ASAP. His last message was left on Monday afternoon.

"I need you, Kae. Call me."

My stomach fluttered as I dialed his cell phone number. It rang and rang until his masculine voice reached me via voicemail.

"Hey this Rick. I'm not available right now but uh…you know what to do so at the beep be like Nike. Just do it."

I did and I waited…and waited…and…damn, I forgot to feed Farrah!

*

Midnight was approaching and I was still lying in my bed in a cutoff t-shirt and an old pair of big booty drawers. I was laid on my back with my ankles crossed and the remote control in my hand. I rolled my eyes as I watched booty-bouncing-black-Barbie-Beyonce glide in slo' mo' across the screen with a Pepsi in hand. *Note to self, don't drink Pepsi.* First Ludacris, now this. Mischka slept comfortably across my belly and Rick had yet to answer any of my four messages.

A soft thud called from below and jarred me. The girls and Janelle had gone to bed around nine-ish as far as I knew. I eased Mischka from my body and laid her beside Farrah. She squinted and quickly found a new spot to rest her fluffy head. I tossed the remote on the bed and eased on a pair of pink DKNY slippers. Whispery voices collaborated from down below. My heart rate quickened as I strained to recognize the voice. I headed down the stairwell and my eyes widened, I nearly lost my balance and tumbled the rest of the way down.

"Rick?" I whispered as though I really were unsure.

He turned to face me and I melted. I ran down the remainder of the stairs and into his arms. My heartbeat doubled as he held me, rocking me from side to side. A chill ran through me when he rubbed his hand through my hair.

"It's growing back already," he whispered.

"Yea, I know. I need a trim already."

"I told you not to go." His lips pressed to mine. Happiness poured over me.

"Goodnight," Janelle said in an icy tone. She glared at me but I didn't care. Screw her. Screw Annie and definitely screw Jewel's ass. It just felt too good in Rick's arms for me to give a damn about any of their feelings and envious opinions.

This Changes Everything

I laughed so hard that my ribs began to ache. The sun was high and the heat was blazing. Perspiration followed the trail down my spine and in between my brown behind cheeks. Dark sunglasses protected my pupils from the bright afternoon sunlight as I tossed my head back. Rick leaned over me smiling and trying to feed me a fresh strawberry that had been dipped in a tub of Cool Whip while at the same time tickling my exposed flesh.

I sensed the jealous vibes that floated through the salt-water air and collided with the positive love struck vibes of onlookers. Rick and I were attractive, young and wealthy African American lovers on display. He and I were having a picnic while getting a tan on Miami Beach.

I was sexy in a yellow, blue, and green metallic triangle top and tie side bottom bikini. My toes and fingers had an elegant French style that exuded classiness. I pressed my hand against Rick's firm chest in a playful attempt to push him away. I was happy again and it felt great. The past few weeks had been like this. All smiles and laughter shared between us. The only dark cloud looming over my happiness was of all people, Janelle, my own sister. By right she was supposed to hurt people for my happiness not try to sabotage me when I finally found some of my own.

I decided to let Annie cool down, I'd stopped trying to contact her and stopped waiting for her to contact me. It didn't matter much anymore, no one else was speaking to me and one more person wouldn't make much of a damn difference. Besides that, who the hell really needed friendship? I had a new man and that was all I needed to get by.

"Ha ha! Stop it!" I laughed. Rick slid his hands down my tummy in slow motion. My body relaxed and I took the fruit into my mouth easy and purposely provocative. After I chewed and digested Rick filled my mouth with his tongue, searching for the remnants of the sweet fruit. I sucked it in and held it, nibbling gently then releasing and embracing his lips between mine.

We kissed slowly and passionately, completely forgetting about the half-dressed beach patrons surrounding us. Slowly we separated but kept our focus on each other. Rick pulled my Dolce Gabanna eyewear away and looked deeply into my eyes. My heart paused as I anticipated the words *I Love You, Kae* slipping from his lips. I held my breath.

"I love days like this. You about ready to go?" he asked.

I exhaled. "Uh, yea. Sure."

"You alright?"

"Yes, of course. Why wouldn't I be?" I put on my traditional fake P.R. smile. "May I have my glasses back please, the sunlight is hurting my eyes."

Rick handed me my glasses and I pushed them on my face. He wouldn't take his eyes off of me. There was a strange look on his face. It was as though he were searching for something, some sort of answer to an unasked question. I kissed his lips quickly and moved away.

*

"Hey! Me likkle gal done finally come see her old aging granpa! Come give me some suga," Pop-Pop said, his thick brown arms extended wide.

"Hi Pop-Pop!" I inhaled deeply before accepting his love. My grandfather held me tight, cutting off all breathing, blood flow, and muscle movement for what felt like a full sixty seconds.

"And who is dis young man 'ere?"

"Pop-Pop this is my friend Ricky. You may not remember him but he went to high school with me. Rick, you remember my Granpa don't you?"

"Yea, vaguely. How are you doing, sir?" Rick extended his arm allowing my grandfather to take a firm grip.

"Just well. 'Ow 'bout ya'self?"

"Good sir. Very good, thank you?" Granpa paused momentarily and nodded while looking back and forth between the two of us. "Well don' jus stand there. Come now. Almost time ta eat."

My grandfather patted Rick on the back roughly with his thick laborers hand. The three of us walked to the back of the house where we were greeted by a few other relatives. I left Rick to mingle with the guys while I went into the kitchen to offer Grandma Daisy a helping hand. Although I burned water and my grandmother didn't hardly need my help it was the polite thing to do.

Janelle was pulling muffins out of the oven when I entered. She looked at me and rolled her eyes. I shrugged it off and reached for a piece of my Grandma's infamous jerk chicken. I'd barely lifted it to my lips before she smacked the back of my hand causing me to drop it back into the pan.

"Why ya come here an ya no tell me hi, hello, nothing? Come now, give ya granma some suga sweetheart. Where ya been hiding these days?" Grandma Daisy and Pop-Pop had been together so long she inevitably picked up on his Jamaican accent and claimed it as hers.

"Working hard-"

"Hanging out with her new stolen boyfriend," Janelle cut in.

My eyes burned holes in the side of her head. She noticed and met my glare unaffected.

"A new boyfriend, eh?"

I quickly smiled and returned my attention to our grandmother. "Well as a matter of fact, yes ma'am. His name is Rick. He's right out there, right there talking to cousin Jesse."

"Oh, he's so cute."

Janelle slapped the towel hard onto the counter. "I know you did not bring him here to a *family* function," she said stressing the word family.

"Why not? He might be family one day."

"Oh, you are insane. Y'know you are just so selfish that sometimes I don't even want to claim you!"

"Don't then, ain't no skin off my back!"

"Janelle. Mikaela. Stop it right this minute," Grandma Daisy stated firmly. She looked at both of us as if challenging us to disobey her. "Now I don' know what gwan but I won't have this nonsense tonight. 'ear?"

"Yes ma'am," we both mumbled.

I grabbed the pan of chicken and carried it out to the patio. I sat it on the table and reached inside the purse strapped around my body. I pulled my cell phone from inside and dialed Rayvon's home number. This wasn't my first attempt to reach out to Rayvon. I'd called him a couple times this evening alone. Lena answered and told me he was busy but she'd give him the message only not near that polite. I was sure she wouldn't deliver it as I was just as certain that he already knew it was me anyway.

I sighed and rubbed my forehead before putting on a happy face and returning my attention to my family and my man.

*

My cell phone rang early enough in the morning to be deemed just rude.

"Hello?" My voice was groggy and my head was spinning. Rick and I had spent the better part of the prior evening trying to outdo each other with shots of Appleton and I was feeling a little better than hung over. "Hello?"

The line was disconnected. I looked at the display but unfortunately the number was unavailable. I shrugged it off and sat the phone back on the nightstand. I rolled over and pressed my naked body against Rick's. My hand eased across his waist and found the shrunken treasure in between his thighs.

I pushed him on his back and climbed on top of him. I kissed his chest and worked my way down. His body began to stir as I neared his happy place. He looked down at me with a tired smile.

"Whatcha doing?" he asked.

"Nothing much, just exploring my options."

"Really now. Come here."

I moved back up until we were eye level. We kissed simply on the lips before he cradled me in his arms. I stroked the hairs on his chest.

"Why are you up so early anyway?" he questioned.

"Not my choice, keep getting these strange calls."

Rick sat up slightly. "Really? What do you mean strange calls?"

"Someone keeps calling from an unavailable number. When I answer they just hang up. "

Rick's demeanor changed as he took his arm back to his side. He suddenly seemed to drift away loosing interest in my presence.

"What time is it?" he asked.

I sighed and rolled away. "About seven. You hungry?

Wanna go to breakfast?"

"Nah, tired."

"Go on back to sleep baby. I'm going to take a shower."

Rick kissed my forehead and turned on his side. I secretly huffed and rolled out of the bed and went to shower.

I heard the faint sound of early a.m. television as I reached the bottom of the stairwell. I shuffled into the kitchen and joined Janelle at the table.

"Good morning."

"Good morning," I answered. "What you watching?"

"Judge Mathis."

"Oh. I like him." I sat quietly listening to the case of the slumlord who threw his pregnant tenant out onto the cold Chicago streets in the middle of the winter. When a commercial came on I told Janelle what I needed to tell her. "I think you ought to know that Rick is going to be moving in."

The only sound in the room was that of the White girl who wanted to share with the world how Keiser College had changed her life.

"Did you hear me?" I asked.

"I heard you."

"Well?"

"Oh what, now you want my opinion?"

"Not really."

"I think it's foolish. You two haven't been together long enough for you to become a live-in couple. You don't even know each other. All you know are the teen and telephone etiquette versions and now you swear you're soul mates. The only real reason you want him is because someone else almost got him. But you don't want my opinion so I'll keep it to myself."

The silence returned. We watched a Target commercial intently as though it were a daytime drama and we were trying

The Miki Starr Storybook

66

to follow the storyline.

"Rick is moving in, Janelle."

"If he moves in, we move out," she said calmly before taking a sip of her Starbucks blend.

"What, so now you're giving me an ultimatum."

"No, I'm giving you notice."

Janelle politely got up from her seat and placed her coffee mug in the sink. She walked past me and left me behind in my kitchen alone.

You Told Me So

I was in a state of disbelief when the car service driver eased on the brakes behind the mini UHAUL that was parked in front of my home. My bottom lip in my lap as angry thoughts, frustration, sadness, and denial piled up and attacked one another inside my mind.

Rick spoke some words, which passed through the breeze aimed at me, but my ears were not receptive. My body slid from the car in what felt like slow motion. I crept toward the truck as though I were afraid it would attack. I peered inside. Bags filled with little girl's clothes, a tot bed, and a handmade dresser. I jumped at Rick's gentle touch. He rubbed my arms as my emotions began to merge together.

"Well, this is awkward," that was Janelle. She was strolling out of my front door, a half eaten apple in one hand, a battered blue suitcase in the other. The same suitcase she came with the night she left her husband for good. "I didn't expect the two of you for another day at least."

"Damn J, how can you possibly be serious about this?" I asked making my aggravation apparent through my tone.

"Why would you think that I were not? You know me better than anyone on this earth. You know that I mean what I say and

I don't do idle threats."

She continued her nonchalant stroll past Rick and I, as if her abandoning me were justified just because I had moved Rick in. She bit into her Granny Smith. Her eyes rolled to the back of head as if it were the sweetest juice that had ever had the honor of gracing her tongue. Part of me wanted to cry while the other wanted to smash that got-damned green apple in her gloating golden face!

My physical took on its own set of socially acceptable rules and I began in Janelle's direction without first clearing it with my good sense. My eyes went past my sister and landed on the tanned faces of Kya and Brianne. The sisters held hands and swung them back and forth as they exited the house, completely oblivious, as children should be to the tension between Mom and Aunt.

I back down. That was near four weeks ago.

*

The house was eerily quiet when I rolled out of bed. The sunlight streamed through my window and fell softly across my empty bed. I slid into my house shoes and wriggled my knee length nightgown down to its proper position. Farrah clawed lightly at my bedroom door. Since Rick moved in, she'd moved out of my room as he didn't want animals in his personal space.

I opened the door and saw Mischka waiting beside her. I took my kitten into my arms and carried her down the curved stairwell as Farrah followed. I pretended that the aroma of turkey bacon, eggs, grits, pancakes, and fresh squeezed orange juice mingled in the air. I closed my eyes and carefully took the last couple of steps. I scratched behind Mischka's ears as I stepped through the archway.

I tried to imagine an early a.m. judge scolding some unruly excuse filled teen. I imagined that Janelle was standing behind the kitchen counter twisting new oranges around an old school juicer. I imagined Kya and Brianne standing at the sliding door teasing Langston. I even imagined Corey sitting at my kitchen table scarfing down fried eggs unaffected by my presence.

A noise coming from behind me caused my visions to disappear instantly. I jumped and turned quickly in time to see Rick entering through the front door, sweat glistening on his forehead.

"Hey," I said.

"Wassup?" he replied with a slight head nod.

We awkwardly watched each other. "Running?"

"Yea. Wanted to…before it got too hot."

"Want breakfast?"

"You cooking?"

I raised and eyebrow and shook my head no.

"I'm good," he said.

"Ok." I turned and carried Mischka to her dish. I listened to Rick's footsteps fade away as he jogged up the stairs.

*

"I've missed you so much girl," I said as I embraced Menisa in a friendly hug.

"Oh mama, I've missed you too. Glad you decided to stop hibernating. How have you been?"

We took a seat across from one another at the Aventura Ruby Tuesdays. "I've been well."

"Kae, don't front. Rayvon already told me Janelle moved out. You're telling me you're okay with that?"

I laughed uncomfortably. "Girl, please. My man is there. We can run through the crib butt-booty ass naked without fear of doing permanent psychological damage to someone's shorty. I'm straight."

"If you say so."

Our waitress came and took our order then left us alone to play catch up.

"Well to answer the unasked question, yes Lena and Rayvon are still together but they decided they wanted to have an open relationship - "

"Which basically means she's messing around on him."

"Basically."

We laughed. It felt much better than great.

"And what about you big sexy?" I asked. I took a sip of my cranberry and Vodka.

"What about me?" she played dumb. She knew what I was asking about. It was the same question I always asked over drinks.

"Still haven't met anyone worthy of replacing Eddie?"

"Hell no. Nothing but jerks and assholes in my circle."

"Really? Or is it that you're just not over Eddie yet?"

"Oh I'm over Eddie. I don't have choice. I just found out he's having a baby."

"Nisa, no."

Menisa nodded. Eddie, or Eduardo Perez, was the love of Menisa's life for three years. Until he went through some mid-twenties crisis and decided he needed time to get to know himself better. She tried everything she could to work through it and get back together but it wasn't until her eventual burn out that he realized what he had in her. He hadn't appreciated her and what they had and so she vowed not to go back to him. That was a year ago and she still had not officially moved on.

Menisa continued taking the conversation down a whole new path. "He'll forgive you, y'know."

I sat my glass on the table and huffed. I'd been wondering when this topic would surface. "He'll forgive me. You say that as if I did something wrong."

"Well ya kinda did shorty. You smacked his girl."

"That trick tried to kiss me again."

"True, true dat. But let's look at it from a different angle. You willingly kissed her in the past-"

"I was drunk. Why does everyone continue to forget that little detail? "

"Yea well, you hit on her knowing that she was into you. You wanted her to come on to you just so you could hit her. In some circles that's called entrapment. "

I opened my mouth to defend myself but our secretly transsexual waitress returned to clear our dishes. I ordered a Long Island, Menisa ordered the same.

"How's he doing? His health holding up? "

Menisa paused before opening her mouth to speak. She smiled. It wasn't a happy smile nor a sad one. One of those empathetic ones.

"Not very well. He's been bedridden for the past couple days and refusing to take his medication. Lena has to literally force it down his throat. I worry but I try not to show it. You know how stubborn your boy can be."

I looked away at the ceiling, at nothing, just trying not to cry. F'king Rayvon. F'king HIV.

"I'll try calling him again."

"Swallow your damn pride and just go see him."

"I will."

Rayvon was diagnosed with HIV two years ago. He was given medication to keep it from progressing. He may already have had full-blown AIDS if I hadn't been there to do what the doctors said. I was the one with the energy to fight him, the one whose stubbornness outmatched his. And then he met Lena and if nothing else she supported him. Either way it was clear that now was a poor time for me to be childish.

"So what about you, Kae? You ready to be honest?" Menisa asked sipping the fresh drink that had been placed before her.

"And just what on Earth are you talking about?"

"I know you're not as happy as you claim to be. I could hear it in your tone when you called."

"Oh really, Ms. Cleo?" Menisa raised an eyebrow and I

opened up. That was the downside to alcohol, worse than hangovers…honesty. "I don't think Rick and I are working out. I mean, everything was gravy the first couple of weeks but then it seemed like overnight life flipped the damn script on me. We were the best of friends and now we hardly speak. We argue over stupid shit. My pussy so freaking backed up I need Drano to unclog it before I even try to get some again!"

Menisa and my eyes met before laughing so hard alcohol damn near flew out our nose. I continued to get everything that had been bugging me off my chest. "Girl he smokes. He didn't smoke when he was with her. He's a slob. He picks his friggin' toenails in the kitchen!"

"No!"

"Yes! Aaargh! Jewel can take his ass back, what the hell was I thinking? I didn't know he'd picked up so many bad habits over the years. Hadn't seen him face to face in over four years before we went to Minnesota. I guess J was right after all." Confessing that made me sick to my stomach but I kept my poker face.

"Okay, alright enough of this depressing crap. Let's talk about birds."

"Sunny days."

"Let's talk about uh, fast cars!"

"Let's talk about money and cute boys we wanna suck in the back seat of fast cars!"

We laughed and drank more. Had Menisa not called it a night I may have drunk myself into a stooper and crashed under my dinner table right there in that restaurant.

*

The house was dark when I entered after 2 a.m. I tossed my keys on the table and went into my kitchen to check on Langston. The sickening stench of cigarette poison consumed my nostrils. I tugged at my hair and walked out onto the patio. Rick was laid back in one of the wooden chairs that Corey built for Janelle. His legs were propped up, a cigarette dangling from his lips. My eyes rolled to the back of my head. Rick spoke up before I could.

"Where you coming from this late?" he asked while simultaneously blowing smoke into the Miami night.

I stooped down and scratched behind Langston's ear. "Out with my girl Menisa."

"You couldn't call?"

"I could have."

Silence.

"Hey, I'm going to take a trip up North for a couple days."

My heart paused. "Up north? For what?"

"I just need a break, Kae. I haven't seen my boys in ages and well…me and you…me and you need a break."

"Are you going to see her?"

"Aaaw hell Kae, come off of that please. I'm sick of hearing about it."

"I know that's her calling my damn phone."

"Probably is."

More silence.

"Well why do you have to go to Minnesota for a break? Of all the places you could go - "

"Because that's where I feel most comfortable."

Again silence.

"Ok…you're right. Well, do what you gotta do. I would never want you to be uncomfortable. I'm going to take a shower and hit the sack."

I turned to walk away. I stopped and looked at the back of his head. He didn't look back. I walked into the house and closed the patio door.

Making Amends

I stood at the front door of the apartment contemplating everything from what to say to how to react once I was received on the other side. My hands were crossed in front of me and my head was down. I took a deep breath and raised my head, held it high and proud and knocked gently. Gently at first but when there was no answer my knock became a bit more anxious, more aggressive.

"I'm coming," came the voice from the other side. "Just hold on a damn minute."

Footsteps slapped hard against the floor. The sound traveled though the floor was carpeted. The locks were undone but the door was not immediately opened.

"Who is it?"

"Mikaela."

After a brief contemplative pause the door swung open.

"Mm. Long time no see."

"It's great to see you too," I grumbled unenthusiastically. I closed and locked the door behind me. I followed Rayvon to his bedroom in the rear of the apartment. He continued through and into his private bathroom. Offering not so much as an "excuse me" he closed the door behind him. I took a seat in the antique-like padded back wooden chair that was set beside his bed.

General Hospital was on the screen. I watched as Sonny sweet-talked his heart and soul, Carly. I could hear Rayvon on the other side of the door coughing, a deep throaty cough before spewing the contents of his contaminated lungs into the toilet. Soon after it flushed and water smacked against the porcelain sink.

The door opened and Rayvon exited. He slow strolled to his bed and crawled beneath the duvet without first removing his robe. He pulled until it was tucked securely beneath his nostrils.

"These so-and-so's is meant for each other, I don't know why they are always trying to front," he spoke suddenly.

"Please. That Carly is such a skank. He need to just leave her alone once and for all."

"Kae, please. Can you see watching this bullshit and not seeing Carly and Sonny getting on each other's nerves? Really, no matter what character flaws exist some people are just meant to be together…no matter what."

Our eyes met, my heart melted. That moment lasted just that long. Abruptly we returned our attention to the television and began to talk about everything from that mentally challenged looking kid Michael, to the dumb ass Maroone commercial, to whatever else came to mind. Basically we just picked up where we'd left off.

*

It was hotter than a son-of-a-I'll-be-got-damned! outside and I had so much on my mind. I didn't want to go home and dwell on things. Tired of being down. Tired of being low. Sick and tired of being the enemy. I parked my car and dreaded to leave my loving air conditioning behind. I took a deep breath and stepped out into the sunshine.

I wore as little as I could get away with and still be the

classy bia-bia that I am. A pair of red thong sandals separated my soft feet from the hard concrete. I wore a white sleeveless button down with matching brand red short-shorts. With a red mini guess purse in hand I headed down Lincoln Rd.

I stopped to get a closer look at the merchandise of the street vendors. I picked up a beautiful Opal necklace and matching ring. I turned off the road and into one of the shops. I hadn't paid any attention to what sort of shop I'd entered, I just knew that the beads of sweat that were trying to make their way from my armpits and down the side of my body was less than appealing.

I strolled through the shop admiring the hand carved Indian artwork. I held a few pieces in my hand, shifted from a yes to a no to yes but then ultimately back to a no. I needed more crafts in my home like a blind man needed a color-chart.

I picked up the sight of a beautiful journal in my peripheral. A lovely wooden case stood solo near the front door, which housed many a variety of wonderful books. Journals to be exact and their pages were crying out to be blessed with the touch of a perfect pen. I took one into my palms, held it like a precious pearl. I gently opened to the center and inhaled every detail of that papyrus used. With one finger I softly brushed the page, became one with the page. I closed the journal and held it to my breast. It had called to me and I had answered. I carried it to the counter to pay. Fifteen dollars but well worth every cent.

Feeling a bit better about things I left the store behind. The heat once again embraced me and at that moment I knew it was time for me to leave. I headed across the street to a 31 Flavors and purchased a small cup of Cookies n' Cream ice cream. I was so engaged in my new tasty treat that I walked directly into a patron as I left the ice cream shop.

"Excuse me," I mumbled and continued on.

"Mikaela."

The voice stopped me in my tracks. I raised my head and

turned to look behind me. Sure enough standing there blocking out all the sunlight was Corey.

"What are you doing down here?" I asked.

"Damn, a nigga can't get a little shopping done without being judged?"

I took a spoonful of ice cream into my mouth. "I wasn't judging, I just didn't expect to see you down here."

"Oh yea. Well, I was just saying wassup. Holla."

Corey turned to walk away. I paused momentarily then started on my route once again.

"Corey," I called, stopping yet again.

"Yea."

"You down here alone?"

"Yea. Why, wassup?"

"Feel like catching a bite to eat?"

Corey paused, said nothing. He appeared like a deer caught in headlights but quickly pulled himself together and returned to his tough guy demeanor.

"Yea, why not? That spot over there got some good ass linguini."

"Cool."

Not many words were spoken as we sat at the outdoor table. It seemed we were both anxious to see our waitress as it gave us an opportunity to speak out. But once she was gone so went our words. Small talk was made. Basically and mostly about how damn hot it was.

Our food was finally delivered giving the both of us a break from trying to be cordial to one another. I found myself full half way through my meal but forced myself to continue to eat just to have something to do with my mouth and my hands.

"When's the last time you talked to Janelle," I asked once I realized my stomach could bear salmon no longer.

"This morning. Kya had a doctor's appointment that I took her to."

"She okay?"

"Who? Janelle?"

"Kya."

"Yea, she's cool."

"A-and Janelle?"

"She's fine. Janelle will be fine in any situation. She does miss you though if that's what you're getting at."

That was what I was getting at. I was silent for a moment.

"Did she say anything?"

"About what?" he asked.

"You know. About what happened between us?"

Corey sat his Long Island on the table and exhaled. "Damn Mikaela, you invited me to lunch so you can find out how much I know. I ain't gettin' in that. That's between you and yo' sister. You want to know how she feel, what she think, then ask her."

"Oh negro, please. You being up in my crib all the damn time make you part of the b'niss," I replied becoming instantly offended.

"Well Janelle don't live there no more so I ain't gotta be all up in yo' shit no mo' do I? Man, forget this. This was a bad idea. How much I owe for this?"

"No worries, it's on me."

"Bet that up. I'm out."

I sighed and swallowed my pride. Corey wasn't my favorite person in the world but next to Janelle he was the realest person I knew and the closest I could get to have my family at this time.

"Corey sit down," I demanded. He gave me a look like I had called out his momma. "Please."

"What's wrong with you girl? Why you wanna be around me all of a sudden?"

"I need to know something Corey. Me and my sister are just alike. We both can be cantankerous bitches with stank attitudes yet you like J and hate me. Why is that?"

Corey laughed. Not quite the response I was expecting. "I don't hate you girl. You just get on my f'kin' nerves."

"Whoa, big difference."

"It is a huge difference. You know what separates you and your sister? You're phony. You're overcompensating for something but you really want people to believe that you're this perfect person that has everything together and all the answers. Janelle will tell you her down falls straight up. She never disguises herself as something that she is not and never puts herself above the rest of the world."

"Oh please. I tell people upfront that I'm a bitch all the time."

"You say it like it's something to be proud of. Like – like it's a badge of honor. Diva-bitch. That don't count for nothing Mikaela."

I wanted to throw the last piece of salmon in his red friggin' face. I wanted to tell him that he didn't know what the hell he was talking about. I wanted to say that but how could I build up enough force to say it when I knew damn well that what he said was true.

I sat back in my chair and played with my fork. I chewed the inside of my lip feeling Corey's eyes on me, judging me though I pretended not to care. I put on a face that said I was disregarding everything he said but somehow I believe he saw right through it.

"Corey, do you have a girlfriend?"

"What?" his expression changed. He smiled and his faint dimples found their way to sunlight. "Where'd that come from? What, you offering?"

"Just wondering. I mean something has to be stopping you and Janelle from hooking up."

"Ah ha. Man, I love Janelle but it's more the way a man loves his l'il sister. I would do anything for her and for Kya and Briane. Anything but give her some of this," he said groping between his legs.

"I see you're just as vulgar as I suspected."

"You damn right," Corey laughed.

I contemplated. "You saying if J wanted some, you would tell her no."

"Couldn't do it."

My lips twisted in doubt. "What if you came by and the girls were gone and she was waiting there, bucket nekkid? You gonna go grab her a robe?"

His eyes moved away for a moment then came back. "Ay, Janelle fine as all get out. I think it might hafta be a l'il incest in the family tree. Nigga can only be so honorable."

I grinned feeling a hint of butterflies as I recognized just how cute Corey really was. I shrugged it off and spent the next fifteen minutes finding a polite way to say this "date" is done.

*

It was still early when I headed home. I was bored and lonely. I already knew that Menisa was working a double shift and I couldn't take sitting around Rayvon for too long when he was sick. I had tickets for a comedy show that was going on for the evening. A long awaited one. I'd bought the tickets so that Rick and I could attend. Alas Rick was still in Minnesota with "Amir".

I turned the key to unlock the door. The sound echoed when it closed. I tossed the keys on the table and headed for my phone. I checked my messages. Not a one from Rick. I hadn't heard from him since he left me the message saying that he'd touched ground seven days ago. I shrugged it off and picked up the receiver. I scanned the list of numbers written on the tiny index paper until I saw the initials C.M. I held my breath.

"Yea?" Corey answered.

"That's how you answer your phone? Yea?"

"Yea."

"Whatever. Sorry to bother you. You busy?"

"Nah, not really. Wassup? "

"Nothin' much. I just have a spare ticket to the comedy show tonight and if you're not busy…well, maybe you want to go."

"Mikaela Johnson askin' me out on a date?"

"Hell naw."

"Well damn you too!" he laughed again. It was a nice laugh. A hearty laugh. "Aiight. You pickin' me up right?"

"No. I told you it ain't a date. You can meet me at the auditorium. 8pm."

"Trifling ass. Aiight, I'a meet you there. Bye."

"Bye."

I returned the phone to its cradle. I don't know why but I felt good, better than I'd felt in a long time. I smiled as I ran up to my bedroom to get dressed. I smiled, a genuine smile and couldn't stop.

Mikaela's Story
As my world turns

"She doesn't want to see me." I shifted in the passenger seat as the car moved along. I ran my fingers through my growing hair repeatedly more out of nervousness than anything else. I hadn't seen nor spoken to Amori in a couple of months. I missed her and missed her fashions even more but after the breakdown in our relationship I didn't know how to come back into her world.

Now here I was in Corey's Avalanche on my way to make a pit stop at Amori's house. Three months ago I would not ever have pictured myself here, with Corey, afraid to see Amori, living alone and having no contact with my best friend Annie.

Now don't get it twisted. I discovered that Corey is not half bad after all. He can even be an entertaining person to be around. But there is no more to our relationship than that. He's pretty cool people but I am not the least bit interested in pursuing anything further with this kat. Quiet as kept I sincerely doubt that he has any intimate feelings toward me.

"Stop trippin'. You need to squash whatever is going on between you two, bottom line. Amori is good people. Jill is good people."

Jill? What the-? "Please do not tell me that Jill is going to be there."

"And so what if she is. Ay man, what's your problem with Jill?"

"Simple. I don't like her and that broad don't like me."

"You got some deep seeded issues Kae, for real. I'll tell you one thing. That's my dog so whatever negative energy you harboring, I'm gone advise you keep that shit on the DL while we at the crib."

He had a lot of damn nerve! Trying to tell me how I need to behave with regards to this heifer that I have never liked. I spat all sorts of profane insults in his direction. Problem was it was all contained within the confine of my mind. I bit my tongue, something I do for no one. I folded my arms defensively across my breast and twisted my lips in an effort to make sure he knew that I was upset and he was the object of my bitter obsession.

"Girl you better fix your face," Corey said as he used one hand to push my arms from my breasts. I fought effortlessly against him and the smile that took up residency upon my face.

My heart seemed to stop as the vehicle pulled into Amori's driveway. I took a deep breath and jumped from the car. I pulled a pair of bug-eye D&G sunglasses from my leather purse and slipped them onto my face. I felt more comfortable that way. Sort of like the kid from Big Daddy, when Adam Sandler slipped those cheap dime store lenses on his ashy little snot-filled nose.

I stood with my back to the door. I heard Belle open it but I remained firm in my position with my head held high until I heard Corey's footsteps move from concrete to marble. I inhaled deeply, turned and followed suit. My stomach fluttered as I walked forward but I refused to let it show on the outside. I took in another breath, shook my short hair back and caught up to Corey, entering the studio side-by-side. Silence fell over everyone in the room. Amori mumble into her cell phone, "Lemme call you back." Jill cut her eyes at Corey, I could see all of her cynical questions forming in her eyes.

Brenda smiled. She moved swiftly from behind her desk and

headed in our direction, her arms spread open wide. And I, Ms. Mikaela Johnson, felt like the biggest ass alive! I removed my glasses from my eyes and returned her love as I returned her embrace. The one person that Corey failed to mention, Brenda was good people too.

"I'm sorry Brenda, for being so mean to you," I spoke into her ear.

"Don't worry about it. You were upset, I'm not bothered."

Though appreciative I began to feel a bit uncomfortable with the affection. I pulled away gently and felt at ease. That feeling didn't last long.

"Welcome home," Amori spoke with a smile on her face.

"Thank you, ma. I have a reading in San Diego next week. You got anything in there for me?"

"I always have and I always will."

"Oh, I don't believe this," Jill spoke up looking at Corey but referring to me.

"Giirl don't start!" I turned to face Jill ready for showdown number two, despite just being reunited with true friends. I hadn't forgot that the bitch had sucker punched me. She was still on notice.

"Was I speaking to you?" Jill retorted.

"Ay!" Our attention immediately went to Corey. "Y'all need to cut this nonsense out. I bet you two don't even remember why y'all don't like each other. You just bicker like hens out of habit!"

I opened my mouth to defend my position but my mind drew a blank. Why was I always so angry with Jill? Did it have anything at all to do with Jill as a person? Not really. It was more about who she reminded me of. That woman that my daddy slept with when he was supposed to be sleeping with my mother. That woman that I blame for my sister and I growing up without parents and without the baby brother that my mother was carrying when she was killed.

But all of that wasn't Jill Lauren's business and it definitely was not Corey's business. It was information that did not need to be shared outside of anyone in a blood circle. No one in the room was connected by blood therefore my secrets were not their business.

I threw my hands up in defeat. What was the use? Carrying a grudge that was powerful enough to come between me and those who cared for me most? Jill Lauren was not that woman. Jill Lauren could bear no blame in what happened to my mother, father and unborn baby brother. I needed something positive in my life again. I'd forgotten what it was like to wake up with a smile on my face and carry that smile until it was time to close my eyes at night. Harboring ill feelings for an innocent bystander was not going to get me there.

"You're right. If I did something to you Jill to cause this conflict, I apologize."

Jill looked at me long and hard. It was as though she was looking for some sort of truth in my eyes, an answer maybe. A reason to believe me possibly. As far as I was concerned she didn't have to believe me. My apology was real, it was true and it took a twenty-pound weight off of my shoulder and I wouldn't trade that for the world.

"Yea okay, so Corey who are you taking with you?" Jill asked reaching inside of her purse. She pulled out what appeared to be two tickets and handed them to him.

"How many is it, four? My cousin want to take his girl so maybe I'll let Kaela roll with me." He grinned in my direction.

I wanted to say, *Forget you negro, I don't want to go anywhere with you.* I didn't. I rolled my eyes and half smiled.

"Mm, you two do make a cute couple," Brenda said as she returned to her work.

Corey and I glanced at one another but shrugged it off. She didn't know what the hell she was talking about.

*

If I were honest I would admit that Corey and I were going out on a double date. But there was no way that I would confess to that if he weren't going to. That wasn't going to stop me from looking sexy as hell! I was going to make him want me even if I didn't want him.

I changed my clothing at least fifteen times but finally settled on a short little number which I'd only worn once before and was sure that by now no one would recall. I shimmied into the sheer Chanel printed lace dress with a satin and gros grain ankle strap Chanel heel. I dabbed fragrance in all the right places and made it downstairs just in time to greet Corey at the front door.

The look on his face said it all. Yea, he tried to be smooth and subtle but he couldn't hide the desire in his eyes. I must admit however, I was digging on his aqua linen suit and open toe leather sandals. We both perpetrated and walked to his car not commenting on how good the other was looking.

I'd grown accustomed to the Theatre. Seeing actors interpret brilliant pieces on Broadway was more than a tad bit different than watching Shemar Moore do his thing in some God or Mama or No-Good Brother play but I enjoyed it nonetheless.

At intermission I parted ways with Corey as I needed to check my face and gear though I told him that I really needed to go. Truth be told I wouldn't dare do my business, one or otherwise, in public facilities. I made my way through a tough crowd as I proceeded back to the auditorium to rejoin my party. I nearly made it without incident but mere steps before the double doors a strong heel met with my expensive shoes.

"Ow! Dammit, watch where you're going," I complained not paying any attention to the fact the person connected to that heel may have the ability to whip my l'il brown ass. Not wanting to entertain that prospect I continued forward.

"Mikaela."

"Yes?" I stopped dead in my tracks. My heart paused for moments and only beat again out of a necessity to keep me alive. I closed my eyes to blink and dreaded reopening them, as I would then be eye to eye with none other than Jibari. I swallowed hard and took on a non-flinching stance.

"Damn you look fine girl. Can I get some love?" he asked.

I chuckled and looked him over. Damn he looked good! "You must be kidding."

"Alright, I deserve that. Ay shorty, can we talk for a moment?" He asked.

"Talk about what Jibari? Didn't your *wife* already do enough talking for you?" I reminded him that I hadn't forgotten why we were no longer together.

"Kae, please. Just give me a few minutes."

I sighed and sucked my teeth. I still harbored feelings of love and desire for Jibari. I didn't want to but how could I not. Just because the bastard is married with kids doesn't change how my heart skips its beats. "You got two minutes, Jibari."

I followed him to a quiet corner near the lobby. He spoke no words immediately. Just licked his lips and looked me over like I was the last pork chop at Sunday dinner. He reached for my hips and though I wanted to stop him, I wanted to push him away and call him a no good, trifling motherf'ker, I didn't. I succumbed to the power that he held over me.

"I see you cut your hair. I like it," he whispered in my ear. I shifted, tightening my love muscles as his tongue traced the outline of my ear.

"Yea. Thanks."

"Kae baby, don't be mad."

"Give me one good reason why I shouldn't be mad."

"I still love you baby. That shit with T, I'm leaving her. I was working on getting out of that relationship back then but with the kid and shorty on the way the bitch kinda had me by the balls. She was refusing to let me go."

He turned my back to him and I could feel his nature rising behind his jeans. He continued to breathe slow and steady against my flesh as his tongue danced in and out. His body gyrated in slow motion, at a rate where no one but us knew for sure what was going on though I am sure passerby's speculated.

"So what's different now?" I asked losing fervor. I swallowed hard.

"We worked it out."

"So what are you saying?" Why do we as women even bother to put ourselves through this sort of bullshit anyway? I knew Jibari was no good for me yet I could not seem to find the courage to resist his touch.

"Who you here with?"

"A friend of mine."

"A nigga no doubt."

"No doubt."

"Call me after the show and I'll meet you at your crib. We can talk some more then."

"I'm on a date." I couldn't believe I said that. "You want I should dump my date to go home to a man that dumped me for his wife?"

"You love that nigga?"

"What does that have to do with anything?"

He turned me to face him. "You love that nigga?"

"No," I answered barely audible.

"Aiight then. Let's say about midnight?" He kissed my lips and disappeared before I could answer.

I stood alone trying to regroup. I adjusted myself and returned to the bathroom to clean myself up before returning to the group with a lame explanation about what had taken me so long. I don't think anyone, not even Corey, really cared.

*

Rick was due to return. He'd called and said that he would be back on Friday and that I was to meet him at the arrival gate at 6:45 pm. I was reluctant about seeing him. He'd already been gone for so long. And with the way things were going before he'd left I wasn't sure what was in store when he came back to me.

*

It was past noon when I awoke the next morning. I shuffled into the kitchen and fixed myself a hot pot of coffee. I thought about Rick and the brief relationship that we'd shared in comparison to the lifetime friendship, which blessed our past. I wondered if we should have left well enough alone. Or maybe things would be better upon his return. Maybe we just needed a break from one another. After all we did move into this aspect of our relationship full steam ahead.

The phone rang interrupting my thoughts. I picked up the receiver from the wall mount.

"Hello?"

"You did the right thing."

"What? Who is this?" I jumped up and two-stepped to the Caller ID. "Annie?"

"Yea. I talked to Jewel. Look sis, I'm sorry about getting so mad at you over this Rick thing. It's just that…well… anyway, I think hat was really big of you."

"What was big of me? What the hell are you talking about?"

"Giving up Rick. Admitting you were wrong and letting him go back to her."

"What?" My face was flushed. That son of a - this bitch! "You're calling to tell me that Rick and Jewel are back together?"

"Well not quite but he's been doing an awful lot of begging. She said he said it was your idea. Oh, don't tell me you didn't know."

I was quiet. Stupefied. He was trying to work it out with Jewel and he hadn't bothered to end things with me first. How could he? This son of a - didn't have the nerve to call me and tell me!

I didn't want to say anything that I may regret to Annie. After all she was still my sister and best friend. I was sure she took some amount of satisfaction in my predicament but I had opted to put up with her bullshit personality traits a long time ago and couldn't start judging her on them now. I slammed the phone back into its cradle and fumed. It rang again, the sound irritating me more than a simple phone ring should be allowed to. I lifted it and slammed it back into its place again.

I returned to the kitchen table, fighting a winning battle with the tears that were forming in my eyes. I huffed and could swear that steam shot from my ears. I folded my arms across my breast as I wished every evil torment to land upon Rick while on his quest to return to Jewel's good graces. I was focused so intently on my makeshift voodoo curse that I didn't hear Jibari until he was right upon me.

"Mikaela," he stressed my name as though it was not the first time he'd called it out.

"What?" I snapped.

"What is wrong with you?" he asked. My answer was rolling my eyes and looking away. "Anyway, I gotta get out of here. I'll check you out later."

That was when I noticed that he was fully dressed. "Where are you going? I thought we were going to spend the day together."

"Yea, my bad. I forgot about some stuff I need to do."

"You mean like get home to your wife before she start asking too many questions."

"Now Kae, you know it ain't even like that."

"Do I? Just get out my house."

"Mikaela, stop trippin'."

"Jibari, get out!"

He stared at me momentarily as though he was trying to decide whether to beat my ass or get turned on and beat his dick. His cell vibrated and he instead opted to leave rather than take the call right there. I kept my eyes glued to his back as he walked to the front door. I vaguely heard his promise to call me later but shoved it someplace in the back of my mind. I twisted the locks on the door and turned my back against it. I slid to the wood earth below. This time I didn't fight the salty water that pushed forward.

What was my life coming too?

Mikaela's Story
No More Drama

I sat back on Janelle's new comfy blue sofa with one foot beneath my behind, the other in front of me as I cleaned old nail polish from my naked toes. It was definitely time for a pedicure. Kya and Brianne sat on either side of me with water-dipped cotton balls imitating Auntie Kae. I smiled to myself. I missed having them around more than I had realized. They were likely the closest that I'd ever get to a child anyway. Them, Farrah, Mischka, and Langston 'cause Lord knows I am not mother material. Maybe when I get old…like forty.

Janelle entered the living room with a tray of ice-cold lemonade. She sat it on the table before us. I stopped what I was doing and picked up the smaller cups first and handed them to my little girls. I then picked up one of the taller ones and swallowed half of it in one gulp. I was thrilled to be back in my sister's good graces but I wasn't going to tell her so. I'm sure she shared my contained excitement.

Things were nearly back as they should be. It was just like old times sitting there in that living room. The only difference being that it was her living room and not my own. I wanted to ask her to move back in with me but I knew that she would decline my offer. The only reason that she had done so in the beginning was to get her mind right after she'd caught her ex husband cheating with her ex best girlfriend. It was never her intent to stay with me long term, it had just sort of turned out that way. As it seemed some good had come out of our falling out after all.

"When are you going to tell me about that brother you went out with the other night?" I asked.

"There isn't anything to tell. Better yet, why don't you tell me what's going on with you and Corey. You two are what now?"

"Are nothing. And it's interesting how you just changed the subject. Fine, if you wanna be like that. We went out a few times. I'm sure he already told you everything anyway."

"Of course but I want to hear it from your lips. I want you to tell me yourself just how you really feel about him."

I rolled my eyes and shook my head from side to side. "He's cool people. I guess I can see why you choose to spend time around him but that is all. I don't want to be confused with someone that gives too much of a damn about the brother however."

"You better care about the language you use around my girls I know that much," Janelle scolded reminding me why I was far from being a mother dearest. My womb would be staying on lockdown for quite a long time, word up!

My PDA chimed from within my purse. Janelle grabbed it from the floor beside her chair and tossed it to me. I reached inside, pulling it out. The message displayed was from Jibari. I blew stress from my body and tried my best to recoup some sense of relaxation. I was sick and tired of these brothers and their bullshit games. Seriously. It's not as though I am one of those ring-chasing heifer's out at the club every payday trying to see how many dicks I could suck but damn, there must come a time in ones life where relationships should be taken seriously.

There had been many guys in and out of my world

throughout my dating career but I believe that Jibari and Rick took the most out of me. I got a call from Rick finally. Friggin' coward. Told me how sorry he was. That he'd made a mistake, that he'd allowed his lust for me to get the better of him. That nonsense was supposed to make me feel better about the situation.

I must say that I did love Rick and I still do. We'll always be friends, I just need time to put this affair behind me. And as much as I hate to admit it I could never love him the same way that Jewel does. I suppose that's the type of love he needs and Janelle was right. And though I intend to maintain a friendship with him, between you and I, I hope Jewel leaves him sitting on the curb Keith Sweat-in' her ass as he deserves!

I stood from the couch being careful not to smudge my polish as I slipped my foot inside of the thong sandals that I'd worn. I had to meet Jibari, needed to hear what he had to say. Since I'd permitted him back into my world my nights were filled with earth shattering orgasms while my days were full of nothing more than straight nigga bullshit.

After weeks of sleeping together we were finally being seen in public once again. Of course we were meeting at places like Las Olas and Fort Lauderdale Beach, far from any place his wife may just so happen to be. All this despite the fact that he and she were supposedly no longer involved. Yea right.

"Is that your *friend*?" Janelle asked.

"If that's what you wanna call him. But if it's Corey you're talking about then no."

"Who is it?"

"You don't even wanna know." I threw my purse on my shoulder. I held it at my side so it would not bump the girls on the head as I kissed them goodbye.

Janelle eyed me with a look of disgust and contempt on her face. "You know what? Nope, never mind. It's your life. You do whatever you want."

"Yea, thank you. I really needed your permission to do that."

Janelle stood from her seat and walked me to the front door of her apartment. We stood and looked at each other both realizing that any effort to make the other understand our position would be in vain. Instead we let our grievances blow with the wind. We hugged and vowed to talk later. It was certain that we wouldn't talk about any of this. It was a closed subject. Though not verbalized, it was clear that finally Janelle and I would just agree to disagree.

*

So many thoughts raced through my mind as I made my way across Highway 95 northbound away from Miami. It was my intent to call things off with Jibari. After all, he'd led me on for months, lied to me, allowed me to look like an idiot in front of his trick wife, and quiet as kept I would have to admit that nothing had changed.

Niggas were something else. There was a guy in high school, Raymond. Damn, Ray was finer than a mutha-whaat! That was back in the days when light skinned brothers were the biznis and Ray was king of the f'king hill. High yellow, green eyes, curly hair and captain of the football team.

The first time I saw him my Vicky's got stuck to the love juice in between my legs. I was a freshman and he was a junior when he approached me. He had barely asked my name before news that Raymond Greene was sexin' a freshie spread all over the school. Damn those females hated me!

Of course I was a virgin when we met but that didn't last very long. By the end of my sophomore year and what was supposed to be our prom night I was six weeks pregnant. I was so in love with Ray and after nearly two years together I swore he was in love with me. I was thrilled when I told him that we were expecting. Long story short he accused me of being *'just like the rest of them greedy ho's, trying to trap a nigga ride his inevitable stardom all the way to the bank'*, and *our* prom night was shared between him and Odette Mason, another sophomore and my nemesis.

Shit don't change, we just get older. I don't know what I expected from Raymond Greene. Maybe I thought that he would do like they do in the EPT commercials. Swoop me up in his arms and swing me around. Then carefully set me down, as he would not want to stir the baby too much, not want to risk causing it harm. But that didn't happen and shortly after that I wound up in our local Planned Parenthood discussing my "options", pretending one of my older cousins was my momma.

Now I'm creeping up on thirty years old and am on my way to a trendy little sports bar to meet another man of my dreams who is more in love with the idea of how wet my cootie gets than how deep my mind flows. And I hope the same thing, the same hope that I had when I was a fifteen year old shorty lying on a sterile bed with silent tears rolling from my eyes after my child had just been gutted from my over-developed young body…that he will choose me.

I drive with the hope that Jibari will take me into his arms and tell me that he loves me and that he is sorry for hurting me and that we can try to make it work. Just how I'd hoped Ray would. But the reality is Ray never showed up and he went away to the University of Michigan without a thought of me or a concern for the child we created. Last I heard he and Odette had a baby girl together and married a year after she and I graduated from high school. He ripped his ACL to shreds during his first year of college footbal.l He never made it to the NFL. Forgive me for taking pleasure in that.

I held my head high as I entered the sports bar where Jibari was waiting for me. He was sipping a beer while watching a U of M game on one of the many overhead televisions. He smiled when he saw me enter. I forced a courtesy smile in return. I took a seat across from him. Damn Jibari was sexy.

"Hey baby girl," he said taking my hand in his. He pulled it to his lips to kiss it.

"Hi."

We made small talk while watching the game and waiting for our order of spicy chicken wings. It wasn't the greatest date. An afternoon at a sports bar famous for chicken, sauce, and titties, but it was good. It was fun and I hated to have to be the one to ruin the moment.

Hand in hand, Jibari and I strolled toward the river. We were silent, taking in the sounds about us. I leaned my head on his shoulder as we approached the rivers edge. We spotted a row of benches only a few steps away, but far enough from the action that it could be considered a quiet spot.

"You straight?" Jibari asked expressing a genuine concern for my emotions.

"Yea, yea I'm fine. Just got a lot on my mind."

"Uh oh. What's up? This is about me and you, ain't it?"

I sighed not looking forward to the conversation ahead of us.

"Damn, it's that bad?" he asked.

"Jibari, what's up with you and your wife?" I asked.

The look on his face said that he was not up for this line of questioning. He removed his arm from around my shoulder and clasped his hands sitting them on his lap. "We've already talked about this, Mikaela."

"We have but I don't believe that you're telling me the whole story."

"Kae, I ain't about to talk about this anymore."

"Jibari, are you still f'king your wife?" I asked, my aggravation mounting.

Although his silence told everything, I needed to hear it from his mouth. I didn't understand why but I couldn't release him unless he gave me that key that I dreaded to hear but needed to let go.

"Why do you keep stressing me about this?" He stood and walked a few steps away before stopping and turning back to me. "I told you me and T are separating. What more do you want from me?"

"Separating. What does that mean separating? If you're still sleeping together it means nothing. If you're still living together it means even less. And if neither of you have filed divorce papers then it's redundant." I locked my gaze upon Jibari's face, assessing his reaction. Hoping that he would run to my side and say *Oh baby, I love you and I will file those papers first thing in the morning*, though knowing that only in my dreams would that happen.

"Kae, why are you doing this? You wanted us to be together and now we are. But I have to say ma, if you keep stressing me about what's going on between me and T then this may not work out."

I chuckled and looked him over. "You're right JB. I apologize for all of this. I shouldn't be stressing you when I already know that this isn't working out."

"Kae, why are you tripping?"

"Bye, Jibari." There was nothing left to be said. I turned my back on that drama.

"Oh hell naw, Kae! I jeopardized my marriage for you and you think you just gone turn yo' muthaf'kin' back on me?" Jibari grabbed my wrist turning me to face him. "What do you want from me Mikaela? You want me to divorce Tamika so I can marry you? You want us to live together and raise a family? What, you wanna be in my arms on the back of the Source with a caption reading 'Jibari Owens and Mikaela Johnson sharing their love with the world at the Art for Life charity in the Hamptons'? I mean dayum."

I sighed and sucked my teeth. "Jibari, I do not want another thing from you. Go on home to your wife."

I did just what I did best, front. I walked all the way to the parking garage that housed my ride dolo, all the while pretending that breaking things off with Jibari didn't bother me one bit. Ignoring the final pleas that lingered on the air between us. On the drive home I pretended that the idea of being without Jibari or Rick didn't offend me. I walked into my empty home and locked my door and walked into my living room and plopped my behind on my sofa and lost the ability to fool myself into believing that I was okay.

I ran my fingers through my hair, digging into my scalp as that first tear created the pathway down my brown face. The floodgates had opened and like obedient little soldiers more pools of salt water followed. I tossed my head back, my arms limp at my side as my face contorted into every ugly crying expression known to man. I cried so hard that my body began to ache, my heart literally hurt. I pushed my purse to the floor and curled my body into the fetal position. And there I wept. And there I slept.

*

Brrrrrrrriiiiiinnnnggggg.

The urgent ring of the telephone awakened me from my slumber. My mind was in a temporary state of confusion as I was seemingly suddenly thrust into 360-degree darkness. I'd been asleep for hours. I didn't want to answer my telephone, as I was certain that it was Jibari calling to beg for me to take him back into my arms. But with two small nieces, aging grandparents, and an ailing friend there wasn't much of an option.

"Hello?" I said with a much huskier voice than I'd hoped to have.

"Ooh, you don't sound too good when you waking up."

"Corey? Did you call just to insult me?"

"Actually I called to invite you to a movie but you don't sound up for it so never mind."

"No, no I need to get out. Thanks. Where should I meet you?"

"Don't worry about that, just be ready in an hour and a half aiight?"

"I'll see you then. Oh, and Corey."

"Wassup?"

"This still ain't a date."

"Aww forget you, just get dressed." He laughed that beautiful hearty laugh.

I disconnected the line and sat with the phone in my hand. I had to smile. It's crazy how things turn out. The one person that I disliked the most would be the same person to pull me out of my rut.

*

I peeled potatoes as Corey cleaned and seasoned fish for dinner. After having gone out a few times this was the first time that he'd invited me to his home. A surprisingly lovely home I must admit. Immaculately clean, African sculptures, priceless paintings of Miles Davis, Lena Horne, Count Basie, etc.

I was surprised when Corey invited me for dinner; such an event seemed rather intimate. And though we had been spending a great deal of time together as of late I didn't think he'd be interested in anything that could be confused with a come on. But he hadn't come on to me yet and I was beginning to think that he never would…I mean not that I cared. After all, Corey was nothing more than a cool person to hang out with.

"Jill's probably gonna stop through later."

Aw, this dude knew how to kill a moment!

"You are not serious," I said firmly setting the potato peeler against the oak wood table.

"Girl, you better cool yo' heels. Now I thought we squashed this between you and Jill."

"We did but that doesn't mean that I want to spend an

evening around her cranky ass."

"Man, what the hell? What's up, Mikaela? What's with this attitude of yours. You be acting so damned phony and it's tired."

"Excuse you. Who the hell do you think you are to be passing judgment on me especially with the funky ass attitude that you crawl out of bed with every morning."

"I for damn shole do but you overcompensating for something. You go out your way to show er'body that you a bad ass bitch and I just don't buy it and neither does Jill and that's why you don't like her."

"Look, I'm the way I am because I have to be."

"Why? Why? Why? That nonsense is so tired and personally I don't need that in my world."

I was taken aback. What did it matter whether I was "overcompensating" for something or not? Why did he care and why did I care what he thought? He sounded as though he were planning on dumping me even though we were not a couple. For some reason the thought of that disturbed me.

He needed an explanation for Mikaela Johnson, then fine he would get one. He wanted to know about when I was nine and Janelle was five and on a day of early release we came home to find my dads car in the driveway. I rang the bell, I knocked on the door, I called out for my father yet was forced to wait at the door.

Did he need to know how I went to the window to see what could be taking my dad so long and saw him yelling at a woman from the neighborhood who sat butt-booty naked on my mother's favorite sofa while he rushed to return his jewels to his soiled draws and jeans? How I took Janelle's hand and ran down the street to Ms. Rose but never said anything to anyone, not even my mother when she came home that night.

Did Corey need to know how that lady that slept with my daddy on momma's favorite sofa harassed Janelle and I every chance she got? Something about Jill Lauren reminded me of that lady. Maybe it was her tone of voice when she spoke. Maybe it was nothing more than the copper skin tone and button nose. I don't know what it was but I know that Momma didn't like it one bit when she found out about that lady and that lady couldn't handle it when daddy broke it off to save his marriage.

Janelle was too young to remember that lady vandalizing our home. She was too young to remember how our first cat Billie Holiday was killed and left on the stoop for me to find on my way to school. Fortunately she wouldn't recall that lady standing in front of our house yelling my daddy's name making Momma so angry that at six months pregnant she wanted to go give her a good kick in the ass. But Daddy didn't let her. He went out to talk to her, to tell her to leave his family alone while Momma called the police.

I heard the sirens at the same time she did. I heard her tell my daddy that he was going to regret messing with her. Janelle was too small to feel the full affect three nights later when Mom and Dad took Daddy's car to go to meet some friends for dinner and that lady showed up and caused a scene that caused an argument in the car that caused the mangled pile of steel that was aired on the nightly news.

I knew that lady murdered my mommy and daddy. That bitch took the life of my baby brother robbing him of any chance of future greatness. So was I supposed to tell Corey how hard it was when I moved in with my grandparents? How they were wonderful but kids are cruel and Janelle and I, the kids without a mommy, the kids whose mommy was killed by a crazy lady, were often the butt of ruthless, childish jokes.

I had to develop thick skin, we had to. I had to protect my baby sister and myself. I had to be tough in case that crazy bitch ever showed up again. Of course she wouldn't, as it turned out she killed herself shortly after she killed my parents and subsequently my spirit.

Yea, as I became older my peers became much more sympathetic but by then my personality had permanently adjusted. I didn't trust anybody then and it's hard to trust now. So I told Corey all of this. Told him secrets that I only shared with people that loved me and that I loved. And all that nigga had to say was –

"That's messed up what happened to your moms and pops but that was damn near twenty years ago, shawty. You can't use that as an excuse for your present life."

What the hell? My face was hot and my throat closed up on me. I pushed that bowl of freshly peeled potatoes onto the floor as I stood from my seat.

"What the hell is wrong with you," he demanded to know adding extra base to his voice.

"What the hell is wrong with me? You're kidding right? What you saying Corey, just forget my momma and daddy? They're dead so forget 'em. Move on like nothing ever happened. No screw that and screw you got-dammit!"

"Who you think you raising your voice at? For one, ain't nobody tell you to forget about yo' momma and daddy but in all honesty don't nobody care at this point. That may sound cold but that's reality. You was nine years old when that shit happened and I'm sure you was messed up back then but when you twenty-whatever don't nobody wanna hear youse a bitch cause yo' peoples got killed back in the day."

"Go to hell Corey! As a matter of fact just take me home!"

"Aw girl, sit yo' sensitive ass down somewhere and calm the hell down."

"Take me home!" I yelled. It had been quite a long time since I had been this angry. I saw spots before my eyes and my flesh must have been warm to the touch.

"Who are you talking to like that?"

"Whatever, Corey! I'll take a cab home." I turned to gather my belongings and head out the door. I didn't hear his footsteps as he quickly came up behind me. I didn't realize that he'd moved until he was on me. Until he'd turned me to face him, taken my purse and thrown it onto the kitchen table. Until he'd pinned me to the wall, his strong hand on my waistline and I was breathless.

"Mikaela, stop trippin'. You need to calm your down for a second. You went through some rough times as a jit no doubt but baby you cannot mistreat people that played no part in that as some sort of revenge."

I said nothing more. I was lost in his eyes, caught up in the rapture of the feel of his warm breath against my cooling flesh. Our bodies were but centimeters apart. I knew at that moment there was no malicious intent behind Corey's words, he was simply not a very tactful person. My lips parted and my breathing remained rapid. I swallowed hard as Corey watched me watching him. I felt all tension flutter from my soul as our lips touched. We kissed slowly, our tongues introducing then becoming better acquainted with one another.

I raised my hands and took his face in my palms as I initiated a kiss deeper and more passionate. I gasped when Corey's hand took on a mind of its own, traveling up my body and finding a home around my breast. My panties became sticky as my love flowed forward at the feel of the bulge forming rapidly behind his jeans.

I panted and moaned and allowed him to unbutton my blouse and trace the curvature with his tongue. I tossed my head back in ecstasy. I would have never thought that someone like Corey could make me feel so good before he ever really did anything. My back slid slowly down the wall as we made our way to kitchen floor. Finally, my practice of carrying condoms in my purse was once again put to good use.

I bit down on my lip when Corey's lips planted sugar sweet kisses on my naked navel. Caught up in the moment I had to pull a Tweet and slid my hand up my thigh and up my skirt until, *oh my*, I found that welcoming spot that craved the feel of Corey's masculinity within.

It was beautiful. Making love to Corey on a kitchen floor amongst sheered potatoes and invisible dust mites. So beautiful, so wonderful that the details are none of your business so go get your own lovin' and quit livin' vicariously through my cootie!

*

It was an amazing thing that happened between Corey and me yet for some reason we couldn't bring ourselves to put a label on it. At least not right away.

Brenda invited us to her daughter Lisa's seventh birthday party near the waters edge. Out of convenience Corey picked me up. Food was plentiful and kids were everywhere, including Kya and Brianne. I loved Lisa, as grown as she was.

"Thank you guys for coming," Brenda said kissing me on the cheek first then Corey.

"What up, jit?" Corey asked addressing little Lisa.

"Nothing. Y'all brought me a present?"

"How you just gone come at yo' guests like that? Yea, we brought you something, l'il momma," Corey said, laughing.

"Let me get it then."

"Lisa!" Brenda scolded. "Quit begging. After cake and ice cream young lady. "

"Yes, Momma. Uncle Corey, is Mikaela your girlfriend now or something?"

From the mouths of babes. And that was it. That was the push that we needed. We looked at one another and the answer was clear. I was happy again, for the first time in a long time. It was unlike what I felt with Jibari or Rick. It was a comfortable feeling. I was relaxed and uninhibited. I had no secrets with Corey. I didn't have to pretend with him and he wouldn't dream of pretending with anyone. We bumped heads, had fun, and made beautiful sweet love at night.

I looked him in the eye and gently stroked his five o'clock shadow before turning my attention back to Lisa. "Yes baby girl, I'm his girlfriend or something."

Corey smiled, then took my hand to his lips and kissed it.

So this is what my life had come to. Not half bad.

Book 2:
Fantasy of Love

*

"You're back live with your girl Ce Ce Kensington on the Quiet Storm. It's just past midnight here in the windy city and the question we're asking everybody is 'Why have you given up on love?' To all my listeners tuned in this early a.m., finding themselves void of sleep give me a call at 866-1234 and tell me what's on your mind. Okay we have a caller now. Hello caller, you're live on the air with Ce Ce during the Quiet Storm. Why don't you tell our listeners your name."

"Kyra."

"Kyra. That's a nice name, girlfriend. So Kyra, tell us. Why have you given up on love?"

Empty silence from a sad and lonely lover took over the airwaves leaving only the sound of the instrumental to Rick James' *Fire & Desire* playing in the background.

"Kyra? Are you still with us?" DJ Ce Ce asked.

"Yes," Kyra sighed. "I'm here."

"Aaww girl, it can't be that bad. Hey, why don't you tell the city of Chicago all about it."

If Ce Ce were to take the time away from the seclusion of the studio and travel to Kyra's uptown neighborhood, up three flights to apt 3B, across the hardwood floors to the corner of the massive living room where she sat with her knees to her chin, embracing them tightly in her arms, she'd see the pain etched across Kyra's oval face. She'd see the water that flooded the brims of her eyes.

Kyra blinked back her tears and scanned the room before her. Her vision fell across the face of a handsome young man, the framed centerpiece above her fireplace. His skin was smooth mocha, his eyes deep-set ebony. His slick playeresque grin showed hints of perfect white, healthy teeth. He'd gotten a fresh haircut that day and Paul had trimmed his beard and mustache to perfection.

"Love isn't real," Kyra finally spoke up. "Love is just the name of a fantasy land that we visit occasionally as a means to escape the painful realities of our retched existence."

The DJ Ce Ce Kensington who was always full of quick wit and catchy commentary found herself at a temporary loss for words.

"That brother hurt you bad, huh?" she muttered, momentarily loosing her trained public persona and falling into sista-girl mode.

Kyra smiled a soft, sad smile and smeared a stray tear from beneath her eye. "Don't they all? But it's cool right? Hey, life happens."

"True, true. And hey girl, we've all been down that lonesome road and we all persevere. What'd he do? Cheat?"

"No, no. He's not a cheater, he's not a batterer. No chemical abuse problems."

"So what did he do that was foul?"

"He hurt my soul."

"Girl, that's deep. Any request I can fill for you tonight to help you cope?"

"As a matter of fact, yes. How about Frankie Beverly's *I Can't Get Over You*."

"Anything. You hang in there girlfriend. We're gonna go ahead and get into that Frankie Beverly…"

Kyra slowly moved the phone away from her ear and placed it in its cradle. The mellow groove of her request wafted through the speakers. With the remote that sat on the floor beside her she returned the volume to an audible level. Kyra slid backwards across the floor until her back was pressed against the wall. She took the photo that she held of her and Jaahai and pressed it against her breast.

She inhaled deeply taking his scent inside of her. She wore one of the oversized, unwashed t-shirts he'd left at her apartment the last time he was there and a pair of his freshly washed boxers. Tears flooded her eyes. She'd been strong for the first couple weeks of their break up but tonight strength was fleeting. Logic and good sense told her tears in the dark were useless but to her heart that was a moot point. Her heart was stubborn and unyielding.

The sound of the telephone ringing interrupted her private pity party. Her breathing ceased as her heart rate accelerated. Her fingers carefully tilted the caller ID to an angle where she could read the LCD display. She exhaled and her body shook with anger. Her spirit uplifted, had been dropped with a heavy thud onto the hardwood, descended another notch when she read the name Tamyra Douglas.

Kyra sighed and answered her sister's call. "Yes, T."

"You need to stop it, Kyra."

"Stop what? I don't know what you're talking about."

"Quit frontin'. You know precisely what I'm talking about. I heard you on the radio."

"What are you doing up this late?"

"Homework. College is kicking my ass. I'm still working on this research paper for Psych. Imagine my surprise when I hear my big sister dogging love on the Quiet Storm."

"You don't understand."

"I've never loved and lost?"

"Well yea but-"

"But what? Ky you have fought for and humbled yourself in this relationship for over three years. If Jaahai isn't willing to meet you half way then you've got to move on. I'm sorry Ky, I just don't like seeing you like this. You broke up with him, you musta had a reason. What reason was that?"

Kyra sighed and looked away. Her eyes went to the ceiling as she held her tears back. "I didn't feel like he was loving me the way I wanted to be loved. I know what he said. He said he loved me, told me he wants me to be his wife and the mother of his children…someday. And I want that."

"So what makes you think he doesn't still feel that way? Maybe he's just being stubborn. You know how men are, especially Jaahai. Maybe he just needs some time."

"Why hasn't he called me, T?"

"Why haven't you called him?"

"I don't really know," she answered honestly. "I think maybe I just wanted to see if he would in fact fight for me. I only want him to be willing to fight for me. For him to not just let me go. How can it be so easy for him?"

"Maybe it's not as easy as it seems to you."

"Cha!" Kyra was instantly angry with her sister. "What? Are you on his side all of a sudden?"

"No. Shit, Ky." Frustration speckled Tamyra's tone. "Why don't you just get closure. Just call the man and tell him how you feel. Make him tell you what's in his heart so you can proceed with or without him. But Ky honey, you have got to be prepared in case he doesn't tell you what you want to hear."

Kyra was done with Tamyra. She had her man and he wasn't emotionally selfish like Jaahai was. He had a pet name for Tamyra. He apologized to her whenever he was wrong. He never wanted to do anything to hurt her and it pained him if he did. He needed to hear her voice everyday and everyday he told her he loved her without provocation. Like Jaahai, Karim was a strong man with a powerful presence but with Tamyra he was gentle and kind. He never cared what anyone thought about it, with his woman he carried no sword and shield. He was putty in her hands.

Those were the qualities that Kyra wished were present in Jaahai. But Jaahai was so guarded and emotionally stingy. Consumed by teenage ideologies of what a man is supposed to be. As a result, he sucked the life out of their relationship. They talked less and romance became nothing more than a myth, an Aesop's Fable of sorts. Sexual desire was preempted by cordial intimidation.

"T, I'm sleepy. I'm going to bed now."

"Okay love. Get some rest and call me tomorrow and let me know you're okay."

Kyra kissed into the phone and hung up. Kem's *Love Calls* surrounded her. She lowered the volume on her stereo then shuffled to her plush sofa. She curled into a fetal position and let the free flow of tears spill forward.

*

T was right, it was true that Kyra had been the one who initiated the break up nearly a month ago. She thought that was the only way to get their relationship back on track. They'd step away for a brief period and date again. Things would improve, they'd get back what they once had and both would be pleased.

She hadn't planned to take it there, it was something that just happened. It happened on a day that he'd asked her to be with him. They were to be spending time together but four personal calls later, Kyra began to feel neglected while Jaahai only made light of the situation. She felt awkward while trying her best to establish a repor but Jaahai's mind was anywhere but on her. A couple tequila's later and he was relaxed in her presence and they were enjoying their time together. That was until a ringing cell phone sent him rushing from the early noon quiet of the bar out to the pedestrian filled and bongo playing atmosphere directly outside its doors.

Kyra wanted to yell, scream, cuss and accuse his shady behavior but she didn't see him often enough and opted to ignore the issue for the time being. It was that evening back at his place when he left her to entertain herself for hours while he made other use with his time that she had the brilliant idea to end their relationship – for the time being.

Kyra hadn't expected Jaahai to put up a fight though she'd have been honored if he had. She hadn't expected to hear from him before she initiated contact and she was right in that belief. He was in control and he knew just how far his power over her stretched. He knew that she'd eventually cave and call to him. And as badly as she wanted to prove him wrong she was weak for him. Two and a half weeks later she two-wayed him opening the door to communication but Jaahai had not yet walked through.

*

Jaahai couldn't understand how much Kyra was in love with him, that love he took for granted. She could hardly understand herself. She'd go to the ends of the earth for him if it would make him smile. When he'd been badly hurt in a car accident she nursed his wounds. When they were both sick with the flu she'd taken care of him. She'd spent time with his mother learning to cook his favorite foods despite the fact that she didn't eat it. None of this was done for bragging rights. No, his pleasure gave her pleasure.

Her body trembled and her heart ached. She wished at that moment that she could be as devoid of emotions as he was at that moment in time. But she couldn't breathe without him. Thoughts of them together consumed her mind from sunrise to sunset. She jumped whenever her phone rang, hoping that it was he. She imagined him appearing uninvited at her front door pleasantly surprising her. She imagined kissing his lips once more and being held in his arms as he smiled down at her. Wherever she went she smelled him. Everything she saw, touched, or heard reminded her of him.

Kyra prayed that God would take away the desire for him thus removing the pain. But every morning she awoke to get dressed for work she packed up her emotional malaise and carried it with her just as her lunch bag and keys went.

Kyra's eyes closed though her tears still pushed out and rolled down her cheek. She sniffed though her trembles subsided. By the time Ginuwine's *Differences* hit the air she'd already drifted into a restless sleep where The Persuaders *Thin Line Between Love & Hate* was her theme song.

*

Kyra felt like a stalker sitting there on the hood of Jaahai's Cadillac. Four times over the past twenty minutes she'd considered rushing back to her own vehicle and driving away, her dust and tire tracks the only memory that she was once there. By her fifth deliberation it was too late as she'd already been spotted.

Like ice on a recently used stovetop she melted at the sight of him walking toward her. He looked good in his urban casual fashions. The matching orange and white Enyce top complimented the Enyce jeans with the orange stitching. On his feet he wore a pair of crisp white Air Force One's. Kyra thought he was sexy in his top of the line three-piece suits, he could have easily knocked Tyson Beckford off the runway. But she knew how he looked forward to his casual Friday's when he could just be himself.

Kyra fought back her urge to smile. She fidgeted discreetly but maintained her stoic appearance. Jaahai walked to her, the corner of his lip turned down. Kyra swallowed hard and made eye contact.

"What are you doing here, Ky?" Jaahai asked letting the

Nike book bag he was carrying fall to his side.

"I thought we needed to talk." Kyra was embarrassed at the slight crack in her voice.

"What's there left to talk about? Didn't you say everything you had to say already?" he asked. An unexpected anger in his tone took Kyra aback. "You shouldn't be coming to my job with this personal shit."

"It's not like I came inside. You're off anyway. Can we just go somewhere and talk?"

"Naw man, naw. I'm tired of talking. It's always the same crap with you. You tellin' me how I ain't good enough for you, how I don't do enough for you. You said you wasn't never gone quit on me but-" Jaahai stopped mid-sentence. He felt funny as soon as the words left his mouth. "Just forget it shorty. Look I got thangs to do so…"

"Jaahai, noo," Kyra pleaded. "Okay, I won't take up too much of your time. I just need to get some type of closure. I need to know from you if we still have a chance."

"I don't know. I just don't know," Jaahai answered honestly.

"What did I ever do to you to make you turn on me like this so suddenly?"

"Kyra," he groaned.

"Are you seeing someone else?"

"Kyra, let's just drop it."

"That's the problem, I can't just drop it. Are you? Seeing someone else?"

"Kyra."

"Jaahai. Well?"

Jaahai shifted slightly. He moved his bag from one hand to the next in a nervous gesture. He didn't really want to hurt Kyra despite what she chose to believe. No matter, he always somehow seemed to do so. She was just too damned sensitive.

"I'm waiting," she pressed.

"Yes Kyra, I met someone."

Kyra stumbled back. She'd been better off had he reached back with his large hand and pimp slapped her across her cheek, it would have stung less. Salty water pushed up but she blinked rapidly not wanting to give him the satisfaction. This confrontation wasn't going as she'd hoped and now she was just pissed.

"She works here? That's why you don't want me here?"

"No, she don't work here. I don't want you here because it's inappropriate."

"Well, I hope you're happy. But you do realize no matter what you think that bitch ain't no better than me," she spat with venom lacing her voice. "It don't matter how good she screwing you right now, I bet once you're with her long enough for her true colors to show the heifer gone give just as many headaches as I did if not more."

"Kyra, calm your ass down. See this is why you shouldn't have brought yo' over emotional ass up here with this. As a matter of fact I'm phenna be up outta here. You can stand here if you want and look like an ass by yourself." Jaahai pushed past Kyra forcing his own anger to the pit of his stomach.

"Screw you, Jaahai! You just as no good as all these other low life ass nigga's out here!"

Jaahai stood upright holding his car door open with one hand, his keys jingling in the other. His breathing picked up and his teeth were clenched behind his lips as he stared at the sky above. Having had enough he slammed his door closed and turned to face Kyra. Startled she jumped at his swiftness and lucid anger.

"I ain't no better, Ky? I ain't no better? I ain't never cheated on you, never hit you, never fuckin' disrespected you. I took care of you and did I ever ask you for shit in return? Anything you needed or wanted I did all I could to provide it to you. But because I ain't got enough bitch in my blood I ain't good enough for you. I tried my best to be more of the man you wanted. Every time you complained about somethin' I ain't do right I tried to make it better. But I see now I can't please you and I just ain't interested in trying no more."

This time Kyra didn't stop the flow of tears, she couldn't if she tried. Before this moment in time she hadn't known he felt that way. She received yet another blow to her ego again for the second time that day. She wanted to tell him how wrong he was, how he had no right to feel that way. But she found herself to be speechless. She couldn't dispute him when he was right. She had convinced herself that it was all his fault but the truth of the matter was she'd also played a major role in the path to the destruction of their relationship.

"So you're saying you don't love me anymore?" she whimpered sounding like a small child.

"That's not at all what I'm saying."

The two stood quietly in each others presence having said all there was to say. Kyra thought quickly. Now that she knew where she went wrong she needed to say something to let him know she understood and that she was sorry and willing to change some of her ways if he continued to work on some of his. Now that she knew the problem they could certainly begin again.

But something inside told her that wouldn't be enough, that he wouldn't break so easily. She needed to try something anyway, something to stop him from leaving her. She wanted to kiss him, yes a kiss would make it right. A kiss would remind him just how much he loved her. She tried to muster all her nerve to, under the circumstances, press her lips to his. The ringing of his cell phone interrupted her thoughts and her planning. Jaahai removed the phone from the clip on his belt and eyed the caller ID.

"It's her isn't it?" Kyra asked just barely above a whisper. Jaahai's failure to respond was all the answer she needed. "Well you wouldn't wanna keep her waiting. Maybe I'll see you around."

Kyra turned away quickly before Jaahai could say anything. She imagined that he would call out to her. That for once he'd come after her as she'd come after him. She was winded at the sound of his engine revving up. It hurt to no end to know he was leaving her to be with another woman. She sped up and rushed to her car and climbed behind the wheel. She didn't want anyone to bear witness to the convulsions moving like waves through her petite frame as she cried. Her tears bore all the force of a waterfall. She struggled to keep her lunch down with one hand covering her mouth, the other pressed against her abdomen.

She recalled all that had been said. Yes, he'd been wrong in the way he handled a lot of situations with her, there was no justification in it, often times giving her the silent treatment rather than expressing himself verbally. But she'd also contributed. He'd needed her to be more aggressive rather than bow down to his whims and attitudes and wait idly by for him to change.

She was now willing to do that. To give him what he'd asked for, to stay on top of him without pressuring him. Not let him shut her out but see that she could be strong for the both of them. She now understood the value of patience and how she should have never expected he'd conform to her ideal man overnight. After all, she knew what she was getting when she got him.

But now it may have been too late for all of her self-discoveries. As she'd sit in her home this evening pining for him, would he be entangled between the sheets with *her*? Sweat and sex funk mixing and mingling in the air, as he's comforted between the thighs of another woman. Would he be thinking about her then?

As Lauryn Hill and D'Angelo's *Nothing Even Matters* played

Kyra thought, *How true*, as she turned up the volume before speeding out of the parking lot.

*

Kyra walked with her back straight and shoulders relaxed, eyes facing the world. She'd spent the morning at the local Korean nail shop getting a manicure and pedicure. Her hair flowed as softly as an exhaled breath on the wind. A DSW bag bounced off of her leg as she trotted along down the Magnificent Mile. Kyra made a quick left and entered the Fireplace Inn. She shook her hand at the hostess who was approaching when she spotted her sister across the restaurant signaling for her to join. Kyra walked easily to the table and slid in across from her.

"Well, don't you just look like a ray of sunshine walking up in here," Tamyra commented.

Kyra blushed and smiled brightly. She was pleased with herself and happy to have impressed her sister. She reached for the menu but Tamyra touched her hand and shook her head no.

"I already ordered for us," she said as she sipped her water. "So how are you doing, as if I really need to ask?"

"I'm really good actually. Just fine."

"Well, you look great. Have you talked to Jaahai lately?"

Kyra frowned slightly and quickly shook her head side to side. "He did send me a text last week though just saying hi and telling me that he hoped I was doing okay."

"You write him back?"

"Nah but Lord knows I was tempted to. Especially since I heard from his Uncle that he stopped seeing that girl."

"Yea? It probably wasn't serious to begin with. Just someone to help pass the time and get his nutt off. So you thinking about trying to get back with him?"

"No. I mean I'd love to but is it really just my choice? I don't even know if I still have a place in his heart and I don't even wanna get my feelings hurt again." Kyra waved over the waitress who was already walking in their direction. She ordered a Vodka and orange juice.

"So you're still not over him, huh?"

"Not hardly. It'll be a long road before I cross that bridge."

"Well you seem fine at least."

"Yea well, dwelling on love lost ain't gone help me find it."

"True."

*

Food being placed before them on the table interrupted the still trying topic. They rather found other entertaining topics to discuss over their meal. The bass of a male voice excusing his way into their conversation interrupted their laughter. Kyra looked into the face from which the voice came. She was impressed. He was tall and well built with locs that hung to his shoulder. He was clean in his appearance with freshly manicured nails.

"I'm sorry to disturb y'all beautiful young ladies while you enjoying your lunch. I just noticed you when you stepped into the spot and thought you was looking kinda fly in your little phatty girl joint. You mind if I get your number so I can call you sometime? I'd love to take you out and show you off."

Kyra blushed and smiled. "I'm real flattered but no, I can't."

"Aiight shorty, that's cool. I ain't surprised someone as fine as you already got a man."

Kyra thought for a second then returned his gaze. He was damn fine. "I don't feel comfortable giving out my number right now but I'll take yours."

"Say word? Cool. My name's Shad, what's yours?"

"Kyra."

Kyra typed his digits into her cell phone.

"Aiight shorty, I'm looking forward to hearing that sweet voice of yours soon. Don't disappoint me."

Kyra smiled and winked. She held her breath as Shad

walked away watching her until he could no more. When he was out of sight Kyra and Tamyra broke out into uncontrollable laughter as they drummed the floor with their feet and pounded the table with their fists.

"Girl, he was fine!" Tamyra exclaimed.

"I'm sayin'." The sisters high fived each other.

"You'd better call that brother tonight."

"Girl I ain't really going to call him," Kyra confessed.

"What? Why in the hell not? Why you take his number then?"

"It just feels good to have options."

"Options huh? Well if you ain't gonna call the brother let me have his number then."

"Hells no. Besides Karim would kick your ass," Kyra said stuffing a forkful of chicken salad in her mouth. Tamyra laughed and playfully tossed a napkin at her sister's head.

*

Kyra tossed her keys on the small wood table nearest the front door after she entered her apartment. She sighed and carried her bag of new discount designer shoes to her bedroom and sat the bag in the closet. A part of her wished that Jaahai were there with her but she had already accepted that he wasn't and wouldn't.

Kyra opened a drawer and shuffled some things around until her fingers grazed the edge of a book. She pulled an old journal out and flipped through its pages. She stopped when she came across entries she'd made when she and Jaahai first began dating. She laughed and smiled and was even surprised at the things she'd written, things she'd forgotten had ever occurred.

Kyra wiped a laugh tear from beneath her eye and gently closed the book. She smiled sweetly at it before setting it in the middle of her bed. She stood from the bed and changed into more comfortable clothes. She glanced at the cutesy blue and green journal with the mirror on it then shook a pillow loose from its case.

Kyra walked to her living room and let the selected jams on WGCI travel throughout her apartment. She walked through and removed anything that reminded her of the former love she still carried in her heart. She replaced pictures of Jaahai with photos of friends and family. She carried her bag of memories to her room with her. Holding a picture of Jaahai in her hand she stared at it and traced the outline of his face with her finger.

Suddenly struck by inspiration Kyra sat the picture by her side and grabbed her journal from the bed. She flipped through until she found the pages describing the first weeks of their relationship. Kyra ripped the pages from her journal then searched a drawer for an envelope. She paused then grabbed a notepad and pen and began to write:

Dear Jaahai,

Hope this letter finds you well and in good spirits. I have to be very honest and say not talking to you or seeing you has been very trying for me. But I accept for now that that's the way things are. And hey maybe I'm not "the one" but I'm still damn sure I'm the prototype. But it's in God's hands and if he wants us together he'll move us in that direction. No matter what though know that I think of you everyday and I love you today as much as I did the last time I told you.

Enclosed you will find a few pages taken from my journal, my gift to you. I give you my heart on those pages. It is yours to keep and know that until the ink fades my heart belongs to you.

Loving you always,

Kyra

Kyra smiled at what she was about to do. She was finally about to gain closure and once again have some sort of piece of mind. She slipped into a pair of K-Swiss and with the letter in hand she grabbed her keys and cell and jogged down the stairs and out into the night air. She reflected as she walked to the end of the block. She giggled when she recalled a playful moment one evening before bed. She smiled and sighed when she recalled the passionate words he expressed to her after experiencing a sudden loss of a loved one.

Kyra opened the mailbox and dropped the letter inside. At that moment as far as she was concerned their negative past was erased. All that would remain would be fond memories of their time together. She didn't know if she'd get a response from him and she didn't assume one way or the other. She was no longer in the business of speculation. She'd just let the chips fall where they may.

Kyra flipped her cell phone open and scrolled through its phonebook. She found the name and number for the cutie named Shad. She contemplated pushing the button and making a date for that evening. After all the best way to get over an old love was with a new one.

"Nah," Kyra said and closed the phone. She wasn't ready for that. True she hadn't spoken to nor seen Jaahai since that fateful day in the parking lot and yes his stubbornness ran deep. But she wasn't completely ready to give up on their love…not yet.

Book 3:

Charitable Taboo
An erotic murder mystery

Prelude

"Today's top breaking story. A man was discovered early this morning shot dead in his Oakland Park home. The identity has not yet been released as his family has not been notified..." The news anchors voice droned on in the background...

I pay no attention to the morning's heartbreaking revelation. I've never been into the news, too much pain and suffering being advertised way too early in the a.m. Actually, there was but one reason I even indulged the dry personality and painted on facades of the media - company. Hearing voices, any voices, diminished the feeling of being solo.

Truth be told I was not actually solo, I never was. David, my gorgeous fiancé, is occupying my bed for the third night in a row. Presently we are in the process of deciding whose home to sell. Believe you me, it's a battle but well worth it if I get to spend the rest of my life with this man.

David. Whew, he is the sexiest man I have met to date and trust when I say I have met a lot of men. He's a woman's dream. Tall, dark, powerful, compassionate - and not to mention, well hung! I swear I can screw him and suck him all at the same time. My, my, my, big dick is a beautiful thing and so is my man but wow, marriage. I never saw myself wearing that hat.

It's a pleasure to meet you, I'm Ima Anne Phelps and that's pronounced E-mah, get it straight. It's German as is my maternal grandmother. How would I describe myself? Well...I'd say beautiful. Five feet, six inches of gorgeous, delectable and delightful candy sweet caramel. My almond shaped brown eyes sparkle in the sun and my pouty lips are one of my best features.

Ok, well have a seat while I get ready for work and let me tell you a little more about who I am. I am dressed in a floral silk blouse and black Renata pants, stylish yet conservative. My brown hair which left untouched hangs well past my shoulders, is swept together neatly in a bun. I am professional when I walk through the doors of one of the largest credit card companies in the US where I am employed as a Business Analyst. Come. Let me tell David bye and then I will tell you why I invited you here.

I pick up the remote and point it at the television, flexing my power to stop Sharron Melton in mid-speak. I sit softly on the edge of the bed leaning forward allowing my warm breath to envelope David's flesh. I part my lips and my tongue traces the outline of David's earlobe. His body shifts and I become more aggressive, nibbling his ear while allowing my hand to find it's way to his happy place. David squirms and moans softly. Mmm, I see you like to watch, huh? Getting that anxious feeling? Well you ain't seen nothing yet.

"Mmm baby, stop teasing me," says David in a cracked husky tone.

"What makes you think I'm teasing this time?" I ask, mischief apparent in my words.

"Ima, now if Mr. Happy starts to smile you're gonna be late for work."

"Alright, alright," I kiss him on the cheek and stand from the bed, pausing to take one last look at the television screen where the news team only moments earlier sat invading the sanctity of my boudoir per my invitation.

It was a morning much like this when a simple news story gone ignored changed my life profoundly. That is why I have invited you here, to share my experience with you in hopes that it can help someone, somehow. I must first, however provide you with my verbal disclaimer:

There is no clear moral to my tale, it is just my experience. I am far from a saint. If you are easily intimidated by such worldly "sins" as sex, profanity, drug and alcohol usage, if you're homophobic or a Jehovah's Witness, under 18, or if you simply have the inability to distinguish fantasy from reality then **STOP**, this just ain't the tale for you.

But for you that are a might bit curious and don't mind opening up yourself to something new nor the possibility of touching yourself when no one's watching, then I am going to back up to only a few weeks ago, to the morning when my world was rocked. A traumatic experience, a wonderful experience, a life altering experience.

Welcome to Charitable Taboo…

1 Missed Messages

"We have a developing story this morning out of South Miami Beach. A man has been discovered brutally murdered and castrated blocks from a hotel where he'd been a guest only hours earlier. Police have not released the identity of the man as his family has not yet been notified..."

I paid no attention to the morning's negative revelations. I instead fussed with the stubborn bun, which I was struggling to roll on top of my head. Finally getting it pinned just right I did my final beauty inspection in the master bathroom's full-length mirror. I smoothed the white twill knee-length Lida Baday skirt and jacket and turned side-to-side to catch my view from different angles. I captured a glimpse of movement beneath the gold satin sheet on my bed and turned off the bathroom light before walking in that direction.

I took a seat on the edge of the bed and lustfully eyed the nude silhouette. I leaned forward and gently nibbled the side of Peta-Gaye's neck. I could feel her body shift slightly. Feeling the moment, I grazed my tongue slowly across her neck taking in its sweet nectar. I allowed my tongue to create a trail to her ear and nibbled her lobe softly while my hand massaged her firm round rear. Peta-Gaye squirmed beneath my advances, an easy moan escaped her parted lips.

"Stop f'king with me Ima," she spoke plainly in her accented voice, fighting against the urge to whip her size B tits out and stuff one in my mouth.

"You know you like it," I whispered in a husky yet sensual tone while my tongue played hide and seek with her eardrum.

"You do this shit to me every morning. Leave me here alone with a wet pussy while you run off and play mama to those over-grown imbeciles."

"I've told you about talking bad about my employees." I playfully bit harder on Peta-Gaye's ear before pushing off the bed and heading out the door.

Peta-Gaye and I had been a live-in couple for near two years. I loved her and always will however commitment was a clear issue for me. She was aware that I'd slept with men throughout our relationship but her desire for me forced her to accept that. As long as I never made love to another woman, in my eyes, I was not cheating. I was well aware that a single lustful act as that would be considered outright disrespect by Peta-Gaye and she would certainly leave me if it ever happened.

But even though she was accepting of men being in my life, still I never shared my sexual escapades with her and she never asked. However there was no doubt that she was aware when I was returning from one, especially when it was with Jonathan my White family man suga-daddy, but you will meet him later.

It was an interesting love that she and I shared. My Jamaican queen matched me in height and beauty with bittersweet cocoa brown skin and the sexiest-bitchiest attitude one could stand. With us there was no such thing as the proverbial "man of the relationship" as we both played that part when it applied.

*

I strolled proudly into my department, which outside of the

distant spaced out whispers of the few employees who were paid to plug in early, was quite empty. I'd barely had an opportunity to log into my computer before Garcelle and Armando, my partners in crime, were over my shoulder nagging me about details of the previous evening.

"Soo, just how big was he?" Armando whispered in excitement.

"Is that all you care about?" I inquired knowing full well the answer was 'hell yes'! Armando simply gave me the 'now you know' look. "Baby he was hung," I proudly announced. I was amused at Garcelle and Armando's obvious envy. I laughed aloud hardly able to contain myself any longer. "Hung like an ant, I tell you it was embarrassing. I was embarrassed for him!"

"Ooh, uh-uhn, you are so wrong," Garcelle said.

Armando asked, "Was he White?"

"No, that's what's so sad, he was a brother."

"Whose brother?"

"A brother, brother."

"Oh, uh-uhn, now that is just sorry." Armando snapped sharply.

"Ok fine, so the thingies teeny-weeny. What about the tongue?" Garcelle questioned.

I only rolled my eyes and shook my head. "It felt like somebody was rubbing a Brillo pad against my clit."

"Ow. And on that note, I'm going to start my day."

"Yes, gurl. Hey, we still on for tonight?" Armando asked.

"As usual." I finger waved my friends good-bye and started my workday.

Garcelle and Armando were great friends who understood me like no one else in my life. Garcelle Washington I've known for ten years, she and I attended college together. Gorgeous Dominicana. There was a time when all I wanted to do was be tangled between the sheets with her while she whispered, 'Te amo', 'Le deseo (I want you)', 'béseme todo encima (kiss me all over)' in my ear. Yea, well she was involved and in love at the time. But during that time she and I became wonderful friends and although she desires more than friendship from me now, I refuse to stray from the righteous path.

Armando is a little different. He was welcomed into our world three years ago but we don't know much about him. He has always been very hush about his past, it was too traumatic I suppose. I have become more familiar with 'Sasha'. By day Armando is a straight-laced, tie-wearing professional but by night he's a flaming homosexual and a shit load of fun.

*

Tension was thicker than Florida's humidity when I arrived home from work. I could hear the voices of my baby sister Natasha and Peta-Gaye before I'd even neared the door.

"Damn the bullshit, you don't need to be flaunting your nasty coochie in front of my man all the time!" Natasha yelled.

"Cho! -mi nuh wa yuh likkle fenke fenke bruk packit man," Peta-Gaye responded.

"Oh, hell no! Don't start that shit!"

"Hey, hey dammit, what's the problem now?" I asked slamming my keys on the kitchen counter frustrated.

"Yu a hear mi, you likkle poil sista wa smadi kick ar bombo rass clate from time to time," Peta-Gay grumbled in her native Patois before sashaying in tank top and thong to our bedroom.

"English, bitch, English," Natasha said to which Peta-Gaye's only response was her middle finger.

"Natasha stop it, please," I tried to reason.

"Ima, no. I'm sick and tired of every time I bring Dre over your damn carpet munching ass bitch is flaunting her stank ass around naked."

"Girl, you betta bite back!" I snapped ready to go off on her junior ass.

"Ima, it's disgusting."

"Natasha, my patience is wearing thin. That's my woman you're talking about. I don't disrespect Dre and thus expect that you won't disrespect Peta-Gaye."

Natasha glanced me over with a vacant, distant look in her eyes. "Like I said, it's disgusting."

My sister and I stood toe to toe, our eyes shooting daggers. Natasha found every possible opportunity to remind me just how trifling she thought my having a physical relationship with a woman was. She backed down when I reminded her that I wouldn't hesitate to put her ass out if she crossed too far over her boundaries. I bumped her shoulder intentionally as I walked past toward my bedroom where a furious Peta-Gaye and some harsh choice words were awaiting me.

*

The line was practically around the corner when Garcelle, 'Sasha' and I arrived at The Whole, a nightclub for hetero's and homo's which we patronized at least three nights a week. My hips moved seductively from side to side as I strolled, licking my lips, toward the head of the line. I was dressed to kill as I always was. Fashion is of high importance to me, something that you cannot put a price on. I wore a David Meister silk satin strapless beaded dress and Vera Wang crystal and silver leather t-strap sandals (heels).

On these occasions I am 'Charity', a single, insatiable creature of the night. On these occasions anything goes and I am guaranteed a good time if not a great one. I am free to be whomever I desire. No one here knows me, not the real me anyway. They do not know the power hungry, German and African ancestry, Catholic prude who is Ima Anne. I do not desire for them to know me intimately. I only desire for them to extinguish the smoldering embers within me. No exchange of numbers, no promise to hook up later. I only love you tonight, by morning light I don't remember your name.

Warren, the built chocolate bouncer from Trinidad, held no shame as he undressed me with his eyes. Surely he was reminiscing about the one and only time that he and I shared together. Romantic? Hardly. I was drunk and frustrated with the evening's selection and thus allowed myself to be hoisted onto his thick long island dick and pressed against a graffiti stained wall while he thrust in and out of my body. Sweat poured from the top of his bald head as my nails gathered up the day's dirt and grime as they dug into his smooth flesh. It was good for me but can never happen again otherwise he may become disoriented and confuse our lustful romps for a relationship.

"Damn girl you look good. Them titties need their own zip code!" he said as I approached the head of the line. The question of when would he be able to bury his face in between them again was obvious yet unspoken.

A small group of females hissed and glared as my trio eased past. I slowly moved my eyes from them and landed them on Warren's handsome brown face, a sly smirk on my glossy lips. I pressed my hand against his cheek and gently moved his lips toward mine. I could sense his little soldiers lining up and preparing to attack as I sensually kissed and nibbled his lips.

"Is my table ready?" I whispered.

Warren's voice was cracked and high pitched when he spoke, "Of course." He cleared his throat and was redeemed as masculine. "Of course."

I pat his cheek and looked back at the bitches to the rear. I looked them up and down before giving Garcelle and 'Sasha' their cue to make our appearance.

*

Cam'ron's "Oh Boy" was bumping in the background. The waitress Sindelle brought to our table a complimentary bottle of Moet and three champagne glasses. It's true that to the general public we aren't important enough to deem such treatment but for all the business we generated helping to get this club off the ground, we deserved to be treated with Mariah status.

'Sasha' lit up the laced joint that he rolled while sitting at our table. He took his hit before handing it off to me. I put the drug to my lips and inhaled deeply. I held the smoke in my lungs while my eyes scanned the crowd hoping that someone would catch my attention. Finding nothing, I twisted my lips sideways and blew the smoke into the air. I took a second hit before passing it on to Garcelle. I'd barely finished off my first glass of Mo' when a club buddy dressed in drag, 'Maccartney', rushed our table.

"Hi babies," Maccartney spoke as 'she' took a seat beside me whilst blowing kisses to each of us. We all answered with our respective smooches. "Charity, you look absolutely fab as usual girl, ravishing."

"Thank you but look at you! Is that Chetta B?" I asked of the long satin red wrap gown Maccartney wore. She was always much too overdressed for the evening but that did not dismiss the fact that she was always stunning.

"Of course darling, you know how I do, O-K?" she snapped sharply in the air. "Anyway there's somebody that I would like for you to meet."

"Oh Maccartney honey, you know I do not do blind dates."

"Bitch please, the picking's is slim tonight and besides this muthaf'ka is fine, y'hear me. Garcelle, darling? You think I can relieve you of babysitting duties?" Garcelle rolled her eyes at Maccartney and passed the joint her way.

"So why don't you screw him?" I asked.

"Bitch stop. Don't play me like this Charity, you know I would not give you no rag dolls to play with. He's straight unfortunately but he's nice though." Maccartney took a healthy puff and passed the remainder of the joint to Sasha.

"Greedy bitch," Sasha grumbled about the minimal remains of the weed he'd invested in.

"Learn to share. Anyway, come. Now."

"Play nice, ladies," I chimed in.

I allowed Maccartney to take my hand and guide me across the floor to a table in the back. I was relieved to see a scrumptious black man sitting behind it. He laughed with friends and craters formed in his cheeks. He was dark with strikingly white teeth, possibly bleached. His style was on point and my coochie contracted. I looked on in lust for a full thirty seconds before Maccartney cleared her throat and got the men's attention.

"Rude. Anyway Steven this is Charity, she's the one I was telling you about." Maccartney reveled in matchmaking heaven as Steven stood and extended his hand in my direction. I turned my attention away from the sexy Negro that I was lusting after and turned to offer a polite 'how are you?' to the attractive European-American Maccartney was determined to connect me with. "Isn't he just scrumptious darling? Well you two go on and play."

I smiled a sweet and courteous smile. The beat for Tweet's "Oops (Oh My)" dropped in and my lace thong began to stick to the sweet sap forming. "It's a pleasure however may I have a moment with this naughty boy over here? My, it's been how long since we've seen each other?"

Picking up on my cue black Adonis chimed in, "Oh damn, I thought that was you. Wow, six maybe seven months. We've really got to catch up."

"Oh yes, let's."

He rose from his chair and must have stood a full foot above me. I felt Maccartney's icy glare on the back of my head but I didn't give her the satisfaction of looking back and acknowledging it. John, as he'd soon introduce himself, clearly impressed by me, led me to a table where we could be alone and talk. The conversation hadn't gone too far before I gave him the go ahead to suggest that we go someplace quiet to get to know each other better.

*

Garcelle, Armando and I had a die-hard rule for our own protection. Anytime we disappeared with anyone we would leave a message with our whereabouts on each other's voice mail. Tonight would be no different. While John waited to be assigned a room by the desk clerk I flipped open my cell and made two phone calls and left two messages. When he was done he took my hand in his and I followed him to our room.

Our tongues had intertwined before we even reached the room. John managed to insert the key card and with his back to the door and his hand firmly gripping my ass, pushed it open. We stumbled backward until the bed became a fortunate obstacle stopping us suddenly. Our breathing was heavy, so anxious to start but being unsure as to where we should begin. John paused and held my face in his hands while staring into my eyes. He scanned my face and slowly down to my breasts, which were spilling forward from the strapless.

John's hands cupped my size D breasts which he massaged while biting the side of my neck. I tossed my head back and went limp in his arms. My own hand touched my thigh and slid up and down slowly while 'oohs' and 'aahs' traveled from my lips. I raised my hand higher and higher until I was touching my own moisture and caressed my swollen lips back and forward becoming more and more aroused.

John stopped suddenly and backed away. There was a sinister look in his eyes. "Take your clothes off," he demanded and I obliged. I slowly slid my dress from over my breasts and allowed it to fall to the carpeted floor below. I stood in my strapless push up bra and lace thong and moved my body in a sexy slow rhythmic motion. I reached back and undid the clasp then pulled the material away from my body revealing perfect round tits. I tossed the bra and it smacked him in the face. I then turned my body away from him and arching my back pushed my ass higher while I slid my thong from my waist. I'd barely stepped out of them before John was up and on me again.

He wrapped his arm around my waist and his mouth around my neck and walked me swiftly to the wall. I stood with my back to him and my hands pressed against the wallpaper with golden glints. John stooped down and pulled my ass to his face. His tongue darted in and out as he searched for something dear to him. I gasped when he found it and caressed and nibbled. I growled and banged my fist against the wall while shaking my head wildly from side to side.

When he was full of my juices, John stood and turned me to face him. He immediately took my breasts into his palms and took turns nursing on each of them. I reached for the crotch of his jeans and unsnapped and unzipped them. I slid my manicured nails from the waistline down until they discovered the opening of his boxers. I reached inside and nearly exploded when I felt the thickness of his hard shaft. I took my hand to my mouth and licked it, gathering as much of my saliva as possible before taking him in my hand and moving it up and down with slow yet strong movements.

A jewel was awarded to me in the form a small pool of pre-cum at the tip of John's dick. Instinctively I licked my lips slowly and eased away from him. His hands were still positioned as if he were holding something dear and hadn't yet come to terms with the fact that it had been taken away. I dropped to my knees before him and licked the love juice from his head. My tongue circled it slowly as my hand moved up and down. I bit down but not hard. John was thick so I had to prepare myself before taking him inside of my mouth. I moved partway south, bobbing my head up and down while rotating my tongue in a counter clockwise direction.

John moaned and his body tightened. He panted and mumbled compliments on my oral expertise. His knees nearly buckled when I moved my mouth down to the patch of hair at the base of his dick. I held my composure and sucked strong and with more ferocity. John squealed like a girl and grabbed my hair guiding at his desired pace. He throbbed in my mouth and his power became stronger. I eased away so that he would not cum before I had the chance to feel him inside of me.

John lifted me into the air and swiftly placed me on my back on the bed. He removed his clothing quickly and I wished I had a camera, as no one would believe how perfect his body was. He pried my legs open and placed his body above mine. Before he reached my opening I pushed him back gently and felt for my small purse. Inside were at least three different varieties of condoms, a travel sized vibrator and a small tube of Astro Glide. John grabbed a Magnum and rolled it on quickly, then slowly pushed himself inside of me. He took my legs and placed them high upon his shoulders, I could feel that he was deep. He moved back and forth slowly at first and then faster and harder.

I banged on the bed and called out to the Father and Son and anyone else who cared to listen in pleasurable agony grateful for this sexy man whose solid chest was clear of all but a tattoo of a snake around a dagger, whose abs one could bounce a quarter off and whose dick was somewhat of a trophy! I grunted and panted and fondled my body determined to show this man that I could hold my own.

John pulled out and taking me by my waist flipped me over onto my stomach. He pressed down on the small of my back and positioned my rear for a perfect entrance. No holding back as he rammed in and out and I held a tight grip on the blanket. He was getting close and I would not miss out. I reached back with one had and rubbed vigorously against my clit and moaned and called as he pulled my waist to him repeatedly.

"Oh shit! Oh shit!" I whispered as I began to reach my

climax. John beat faster and faster and reaching the culmination of all his efforts, collapsed on top of me.

It was after two more rounds of *getting to know each other better*, that I freshened up and headed out the door without so much as offering a thank you peck on the cheek while John, naked and sweaty, slept like a baby…

2 The Other Ones

The negative of partying during the business week is the issue of needing to arrive at one's employment the following day as a fully functional, profitable employee. Consider this, hit a club by midnight, meet a man by one and if the sex is worthwhile you may not see your own bedside 'til somewhere around four o'clock in the morning. I'm lucky if I even get a good three hours of rest before I must be up with the morning news in the background, struggling with a bun and finding the perfect fit-out for the day.

Sleep was necessary but my body was unconcerned with that fact. I was restless as I lay in bed beside Peta-Gaye. My mind continued to wander and reflect on the time that I'd shared with a beautiful stranger named John only an hour earlier. I rolled onto my back and stared into the darkness toward the ceiling above. His sexy chocolate body continued to appear before me no matter how hard I fought against it. My nipples hardened and my vaginal walls began to close in against each other.

I turned my eyes to the right and met the back of Peta-Gaye's head. She slept so soundly I did not want to wake her. I closed my eyes tight and struggled to find relief in sleep. I pictured everything from baseball to Sister Hattie my old evil

Sunday school teacher. I realized my efforts were in vain when warm moisture spewed forward.

My hands took on a life force of their own. I slowly and tenderly caressed my flesh. I rubbed a hard nipple between my thumb and forefinger while my other set of digits crept in between my thighs. I pressed hard against my clitoris while my middle finger played hide and seek gathering sticky moisture along its route.

I moved my fingers faster and faster stifling my moans. I was becoming closer to orgasm yet could not quite find the freedom to climax. Unable to take the stress any longer I turned onto my side facing Peta-Gayes' sleeping body. I moved in closer until I was pressed against her backside. I softly kissed the top of her spine. I looped my arm around her waist and planted more kisses up and down. My fingers crept slowly down her abdomen as if attracted by its warmth. I massaged slowly and bit her soft shoulders. Her body began to come alive and her pussy moist.

I gently pulled her toward me, rolling her onto her back. I placed my body between her legs and hovered. I kissed each individual section of her pretty face while rocking back and forth causing our hard nipples to rub. Peta-Gaye's hands slid down my back in slow motion. She grasped my ass and held it firmly, biting down on the side of her lip. I paused and gazed into her eyes.

"Good morning sunshine," I whispered.

"F'k you, Ima. I hope you didn't wake me just to tease me."

"Sshhh, temper, temper." I leaned forward and pressed my lips against hers. She allowed my tongue to enter her mouth and entangled itself with hers. I kissed her chin and backed away. I held her breasts together and took turns sucking each hard nipple.

"Oh shit," Peta-Gaye moaned softly. Her body began to squirm and she flailed her arms in the air behind her, reaching out for the headboard for support.

I continued to hold that soft pillowy flesh together caressing them with my thumbs as I kissed down her tummy. I licked and nibbled her sides and took pleasure in her kisses. I made my way toward the creamy filled center but Peta-Gaye caught my wrist and pulled me up.

Together we sat up on our knees with our breasts brushing lightly against each other. Morning breath belonging to her, alcohol scented breath belonging to moi, we kissed deeply and passionately while our hands roamed freely. I walked on my knees backing her against the headboard digging for her tonsils with my tongue.

I pulled back permitting her to come up for a breath. Slowly I eased her thighs apart and focused my vision on the tattoo on the upper section of her inner thigh, which matched mine, the image of a cherry Blow Pop with a chunk bit out of the top. I licked the Pop vigorously as though I could actually taste its sweetness. My tongue glided to Peta-Gayes' own sweetness. The thick scent of sex floated forth enticing me even more. My tongue visited her insides and made a decision to stick around.

Peta-Gaye gyrated her hips. She grabbed a handful of my hair pulling me into her more. She moaned and squealed and spread her legs as wide as she possibly could. Her hips moved faster and faster as I focused on applying pressure to her clitoris.

"Oh shit baby, that feels so damned good!"

The tension in her body relaxed as warm fluid gushed forward from her pussy onto my mouth. I sat up and slid a finger easily inside and gather the moisture. I straddled her waist and placed the guilty fingers into her mouth and allowed her to savor her own loveliness.

I moved my body up until I was hovering above Peta-Gayes' face allowing her the pleasure of returning the favor. I banged the headboard against the wall violently as Peta-Gaye spread my cheeks wide and buried her face amongst the few soft hairs I decided to let remain. She reached up and caressed my solid nipple while she licked and sucked and I went wild.

"Oh shit! Oh f'k!" I screamed and banged and shook until I came and collapsed.

*

"Girl, you heard about those murders?" Garcelle asked walking up beside me at the copier, a stack of papers in her hand.

"What murders?" I asked not looking in her direction.

"Damn, do you not watch the news?"

"Actually no, not really. I hate the news. Depressing."

"Well read a newspaper sometime, damn. The day before yesterday they found this guys body castrated. Today they found another one."

"Whaat?" I said in astonishment turning to face Garcelle. Damn, she was fine.

"I can't believe you hadn't heard about that. Yea, some guy John something or other. What's really insane is that his body was found not too far from the club."

Butterflies sprouted inside my stomach. Could it be? Nah, of course not. I never bothered getting numbers so I was unable to call my John from the night before.

"Garcelle, that guy I was with last nights name is John. You don't think it could be him do you?" I asked, my eyes wide.

Garcelle pursed her lips. "Stop tripping. I mean dawg Ima, John is a very common name. It could be any John. Hell, we're in Florida, it could be Jean."

"You think?"

"Absolutely. Hey, do me a favor and let me know when you're done with this machine please."

Not giving the outlandish suggestion a second thought, Garcelle turned and headed back inside her cubicle.

I shrugged it off and refocused on what I was doing.

*

My cell phone began to ring before I had an opportunity to pull from my parking space. It was a Friday and I knew exactly who it was before I even eyeballed the caller ID.

"Hi, Jonny," I greeted with a smile in my voice.

"Hi, baby. Leaving work now?" Jonathan asked.

"As a matter of fact I am." I backed the new mineral green Lexus RX, which Jonathan paid for, out of the space. I pulled up to the mouth of the parking lot and made a left as opposed to my normal right.

"I need to see you. Do you think you could meet me?"

"When Jonathan? I'm actually pretty busy right now. I have errands to run." That was a lie, the truth was I was already on my way to meet him at our private hideout.

"Well drop it, for me babe, please."

I sighed and paused as though I was actually debating the issue mentally. "Sure. For you, anything. See you soon. Smooches."

I flipped the Motorola closed and tossed it on the passenger seat. I hit the highway and drove north to West Palm Beach. I knew Peta-Gaye would be pissed at me when I didn't come home, especially since I'd told her we could catch a film together that night but I really needed some pocket money.

As I said before, Jonathan was my White family man suga daddy. An investment broker for a large New York based firm and is great at what he does. He therefore owns a pretty attractive bank account. In his world he has the perfect White American life. Blonde wife who bakes brownies, six-year-old namesake Jonathan Jr. who expresses a passion for baseball and a four-year old princess Victoria, not to mention the families Golden Retriever conveniently named Lassie.

But like most White men, though they'd probably not ever admit to it, he needed some real ass to smack his dick on from time to time. That's where I came in. I fulfilled that massa/slave girl relationship desire passed down for generations and he fulfilled all of my materialistic desires from my cell phone, to my closet to my ride to my crib. Shit, I know you didn't think my paycheck afforded me the luxury of wearing $360 Vera Wang shoes to a nightclub.

The door to the small secret three-bedroom home opened wide as I approached. The home itself was actually no real secret, it belonged to his family…it was their vacation home. The fact that he entertained here throughout the year was however.

Jonathan stood in the doorway smiling, dressed in a cream and black sweater and Dockers. He spread his arms and pulled me into a tight embrace. He kissed my forehead and rocked side to side as he closed the door behind me. Jonathan took my hand in his and led me to the master bedroom. He kissed my lips softly before easing me onto my back where he made sweet love to me.

*

I glanced at the clock; it read 7:46 am. My head fell back onto the pillow and I rubbed my eyes with the tips of my finger. Peta-Gaye would definitely have a conniption. I slowly raised my body from the bed and sat on its edge holding a sheet to my chest. My toes bumped against an empty Veuve Clicquot bottle, with my foot I pushed it away. I felt movement behind me as Jonathan began to awaken from his slumber.

"Good morning sunshine," he said.

I rolled my eyes before looking back at him. Peta-Gaye would kill me if she ever found out I got that early morning saying from Jonathan. I took a quick breath and turned to face him with my plastered smile already residing on my face. "Good morning."

"I know you're not leaving already. It's still so early."

"Yea, I know. I promised my mom I'd go antiquing with her today," I lied.

"Yea? Well un-promise her." Jonathan pushed his body up from the bed and rested the side of his face on his open palm. With the silly grin on his face, which was his version of a sexual advance and the morning sunlight bouncing off his balding head, he appeared humorous but I held back my urge to break out into uncontrollable laughter.

"Oh baby, you don't know my mom."

"Alright fine. Maybe I'll be able to break away and see you next week."

Jonathan rolled over onto his side and closed his eyes while I went to bathe and get dressed. I was on my way out the door when on cue he muttered my name. I turned back.

"Go inside my wallet and take what you need to buy some antiques for yourself."

I nodded. I found $1700 in his wallet. This meant $1600 was for me. I rolled it and slid it inside my bra, blew Jonathan a kiss, then headed home.

*

The house was quiet when I entered. I made the assumption that as it was a Saturday morning, Peta-Gaye and Natasha must have still been fast asleep. I walked into my kitchen tired and still a mite bit tipsy. I paused before opening the refrigerator. There was a note from my sister that was placed beneath a magnet. She'd left it behind to inform me that my mother was expecting me a.s.a.p and that she had already gone to see her. I grunted then took a carton of juice and a swig before placing it back on the shelf.

My mother is a very strict woman and quite intolerant of changes in the world. Her harsh ways caused many a fights between her and my sister. It was somewhat of a struggle but we convinced her to allow Natasha to live with me. That, I must mention, was quite a difficult issue to debate considering the fact that my sister and I have never gotten along.

My goal, however was to try to keep my sister on track by allowing her some of the freedoms I did without. The lack of such freedoms I believe is why I am so "free" today. My sister's main objective, on the other hand, was just freedom. Mom required Natasha and I to spend the weekends as a family in exchange for keeping the arrangement as is.

I sighed and headed to my room to get dressed and heard the front door open. I turned the corner and came face to face with Peta-Gaye. If she weren't so brown I swear she would have been red. She walked up as close as she could get to me without blinking. Beginning at my neck and moving down slowly she inhaled deeply through her nose.

"Jonathan," she said plainly.

I ran my tongue across my teeth but said nothing for a moment. "You need some money?"

"I don't want his f'king pussy payment."

"Ok, fine."

"Why do I even bother? You're turning into nothing but a high priced whore," she spat at me.

"If that's how you feel then leave."

"Don't tempt me."

Peta-Gaye pushed past me and charged into our bedroom. I could hear bumping and a drawer open and closed. Just as suddenly as she'd left the room, she returned and headed for the front door.

"Where are you going?" I asked concerned. She was letting me off too easy and it worried me.

"Teddy's waiting for me."

"Teddy?" My blood boiled instantly. "Where's that bitch taking you?"

"Why are you worried about it? Jealous?"

"Of that dyke bitch? Hell naw."

Peta-Gaye looked my body up and down as though she was disgusted by it. She mumbled the word 'sorry' then turned her back to me. It was an insult, not an apology.

"Bitch," I said just loud enough for her to hear.

She only laughed and walked out slamming the door behind her. I tried to shrug it off…she would never leave me I thought. My ego kicked in providing me with the security that I needed to go about my day without worrying about my relationship with Peta-Gaye. I rolled my eyes and shook my head and went to get dressed…

3 Humping Around

I paused before putting my keys onto the table and closing the front door. I leaned forward and listened carefully. I tuned out the sound of the wind whipping through the trees, the birds chirping in the air, my own breathing. The sounds of stifled moans and groans drifted in my direction. I'd left work early and judging by the time on the small watch on my wrist no one should have been home except Peta-Gaye. There were no strange cars in my driveway and my concern and curiosity as well as anger began to peak.

I inhaled deeply, closed the door, and continued on into my crib. I chewed carefully the inside of my mouth and my eyes squinted. I pulled my heels off and kicked them into the corner and charged into the living room. I stood in the archway with my eyes wide and damn near crossed and my purse dangling from my fingers. I blinked several times to focus because surely my eyes were deceiving me.

They hadn't noticed that I'd entered the house. His narrow ass was still pumping with all his life force. She was bent over my cream sofa with her cheek pressed into it moaning and sighing. The same cream sofa that I'd just purchased only a few weeks back and hadn't myself made love on.

"Get y'all asses up!" I yelled and placed my hands on my hips for emphasis. The two jumped and scattered like roaches when the lights came on. I lifted up a Roc-A-Wear t-shirt that was clearly too big for him and tossed it at him. Natasha quickly stepped into her skirt and struggled to button her blouse. My eyes scanned the floor set on a specific inanimate object, which had not yet turned up. The boy mumbled a 'bye' to my sister and rushed past me and out the door.

"Who was that?"

"None of your business," she snapped like I was the minor caught freaking on the couch.

"Fair enough. Whoever he was why was he f'king you in my living room on my brand new sofa?"

"Aren't you home early?"

"Now that's not your business, now is it? But I'll tell you one thing that is my business. Where's the condom?" I asked in all seriousness.

"What?"

"You heard me. I don't see a wrapper, no nasty used rubber, I didn't see that little nigga snatch anything off. How many times I gotta tell you to protect yourself out here little girl?"

"I'm sorry but I don't believe that's any of your business either."

"Seriously? You don't? You're in my home and I've told you on numerous occasions that I ain't no nanny or no f'kin' nurse. You bring a shorty or a disease up in here and trust you will go back home to Mommy with the quickness."

Having this conversation with Natasha was getting old fast. I made it a rule that every six months when I went to get a check up she would as well. Those semi-annual gyno appointments were the closest thing to bonding she and I were gonna get. Yes, we were both clean but if she continued on her destructive path of sleeping around unprotected one day she would get that phone call saying the STD test is positive. I made it a point to also make sure that she was prescribed birth control pills but there was no guarantee that she was consistent in taking them. And my plate was too full to hawk some young adult every morning about popping pills. I followed Natasha to her room and stood in the doorway.

"Why are you always sleeping around on Dre anyway? He seems like such a great guy," I asked trying my best to ease the tension.

"What? I know you are not trying to get all girlfriend with me now. Not after all these years."

"Well damn I am your sister."

Silence consumed the room, so quiet you could hear a pin drop on carpet. I decided it was useless and prepared to turn away. She spoke up.

"Don't you cheat on her?"

Her? Not *her* name but a start nonetheless. I sighed and turned to face Natasha once again. "I do involve myself in physical relationships with other people from time to time but Peta-Gaye is aware of that. We may not discuss it but it's still not a secret."

"Don't try to get all psychological on me, cheating is cheating. How can you judge me for cheating on Dre if you do the same thing in your relationship? Yea, I'll admit that Dre is nice and all and I do believe I love him but…" her voice trailed off.

"You're still missing something and hoping to find fulfillment in one of the frivolous affairs you have," I finished.

Natasha gave me a curious look but then nodded in agreement. It's funny to me how she despised me because of my lifestyle but with the exception of women she emulated it. I had an insatiable sexual hunger that I didn't bother to control. It wasn't until that very moment did I wonder if I even had the ability to control it. One thing I knew for certain, if I couldn't help me then I couldn't condemn her. I gave her the I-don't-know-what-to-tell-you half smirk and shrug and closed her door gently as I left her domain.

*

"An accident this afternoon on I95 left rush hour traffic paralyzed as two lanes had to be shut down...."

"I think Seinfeld is on," I said fishing for the remote.

Garcelle pulled it away and set it behind her. "No, Seinfeld comes on at 10:30, nice try."

"Well Comic View is on, hell M*A*S*H is probably on."

"Anything but the news, huh?" Garcelle shook her head from side to side. Her jaws moving from the Bubbalicious she was chewing. She was seated across from me on the bed with one of my size 9's propped on her lap making it easier for her to paint my naked toenails rouge. She slid the remote across the bed back in my direction. I leaned back on my elbows and channel surfed.

We were granted a few moments more of relaxation before my bedroom door eased opened. Peta-Gaye bumbled in with shopping bags not noticing Garcelle and I. She set her bags against the wall and turned to speak to me but her words switched immediately at the sight of Garcelle.

"What is this?" she called out.

Neither Garcelle nor I flinched. I was not in the mood for Peta-Gaye's bullshit, especially when she was coming home from being with her dyke bitch Teddy. Teddy smiled in my face and claimed to desire no more than friendship from my girl but I wasn't buying it. She was a big intimidating broad at about 6 feet tall, tattooed White hoe but she didn't scare me.

I sighed and sat up on my elbows and shook my hair back from my face. Peta-Gaye exercised great restraint and stood with her hands on her hip awaiting a reason to attack.

"Don't come in here with that nonsense, it is too late at night," I sighed.

"Nonsense? I come home and find this bitch feeling up your f'king feet and I'm not supposed to get upset?"

"No, because you know there is nothing between Garcelle and I but friendship."

"Friendship my ass."

"Who were you out with Peta? Teddy maybe?" Garcelle asked mischievously.

My eyes became saucers and my mouth dropped open. There would definitely be no peace in my home tonight. I jumped up and covered Garcelle's mouth with my hand.

"What did you say to me?" Peta-Gaye's icy glare landed on Garcelle's face. "You wicked likkle bitch, do not dare come in my home and accuse me of cheating on my woman because you want her for yourself."

As Garcelle rose from the bed Peta-Gaye moved in closer. I jumped between trying to prevent them from coming to blows while still struggling to cover Garcelle's slick mouth. She jerked her head from side to side and bit at my hand.

"You don't deserve to be with a woman like Ima and hell yea, if she would wake up and leave your ass I would be there for her I ain't going to lie."

"Aye gal - mi wi kick yu inna yu rass. Mi no know who yu tink yu a chat to. No ramp wid mi!"

"Okay, you know what? Both of you need to just stop." I intervened holding a hand in front of both of their faces. "This mess is so old and frankly I'm tired of it. Tired." I looked directly into Peta-Gaye's eyes as I stressed my exhaustion since she was the biggest instigator. Peta-Gaye challenged me with her eyes and in them I saw a long night ahead of me. I turned to face Garcelle.

"You ready?" I asked.

"The Whole?"

"Yea."

"Let's ride." Garcelle pepped up and turned to walk away as if nothing had ever happened.

"Uh hell no, you're not going anywhere." Peta-Gaye stepped around blocking my path.

"What? Girl I'm grown and am not about to sit around here while you scowl and bitch all night." I started to throw some things in a travel bag but anxious to get out I decided to just borrow something from Gracelle's closet. I followed Garcelle out of my bedroom and across the living room to the front door, Peta-Gaye close on my heels. Casually, I took my keys from the kitchen counter and walked to the door while trying to tune out Peta-Gaye's irritated tone.

"Ima, you can't just leave with her and expect me to be okay with that," she told me.

"I'm going out baby." I reached for her face to kiss it but she smacked my hand away. "I just need to leave for awhile so you can calm down."

"You need to stay here and work this out."

"We'll talk tomorrow."

"Eigh ehh- Galang wid yu dutty rass gal den. Gwaan tes mi, mi wi fix yu rass. Mi should-a gu-weh so wen yu come back mi gone. Cho blood clate! Mi ca tek yu!" she grumbled as she sashayed away. I shrugged my shoulders and walked out of the door behind Garcelle.

*

Kadir wasn't all that physically attractive but all the money he flashed at The Whole that night was a plus for him. His home was magnificent but judging from its décor I got the impression that not only did a woman decorate it but may have also lived in it. Naked in all of my brown glory I strolled around his bedroom waiting and taking it all in. The Phillips flat screen, the campari Calvin Klein bedspread and sheets, the plush carpeting felt good between my toes.

I wandered over to his bureau and inspected the Rolex and diamond embedded pinky ring for authenticity. An object caught the corner of my eye. I reached to pick it up and discovered it to be a framed wedding photo. My suspicions were confirmed and the night became more interesting.

I stretched my nude frame across the bed awaiting his return and trying to determine how much money I'd get out of this sucker. The sound of footsteps came closer and soon he was in the doorway. He was short, could not have been more than 5'7". His pudgy round belly hung over his boxers and coarse hairs were peppered across his chest. His thick thighs rested against one another. He held in his hands a bottle of Cristal and two flutes.

I stood from the bed and swayed my hips as I walked to him. I wrapped my arms around his neck and traced his lips with my tongue before easing it inside of his mouth. I took the alcohol from him and led him to the bed. I set the bottle aside and climbed onto the comfy bed on all fours, my back low and my ass perched high in the air. I grabbed Kadir by the front of his boxers and led him to me and pulled his little pilot from the cockpit. His size was decent, big enough to offer some feeling but small enough to have some oral fun with.

"Come closer," I whispered. I kissed the head then licked slowly building up moisture. I moved further and further down with each suck allowing my tongue to slide up and down his shaft, moving my hand in rhythm. Saliva dripped from my lips as I worked him faster and steadier. Kadir struggled to set the glasses on the nightstand, one missed and landed on the carpeted floor. He moaned and his butt cheeks tensed. He grabbed a handful of my hair and pulled me to him faster and faster.

"Oh damn, girl. Oh shit you know what you doing," he

moaned as my tongue trailed along the base of his penis. "Shit girl, lemme taste that pussy."

I backed away and Kadir charged at me. He dropped to his knees and tossed my legs upon his shoulders. I shuddered when his tongue touched my open vagina. I could feel its thickness as he darted it in and out of me. I twist my hard nipples between my fingers and gasped as he sucked my swollen clit. My hips rocked back and forth against him.

His hands held firmly on my waistline. Without depriving me of his wonderful tongue I heard him feel around on his nightstand. He moved away and fidgeted for a few moments with the condom that he'd pulled out. He then stood and hovered, thrusting himself inside of me. The initial move seemed to be worthwhile but every pump following was awkward and offbeat. I was quite disappointed that he'd chosen to substitute his amazing tongue with his whack dick.

Kadir pumped hard and fast and somewhere near four minutes into our adventure in intercourse he collapsed all three-hundred sweaty pounds against me. I fought for a simple breath while hoping there was something more to look forward to than what'd just happened; maybe he just needed to rest.

Eventually 'Humpty' rolled off of me and onto his back, it didn't take long before his snores were rocking the bed more than he had. My eyes rolled to the back of my head and I mumbled obscenities to myself. I looked at him and smirked. I snuggled closer and nibbled his neck as my fingers strummed across his chest. Kadir grumbled and rolled away.

In awe, disgust and sexual frustration, I eased out of the bed and into the bathroom. I freshened and dressed. Kadir remained fast asleep when I returned to the room. I shook his chubby arm gently.

"What, what?" he snorted and growled.

I took a deep breath before I spoke. "Hey, I need cab fare. Hey, wake up I need cab fare."

"Hell naw, man. Gone and crash on the couch and I'll drive you to the bus stop in the morning." Kadir grunted and rolled onto his side.

My cheeks became flushed as my anger surfaced. I took a deep breath and smiled. "Yes baby." I turned and left the room and headed down to the lower level and called Yellow Cab, then returned up the stairs and to the bedroom. "Kadir. Kadir?"

The only response was his bear-like snores. I crept across the room to the bureau and carefully eased the Rolex into my purse. I turned toward the door but paused. I opened and sifted through a couple of drawers, third one a charm. There amongst a pile of tighty-whities I found $725 in cash.

"Bingo."

I pocketed the money and quickly walked out of the room and out of his home just in time to see my cab puling up...

4 Third Times A Charm

"A third Miami slaying in the past four days. Miami-Dade County police have reported the murder of twenty-nine year old Kadir Watson. His body was found near a dumpster only two blocks from his home in the South Miami Beach area..." The radio anchor announced.

My heart literally paused as each and every inch of my body froze from shock. A car horn blared loudly in its urgency. Realizing that I was veering into oncoming traffic, I swerved back into my place in my lane. As soon as I could take the opportunity I pulled over to the curb and put the ride in park. My heart raced and my breath was ragged. I grabbed my small LV purse off the passenger's seat and rummaged through. Impatiently I dumped the contents on the seat and shuffled them with my palm. I took the gold and diamond studded Rolex into my hand and stared at it, then the radio.

"It can't be," I spoke to no one. I breathed in and out trying to regain my composure. I tossed all of my belongings back into my purse and sat it on my lap. My hands trembled as I tried to grip the steering wheel. I took several deep breaths and blinked back the onset of tears. I focused and controlled my body enough to finish the last ten minutes of my drive to the office.

Normally I'd strut into the building in much the manner of a fashion model, swaying my hips and teasing security with the sight of a real diva. Today I moved like my life depended on it barely flashing my badge, for all I knew it did. In rose BCB Kinte pumps I ran up the five flights on the escalator as if I was rocking a pair of Air Jordans. I dropped my purse and bag on the floor beside my desk and pushed the button to start my computer. My legs shook and I moved nervously as I waited.

"Hey mamita," Garcelle greeted but I was elsewhere and did not respond. When the various icons finally came alive on my screen, I double clicked the IE identity and typed into the browser www.miamiherald.com and there smiling at me was the face of one "Humpty" known to his friends and family and the Dade County coroner as Kadir Watson whose gold and diamond bezel Rollie was resting in the bottom of my purse!

"Oh my God," I gasped. "Oh no…no…"

My hands trembled uncontrollably but I managed to hit the correct keys on my keyboard. I heard sound coming from Garcelle but I couldn't decipher what she was saying and at the moment couldn't care less. I typed vigorously until I found what I'd been looking for. Quickly, I stood from my chair pushing it back to land on its side. The images of the original two victims were before me. Andor Johnson, the weak tongue brother with the small Johnson that I'd spent my Wednesday night with. John Daniel, the beautiful and sensual chocolate lover who'd sent shivers through me on Thursday.

My throat closed and my body was suddenly weak. I could feel my legs beginning to give way beneath me. My fall was broken by the tumbled chair. Sounds went up around me as I was pulled to my feet. Garcelle held me up while someone turned my chair upright. She sat me down gently, speaking words that I just could not comprehend. My eyes remained transfixed on the screen before me. My body was being shaken but I refused to respond.

"Ima!" Armando said with force. He was standing before me.

"Huh?"

"What happened?"

Tears streamed down my cheeks, ruining my carefully applied makeup. I dropped my face into my palms and cried.

Garcelle stooped beside me, draping an arm around my shoulder and rubbing gently. I could feel her warm breath against the side of my face. "Sweetie, talk to us. What happened?"

I looked up. My eyes roamed from one face to the next. My response was barely audible, "I think someone is after me."

"What?"

"What are you talking about, girl?" Armando asked stooping down on the other side of me.

"Look at this," I instructed directing their attention to the Gateway monitor. "Andor, John, Kadir. Dead. Dead. Dead. Murdered and castrated." I looked to each face but there were only blank expressions. "These are the guys I was with last week, him last night. All three of them!"

Garcelle covered her mouth with her hands. Armando stood, a horrified expression on his face. There was no misunderstanding. Armando and Garcelle looked to each other to come up with words of encouragement, a simple explanation. Armando took my hand in his and rubbed his thumb across my fingers.

He said, "Oh girlfriend, I'm…I'm sure there is a logical explanation for this. It's certainly just some weird and morbid coincidence."

My eyes widened. I took my hand back and spoke in a hushed tone, "What am I an idiot? I was with those three men and in the span of a few days all three are dead and killed in the same way?"

Disgusted, scared, and annoyed I stood from my chair and

paced my little cubicle. I had to think…think. What could this – my eyes grew to the size of saucers. I placed my hand to my open mouth as the realization sunk in. "Oh my God you know what this means? I'm a suspect! The police are going to be looking for me. Shit, my fingerprints are all over Kadir's bedroom!"

My peripheral picked up the presence of a couple nosey employees who detected a problem with their normally cool, cocky and confident leader and was trying hard to sort out the details of it. I stepped from any outsider's line of vision. I leaned against a file cabinet with one arm folded around my waist. I chewed my thumb as my leg jerked wildly as I thought and wondered what could have brought this on. "I gotta get out of here," I decided.

I threw my leather bag around my shoulder and grabbed my purse and keys and charged from the office. Armando and Garcelle followed quickly on my heels containing all line of questioning until we'd reached the atrium.

"Ima, honey, where are you going?" Garcelle asked.

"To my mommy's for awhile. Maybe they won't look there right away."

"Wait, wait, wait a minute," Armando demanded. "Chile this is crazy. I mean, I know it seems suspect but…"

"But you don't have a reasonable explanation for me. I gotta get out of here now."

I mashed the button for the elevator and waited impatiently. I saw the wheels of the minds of my friends whirling but no conclusion could be drawn by the time the elevator doors opened and I jumped inside.

*

I concentrated on steadying my hands as I drove to my mother's private community. As a precaution I got out and opened the garage and parked inside beside her Acura and closed it once again. The scent of Pine-Sol assaulted my nostrils the moment I entered the side door. Mommy's twin tea cup poodles barked in a high pitch squeal. My eyes squinted, threatening them with my expression. They quickly retreated as my mother entered from the guest bathroom wiping her hands on the apron tied around her waist. She was beautifully overdressed for housework in olive green slacks and a satin cream blouse.

"Oh! Zucker!" she exclaimed when she spotted me. She reached out and taking my hands into hers pulled me into an easy embrace and kissed both of my cheeks. "To what do I owe this surprise?" she asked unenthused.

I lied. "Oh, I just wanted to spend some time with my mommy."

"That's sweet honey but shouldn't you be working?"

"I took the day off. I've been working so hard, I needed a little break."

My mother looked at me up and down with suspicion. She took my chin into her hand and looked into my eyes. "Are you okay sweetheart?"

Not wanting her to detect too much I covered. "Well to tell the truth Mommy, I haven't been feeling very well. I think I may be coming down with something."

My mother placed a hand on my forehead then my neck. "Well come Zucker, I'll make you some soup. Turn on the television if you like, the remote is right there."

I sighed relief and took a seat on the sofa and aimed the remote at the television. I'd forgotten that it was still very early and the morning news was still on. Panic and fear gripped me as the anchorwoman recapped the details of the morning's gruesome discovery. Trying hastily to change stations I fumbled with the remote. My mother, oblivious to my plight made small talk. "It's terrible about those boys that were found murdered, don't you think honey?"

"Huh? I, I-uh, I don't know anything about it." I finally managed to power off the television. I turned to look at my mother who'd paused placing a hand on her hip, eyeing me.

"Zucker, darling, you've really got to keep up on current events. How many times does Mommy need to tell you this?" She smiled. And I smiled. But there were a plethora of unspoken words behind those smiles.

*

I spent the entire day with Mommy watching her soaps and napping on the couch. Her eldest child, I'd never disappointed and though she constantly pointed out little flaws and behaved as though I couldn't do anything right, she really didn't believe that I could do any wrong. I wondered what she would think of me once she inevitably became privy to why I was really there that afternoon. How would she react when I became a murder suspect and a media spectacle? Oh, her reputation!

The sun had begun to set over the city and I still had not built up the courage to leave the security of Mommy's domain. I sat curled in the corner of the sofa snuggled beneath a multi-colored hand me down throw when much to my dismay Garcelle appeared from around the corner.

"Not happy to see me are you?" I didn't answer. "You're not answering the phone and me and Mando were worried, so what did you expect?"

I quietly reached for her. She took my hand and leaning forward brushed my hair back and kissed me softly on the forehead. I didn't stop her when she flipped her phone open and called Armando. Not fifteen minutes later my conservative-Catholic mother escorted him in with a strained smile plastered on her face and a box of doughnuts in his hand.

The three of us sat quietly watching a rerun of Seinfeld. My mind wasn't there. I prayed inside that the entire ordeal was some sort of insane coincidence though I found it impossible to convince myself that that could be true. I was never one for fear but this thing had its grip on me. I couldn't see my way out of this situation. On the one hand there was clearly a serial killer on the loose and he may have been after me. On the other hand my DNA was all over three murder victims and if the killer didn't get to me first I'd likely be jailed by the end of the week.

I'd fallen asleep but stirred at the faint sound of ringing. A voice carried into my dreams. "This is Garcelle and this is?....Oh hi...Well I'm sorry, she's asleep...I can't, she is asleep."

My brow furrowed in my state of partial consciousness. I adjusted to my surroundings. I blinked Garcelle into focus and saw that she was talking into my phone. Peta-Gaye! "Garcelle give me the phone," I commanded.

"She's at her mothers, she'll be home soon enough. No worries, Mando and me are taking care of her, something you should be doing. Oh that's right, you're not allowed here. Hello?"

"Garcelle!" I said through gritted teeth. But it was too late. Garcelle snapped the phone shut and sat it back on the coffee table. My eyes were slits.

"Sorry," she smiled.

"Bitch."

I readjusted and pulled the cover to my chin and closed my eyes.

*

In the five years that I'd been employed with my company, I had not taken one sick day before this particular week. I'd already called in two consecutive days and was unsure when I'd return. I was jittery and nervous, every few minutes I looked around or peered out the window. I jumped at every noise. My heart felt as though it'd shot up into my throat when I heard my front door open and close. My body tensed and I scurried into the corner of the sofa shielding myself from danger with a cozy comforter. The sounds of footsteps came closer becoming louder, I held my breath. Natasha paused beneath the archway and made a face.

"What the hell is wrong with you?" she asked with deep aggravation.

I answered, "Nothing. I just thought you may have been someone else."

"Oooookay." She rolled her eyes and adjusted the bag on her shoulder. "So what's up? You sick or something?"

"Or something."

"Alright. Well you haven't worked in days and that's not like you. Look, I'm not trying to sweat you or get all up in your biz or nothing like that. I'm just saying it's obvious something is wrong. And I know we don't click like that all the time but I'm your sister. You can tell me if you need help with something."

I took a deep breath and looked at my baby sister. She stood at the end of the couch in her white blouse and hemmed-a-bit-to-high-up-the-thigh plaid uniform skirt. Her body was much too overdeveloped to do her any good.

"I appreciate your concern Tash really, but I'm fine. I've just got a lot on my mind."

She pursed her lips. After a pause she said, "Yea sure," and without another word turned and headed for her bedroom, her long brown ponytail bouncing off her back. Only minutes later Peta-Gaye entered carrying two plastic grocery bags, which she sat on the kitchen counter. She walked over and took a seat beside me. She smoothed my hair and looked in my face smiling, I smiled in return.

"You still don't want to speak about it?" She asked. I shook my head. She caressed the side of my face before standing. "Okay. Fine. I will go and fix ya up some Ginger Tea and soup and I promise that will make you feel alright."

Peta-Gaye leaned in and kissed my lips softly and stood. She turned to walk away but I caught her wrist and pulled her to me. I kissed her again, slowly and passionately. My fingers interlocked in her majestic dreds. I held them tight with her lips to mine, I wanted to cry. I held tightly onto those tears as I reluctantly pried myself from her.

"I love you," I whispered.

"I know baby. I know," she replied...

5 Three's A Crowd

"Three lives were claimed today in South Florida by a silent but deadly killer. Carbon Monoxide poisoning took the lives of..."

I awoke with a start. I sat upright on my sofa as small beads of sweat formed on my nose. I looked around the living room. All was quiet with the exception of the channel 7 news re-broadcasting the same sour information from earlier. With the remote I turned off the television. I slumped into the corner and ran my nails across my scalp. My quickened heartbeat began to slow down to normal speed.

I tossed the blanket from my body and placed my bare feet on the cool floor and walked to the kitchen. The house was warm so I pulled my tee-shirt up and over my head and stood at the stove boiling water for tea in nothing but my Joe Boxers. I was dozing on the counter when the kettle whistled. I jumped with a start and rushed to turn the eye off. I paused to do a breathing exercise to calm my self then turned to reach for my mug.

"What the - !"

"Oh man Ima, my bad. I'm sorry, I ain't realize nobody was up. I'm sorry," Dre apologized though he didn't bother to turn his head. I didn't say anything, if the little boy liked what he saw who was I to deprive him?

"Andre, its two o'clock in the morning on a school night. What are you still doing here?"

He stammered to get his words out, "W-well Tash said if I could stay...I mean that it was okay if I could stay..." He took a deep breath finally looking into my face. "She said I could stay the night. If that ain't aiight with you I'll bounce to the crib right now."

I had enough stress. I shrugged my shoulders and turned to make my tea. "Whatever, just don't get my sister pregnant or I'll break your dick, do you understand?"

"Y-yea. I feel you. I keep Magnums."

I turned slightly. "Magnums?"

He stood straighter and puffed out his chest. A little on the slim side but he was attractive. "Yea."

"Very well. Was there something you wanted in here?"

"Huh? Well yea but...nah I'm good. Gonna get some sleep."

"Okay." I turned to face him. I leaned against the sink and moved my mug to my lips. "And Dre, just one more thing. Though I'm very sure you enjoy running into Peta and me naked every now and then, you'd better make damn certain my sister never catches you enjoying the view. If she does all hell is going to break loose."

I moved my arms which were obstructing his view of my lovely twins and sipped my Chamomile. He smirked and nodded. I could only laugh.

*

I'd been laid up "sick" for three days. Much to Peta-Gaye's dismay Garcelle and Armando showed up at my door unannounced and fully dressed and ready for a night at The Whole.

"Bitch get up," Armando ordered.

I growled, "What are you two doing here?"

"Coming to get you out of the house. You cannot just become a recluse now, I won't allow it."

"Puh-leeze, I'm not going anywhere." I rolled my eyes and flipped through channels.

"Get up and get dressed. You're going. We're not leaving here without you," Garcelle stated.

"Garcelle are you sure we should do this?" Armando asked, turning his nose up. "This heifer looks a certified mess."

"Don't she?"

"Mmhm."

"Screw both of y'all in the ass with the broomsticks you witches flew in on."

Peta-Gaye could be heard slamming things in the kitchen. Garcelle stuck out her tongue and up her middle finger. "What kind of bug crawled up her ass and died?"

"Don't come here instigating shit, Garcelle."

"If you just get up and dressed then everyone will be happy."

"Well I thank you for your concern but I'm really not in the mood. Besides that I don't think it's a good idea," I said through gritted teeth.

"I got this," Armando addressed Garcelle. He took a seat beside me and took my hand in his. "Ima. Sweetie. Listen to me. No, listen. Stop worrying, nothing is going to happen to you I promise. We're going to go out and have a good time. You'll come home to Peta-Gaye and it'll all be just fine."

I sighed exhaustively. I hadn't heard of any related murders since Kadir. How was I to know that this creep wasn't just laying in wait for me to slip up so he could slit my throat? But what if this was what he wanted, for me to reside in a constant state of fear not enjoying my youth as I chose? Armando could have very well been right. Yes, of course. I could go out and have fun, I just wouldn't pick anyone up. I would party, have a great time, and come home to wifey.

I sighed and crawled from the sofa. "Fine. You do my hair after I bathe while this Queen finds me something to wear."

*

My two friends helped me to look my ravishing self once again. I felt like a twenty-pound weight had been lifted the moment I looked over my body in the black ABS Chiffon dress and Carlos Santana Retro pumps. Despite Peta-Gaye's objections I went out and was happy that I had done so.

The second I inhaled the night air I'd forgotten why I'd hibernated in the first place. My glass was full from the moment I walked into the club and was soon on the verge of being drunk. Maccartney slipped into the booth beside me.

"I heard you were here! We missed you, what happened?" she asked.

"Damn, I've only been off the scene for a couple of days!"

"Well, whatever! I have a little welcome back gift for you!" Maccartney pulled a small tin package forward and eased it open. She poured the coke on the table and cut it into smooth lines before me. "Ready, mama?"

With rolled up fifties we snorted the powder until it was gone. Feeling right we slumped into each other and listened to the music. Garcelle was a blur when she eased in on my left.

"Having a good time?" she asked into my ear. I nodded. "Good. Where's Sasha?"

I pointed him out near the edge of the dance floor. He was grinding and kissing a young blonde kid. She nodded. With her fingers she very easily turned me to face her. She took her free hand and seductively slipped it into my mouth. I felt the small pill begin to dissolve on my tongue.

I poured myself a glass of Cristal and drank it down. Beginning to feel antsy I climbed over Garcelle and tried to exit the booth. I felt her hands firmly on my waist. I glared at her but she smiled and handed me a Charms.

I moved onto the dance floor and swayed my hips to the DJ's beats. My eyes locked on the face of a gorgeous black man. I scanned the length of his tall frame down to the crotch of his pants and back up. His lips were thick and wet with moisture. His skin was the color of steaming hot chocolate. The cornrows he wore nearly touched his shoulders. He walked in my direction. One of his strong arms slid around my waist and he spoke into my ear. His breath smelled sweet like Sour Apple Martini.

"Wassup, Ima?" he asked.

I blinked in the darkness and attempted to focus. "Do I know you?"

"Not exactly. We met last Memorial Day weekend."

"And you remember me?"

"Of course. A nigga could never forget a face as fine as yours."

I tilted my head in wonderment. "Did we f'k?" I asked.

His eyes widened. "No, no we didn't!"

"Oh. So what's your name?"

"Rell! Yo, it's kinda loud in here shorty! Come over here and let me holla at you!"

Twenty minutes later I was anxiously hunting down Garcelle or Armando. I found Garcelle first. "Come here, quick! You see that guy at the end of the bar? There. He's fine isn't he?"

"That's the under-statement of the year. And? You wanna get with him, then get with him!"

"But Garcelle what if…you know."

"Girl please, nothing is going to happen. Don't be paranoid. Go to Brucie's Holiday. It's familiar there and you know they'll look out!"

I paused to ponder my options. I wanted the man but how could I feel confident that nothing would happen? And not only to him but to me as well. "Garcelle, come with me. Please."

"Oh, you can't be serious. You're serious? This is ridiculous, Ima. You can't spend your life being paranoid."

"Forgive me if I'm a little on edge, look at what's happened. I'd just feel safer if you were with me."

She made a frustrated noise. "Fine! If it'll make you feel better! You are so lucky I didn't meet anyone interesting tonight! Wait for me, let me tell Mando!"

I was relieved and relaxed. I told Rell that Garcelle would be joining us as we'd come together. When he saw her any concerns he may have harbored were immediately alleviated. Surely he was hopeful that he would have both of us but it was not that type of party.

A friend of ours, Bruce Buckey or Brucie, ran a local Holiday Inn Express which we often frequented. We were known on a first name basis by staffers and for a small tip were given the best room available for a few passionate hours. Fortunately the Executive Suite was available which gave Garcelle a place to entertain herself while Rell entertained me.

I wasted no time. I pushed Rell against the door and went straight for his zipper. I pulled his less than impressive penis (even at full erection) from his red silk boxers and teased it with my tongue with the hopes that it would flourish under my attention. I watched the contortions on his face as I tried swallowing him whole. He was so lovely that I forgave his "short cummings".

"Oh yea, suck this dick, baby. Suck it," he instructed breathlessly to which I obliged until I became bored with the lack of challenge.

I eased away and his knees buckled. He looked as though he'd been running a marathon. I took his hand in mine and led him to the queen size bed and sat him upon it. I pulled the terry cloth polo-style Ecko shirt and "wife beater" over his head. I ran my fingers across the coarse hairs on his chest before planting soft kisses. I turned so that he could unzip my dress. I swayed gently allowing it to fall to the floor.

I stood before him in my black lace thong and pumps. I pulled his face to me and nibbled his ear and traced it with my tongue. Rell cupped one of my breasts and placed it inside the warmth of his mouth and nibbled. He placed his hands firmly on my waist and moved me away. He quickly kicked off his Timbs and stood to remove his black jeans, recklessly throwing them in the corner. I'd moved away and sat myself on the desk with my legs cocked open.

"Got-damn!" Rell exclaimed while massaging his dick.

"Do you want me?"

"Hell yea!"

"You want to f'k me?"

"Shit yea!"

"You want to taste me don't you?"

"I wanna suck that pussy dry and lick it wet again!"

I signaled for him to come to me. Standing between my thighs and lifting my body slightly he slipped my panties from my body. He held them to his nose and inhaled their scent before tossing them to the floor.

Rell dropped to his knees before me and buried his face in my mother earth. I moaned and groaned as he dashed his tongue in and out. I straddled my legs around his neck. I tossed my head back and jerked against him faster and faster until a warm coolness moved through my body. I rested my weight on my forearms and gasped for air. Rell took me into his arms and carried me to the bed. He kissed and sucked my neck as I worked to regain my composure.

I pushed him away and he lay on his back. I straddled his waist allowing my breast to spill forward into his face. I rubbed my coochie back and forth against him as he took turns with each nipple. My moans increased becoming more erotic. I was surprised, though I didn't flinch, when I felt warm breath and soft lips on my spine. When I turned my head Garcelle was nibbling my shoulder blade. I opened my mouth to protest but she quickly silenced me with her tongue. My mind yelled, screamed, cursed and told me how wrong this was but the desires of my flesh and sexuality drowned them out.

Garcelle crept around me and straddled Rell's waist facing me. Rell's stiffness was unexpectedly caught between two throbbing, wet pussy's. We kissed deeply and passionately. I leaned my body back and allowed Garcelle's tongue to travel down the valley between my breasts. She teased my nipples with her tongue. My breathing was heavy and my body ran warm. She placed her hand firmly around my neck and guided me to her as she bit into me. She was in control. Submission was a role I never played but my shock was too great to fight.

"Touch me," she commanded and I obliged.

I sucked her finger like it was a dick and caressed her clean shaven cooch. We'd completely forgotten Rell's presence. Garcelle took my hand in her hands and guided me from the bed and to the shower. The water ran warm and we stepped inside. My back was pressed against the cold linoleum.

Garcelle fondled my breasts and kissed me, encircling my tongue with hers. She nibbled my bottom lip and pressed her body deeper into mine. I opened my eyes and mine met Rell's as he sat on the toilet top salivating with dick in hand. Garcelle slid down my body and nibbled my inner thighs. She licked me slowly before inserting her tongue inside.

"Oh!" I gasped grabbing a handful of her hair. I whispered in a hoarse voice, "Oh shit…"

Garcelle touched parts of me that no man, nor Peta for that matter, had ever explored, parts I hardly knew existed. It wasn't long before I was bursting fluids into her mouth to spill forth down her pouty lips. My body writhed in ecstasy. I begged her to stop but didn't want her to and she didn't. I moaned and my body shook. Tears streamed from my eyes. I could no longer support my own weight and slipped down into the tub. Garcelle helped me out and took Rell's hand in hers. She led the both of us back into the bedroom. She climbed onto the bed on all fours and head gestured to me, I positioned myself beside her. She leaned in and kissed me again.

Rell took turns pushing in and out of both of us. It felt as though his dick had grown a couple inches wider. I suppose an unexpected ménage could do that to a man. He continued to work us as we moaned and screamed until he was satisfied and exploded all over our bodies.

*

I had, as was tradition, denied Rell's request to exchange numbers but growing tired of his incessant whining and begging I took his before leaving him to replay the events in his own mind. I was deathly silent as we left the hotel. I kept at least two paces between Garcelle and I as we walked.

"Hey, slow down!" she called. "What's the matter with you?"

"What you pulled back there was foul," I snapped.

"Oh now I know you're not tripping. You're not mad at me for what happened back there!"

"You were wrong for that! You totally took advantage of me! I've never messed around on Peta-Gaye and you know it."

Garcelle laughed coldly. "What kind of twisted reality do you live in? Even if I hadn't come in that room, the fact that you were there with that man defines you screwing around on Peta-Gaye."

"You know what I mean."

"Nooo, I really don't. You screw around on her damn near every night and the fact that it's only with men makes it no better. And as far as you and I, you didn't stop me nor hesitate to pop your pussy all up in my face so don't you dare try to make yourself feel better about what you do by placing the blame on me."

"You knew what you were doing when you agreed to come to the hotel with us!"

"Bitch, you begged me to go!"

"Because I thought I could trust you!"

Garcelle's eyes were wide. "Oh so now I'm not trustworthy? Well you can kiss my non-trustworthy ass or did you do that already? Hmm. I'll catch me a cab."

"Yea you do that."

Angry and embarrassed I power walked down the street in search of my ride...

6 All Falls Down

I shuffled to my bathroom and closed the door behind me. I stood with my back to the door and my eyes closed tightly. I was emotionally drained. I ran my nails vigorously back and forth across my scalp and slipped slowly to the tile floor. I was feeling awful, like a terrible person. For the first time, I'd gotten higher than I could handle and cheated on Peta-Gaye with my best friend and placed the blame for it on her. My God, I hadn't even used protection. I felt so much shame but at least nothing happened to Rell and I'd awakened to see another day.

I stood upright and rested my palms on the sink and looked at my reflection. I sighed deeply and filled my palms with warm water and splashed it on my face. I thoroughly brushed my teeth and scraped my tongue. I had to put on my poker face. I brushed my hair back and tied a scarf around it, then returned to my bedroom. Peta was still sound asleep. My head was pounding and I was nauseous.

I slipped my feet into a pair of battered, yellow house slippers and shuffled to the kitchen. I clicked on the small television and turned the volume way down. I searched the cabinet for tea and honey. The lazy shuffling of house shoes made their way across the kitchen floor. I turned disinterested yet instinctively to see

Natasha looking to the floor and scratching her scalp.

"Morning," she mumbled as she opened the refrigerator.

"Morning."

The chime of the doorbell echoed through the house.

"I'll get it. It should be Dre." Natasha shuffled toward the front door as I began filling a kettle with warm water. Moments later she returned much more alert than she'd been when she left me. Unfortunately it was not Dre ringing my bell way too early. I stood face to face with a gorgeous man who was flashing a badge at me and his short, clunky sidekick.

Natasha's voice quivered when she spoke to me. "Ima, these *homicide* detectives are here to see you. Um. Why?"

"Oh my God." The tea kettle slipped from my grip and crash landed at my feet, splashing water all over.

"I take it you know why we're here," the sexy one spoke.

"Uh, no. not exactly but I have an idea."

"Is that so?" His eyes scanned the length of my body and his lips curled into a sexy smirk. "Well I'm Detective Crane, this is my partner Detective Lawrence. May we have a seat Mrs. Phelps?"

"Miss."

"Miss."

"Please." I gestured for them to make themselves comfortable. "I was…I was uh, going to make tea. Red Zinger but there's also Peppermint…or Chamomile. Do you prefer coffee? I can make coffee."

"Ms. Phelps, please. We had coffee and doughnuts on the way over. Joking, relax. Join us."

I sighed and momentarily turned my back to the officers. I closed my eyes tightly, fighting the urge to cry. I took a deep breath, inhaling every ounce of strength floating in the cosmos. As if everything were suddenly peachy, I turned with a smile on my face. I stooped low and picked up the tea kettle and set it in the sink.

"Ima, are you okay?" Natasha asked.

"Huh? Oh, yea. Yea. Of course. Go on back to bed Tash, it's early."

She nodded but looked confused. "Yea. Okay."

I took a seat at the table with the officers. I folded my hands on the table before me then decided that I'd rather sit them on my lap. I changed my mind and unlatched them. I used one hand to move my hair behind my ear.

"Nervous?" he asked.

"Why-why would I be?"

"Exactly Ms. Phelps. Why would you be?" asked Clunky.

I scowled in his direction and then inhaled deeply to regain a sense of control. I tossed my head back (forgetting that it was tied down) and placed my palms flat on the table.

"What is this regarding Officers?" I asked in the most controlled tone possible. Clunky pulled seemingly from thin air a photo and placed it before me. A knot formed in the pit of my stomach and my throat closed, my head swam from a lack of oxygen. My armpits itched and felt moist.

The sexy Detective Crane spoke, "Do you recognize this gentleman?"

Water flooded my eyes. I tried blinking them away but one escaped. Fear gripped me by the throat and refused to let loose. I didn't know how to answer. So being without the advice of a lawyer, I said nothing. The cop continued.

"His name is Aurelius Carter. People that knew him called him Rell. We have reason to believe that you and a Ms. Garcelle Washington were with him around the time of his death."

"What?" I asked in shock and disbelief. The room was spinning.

"Ms. Phelps," Clunky addressed me. "What were you and Ms. Washington doing with Mr. Carter last night?"

"I don't know-" I began.

He continued, "The three of you were seen checking into a

Holiday Inn Express together but only you and Ms. Washington were seen leaving."

"That's because Rell left after us," I uttered.

"Oh, yes he did. He left in a body bag. What we want to know Ms. Phelps, is exactly what happened in that room between you, Mr. Carter, and Ms. Washington."

"Yes, Ima. Inquiring minds want to know. Just what happened between you and Garcelle last night?"

There were no more surprises at this point. Nothing could shake me. I closed my eyes and dropped my head. I whispered an apology to Peta-Gaye, said something typical like, it's not what you think.

"Don't you dare."

I looked pleadingly into her eyes. "Peta, please."

There was an old fashioned alarm clock that I kept on the shelf nearby. The kind that's gold with two loud ringing bells. Peta took it in her hand.

"You f'kn bitch!" she screamed aiming the clock at my head. I was used to her tantrums, I ducked and she charged. Officer Clunky was on her but despite his girth, my feisty little Jamaican woman was almost too much for him to handle. He took Peta-Gaye outside of the kitchen. I watched until I could see them no more. Officer Crane placed a strong hand on mine and I shifted my line of vision.

"Are you okay?" he asked.

"Am I a murder suspect?" I asked to which he nodded. "Then I'm not okay."

"You know about the others I'm sure." I nodded. "Your DNA was found on each of the victims."

"That doesn't make me a murderer."

"No, but it does make you suspicious."

We were silent for a moment.

"So are you going to take me in?"

"Likely. But not today."

"So you're just going to let me go?"

"Would you rather I take you in?"

I was quiet. Detective Crane stood and I followed his lead. He held his hand out to me and I took it in mine and shook. He continued to hold even as I prepared to break, his eyes locked on mine. "I'm going to ask you a question Ms. Phelps and hope that you will be honest with me. Did you do it?"

I looked him directly in his eyes, keeping my gaze steady, stern and unflinching answered, "No."

He nodded and released my hand. I followed him out of the kitchen and through to the living room. Peta-Gaye screamed and lunged the moment our eyes locked. Detective Crane stepped in her path keeping me safe from her wrath. Emotionless I looked past him and at the small neatly packaged bag that sat by the door.

"Where are you going?" I called over his body but her response was only incessant, incoherent ramblings. "Peta, where are you going?"

"Getting the f'k outta here."

"Are you going to Teddy? Sweetie, I need you here with me, you can't go to Teddy!" My voice was thick with suppressed tears. "Baby, I'm sorry. I'm really sorry."

I pushed my way past the Detective and took my chances on a face to face with my woman. I needed her to look into my face...to see the hurt, grief, and guilt in my eyes. I reached for her but hesitated.

"Baby, I didn't mean for it to happen, you gotta believe me. I hate to use a stupid cliché like 'It just happened' but that's the truth, it did. She was only there for protection and she took advantage of the moment and I was so out of it that...that I didn't stop her."

Detective Crane took my arm in his and gently tried to persuade me to come toward him. Peta-Gaye's gaze locked on mine and I remained still in my position.

Clunky glared at us through his beady little eyes. "Ms. Phelps, Ms. Sinclair must leave the premises in order to avoid a domestic situation. Besides, you're in enough hot shit already." He about faced, instructing Peta-Gaye to get her bag and leave.

Her eyes never moved, nor did mine. I tuned everything out and prayed internally that she would find a way to forgive me and stay by my side. I was so focused that I didn't see it coming, only felt the burning sting of the flesh of her palm landing hard against my cheek. Detective Crane immediately pulled me to safety whilst his partner escorted the love of my life away, possibly forever.

Detective Crane held my shoulders in his large hand, obstructing my view of Peta-Gaye with his frame. He looked deep into my eyes. "If you can think of anything…anything that may help your case, call me. In the meantime, if you haven't already, I strongly suggest you consult a lawyer."

I nodded and my eyes followed them toward the door. Detective Crane paused and returned to me, extending his business card. Natasha closed and locked the door behind them and returned to my living room. She stood staring, with a million plus one questions on her tongue. I shook my head 'no' and threw my hands defensively in the air.

"Ima!" she screamed.

I sat on the sofa in silence and took up the remote. I tuned in to CNN and dropped the remote on the floor. I needed to know if my face was plastered all over television as a suspected murderer. Natasha sat beside me.

"Ima what's going on?" she asked with a shaky voice.

"It's nothing. Don't worry about it."

"Don't do this to me."

"Do what?"

"Treat me like I'm some stupid seven year old child who doesn't have the mental capacity to comprehend that mommy and daddy are getting a divorce because mommy's a whore!"

Without thinking about my actions, I slapped my sister hard across her face. She raised a hand to touch the spot and her eyes became slits but quickly softened.

"All I'm saying is that there were homicide detectives here. You can't tell me it's nothing."

I wanted to tell her something, anything, hell everything but I instead shushed her. "Please, just hand me the phone. Hand me the phone!"

Natasha quietly did as instructed.

I dialed Garcelle's home number, it was busy. I dialed her cell phone number and she answered, "I cannot believe it, I cannot believe it, I cannot believe it!"

"I called the house. The line was busy."

"I took the phone off the hook."

"Police were at my house this morning. Detectives."

"Ima, no."

I looked at Natasha. She was listening to the anchorman recap the discovery of the body of Aurelius Carter, listening and trying to decode my conversation with Garcelle, and watching my face. A look of horror crossed her face.

"Ima, you didn't!" she exclaimed jumping from her seat.

"Of course I didn't!"

"Then why do they think you did?"

"What's going on, Ima? Who are you talking to?" Garcelle asked in panic.

"Because me and Garcelle were with him last night."

"Ima!!" Garcelle screamed into the phone.

"What?!"

"So, do you have any idea who did it?"

"No, I don't. Obviously. If I did, I would have said something!"

"Ima Anne Phelps, bitch you better talk to me right now and tell me what the hell is going on over there! I'm coming over."

"No! No, meet me at Armando's house, we'll talk about it

there." The line was silent. "Garcelle. Did you hear me?"

"We're going to need a lawyer," she spoke softly.

I sniffed. "Yea, yea I know."

I disconnected the line and turned off the television. Natasha followed me silently with her arms folded across her chest. I rushed about my room snatching open and closing drawers, removing items and tossing them on the bed. I grabbed a large Nike duffle bag and haphazardly tossed random things inside.

"Go pack you a bag, I'm dropping you off at Mommy's."

I could sense her rolling her neck and eyes as she spoke, "Uh uh, I'm not going anywhere until I have an understanding of what the hell this is all about. You need to tell me what's going on? What kind of mess are you getting into out there? Are me and Mommy in danger? Ima!"

I threw the brush that I was holding in my hand hard into the wall, peeling away flecks of paint and leaving a small indentation, before turning to face her. She swallowed and tried hard to conceal her fear but it was transparent. Rage had swelled within me like rotted wood at a dam about to burst. I had enough to contemplate and deal with, what I didn't need was some little ornery, spoiled brat questioning my authority.

"I don't know what is going on, Tasha! You wanna know what I know? I'll tell you what I know, I know four people are dead and I am suspected of killing them. I have no clue why I'm not in jail now but I have a sneaking suspicion that I will be very soon.

"But wait, it gets deeper. I also suspect that somebody is deliberately out to get me, maybe even kill me. The downside is I don't know the who nor the why! I can't control this and it's snowballing. But there is one thing left that I can control and that's what goes on in this house! So you little snot nose bitch, get your shit and meet me in the f'king car!"

Natasha turned on her heels immediately, slamming the door hard behind her...

187

7 Can't Keep Running Away

I awoke at sunrise in unfamiliar surroundings. The faint light of day streamed through the window and fell across the cream carpeting. I furrowed my brow in confusion as I blinked to adjust my eyes. The Mexican art hanging on the walls reminded me that I'd slept over Armando's house. The sound of a car pulling up outside sent my heart rate up a notch. Something just didn't feel right.

I flung the thin covering from my legs and jumped up and crept quickly across the room, staying low and close to the wall. Slowly and cautiously, I peered from behind the beige floor length curtain. My heart pounded so loud that I was almost certain I'd be heard. I quickly moved out of view and very carefully eased the curtain back just enough for me to see Detective Crane standing beside his car talking into a cell phone. A moment later his pudgy partner emerged from the passenger's side. I moved back and let the curtain fall back in place.

"Shit," I whispered harshly hoping that neither had noticed the movement. I had no time to think and little time to act. I moved into action. Keeping low to prevent anyone from seeing my shadow, I crawled across the floor to the opposite end of the couch. I grabbed my Nike's and gym bag and crept carefully toward Armando's room. The door was ajar and I could hear his soft snore. I detoured and went to the kitchen praying there was no one on the other side of the door. I quietly undid the locks and easily moved into the backyard, closing the door softly behind me.

Keeping low and out of the line of sight from the front of the house, I moved to the end of the yard and tossed my things over the short fence. I climbed over and put my sneakers on my feet, the bag on my shoulder and took off running, keeping near houses at all times. I'd never needed to the dodge the law before and had no idea how it worked. For all I knew my every move was being broadcast over national television and someone would be waiting around the corner ready to haul me in.

My adrenaline pumped. Sweat mixed with my hair, matting it to my forehead. I could feel the perspiration leaking from my armpits. I'd kept moving until I came out on 163rd. I paused and looked both ways trying to determine which way to go. I was too far to get anywhere without my vehicle which was left sleeping soundly on Armando's property. They'd know I'd been there and that I ran. This would make me more suspicious.

I tried to think…think…think… Fearful of using my cell phone, I moved fast and headed south toward the Amoco on the corner. There was a payphone but who would I call? Likely it was unsafe to take a cab home. If the cops were looking for me at Armando's, when they discovered I was gone they would likely check the homes of everyone else close to me. Who could I call that I could trust but that no one would suspect I'd turn to? Maccartney!

I dropped the awkward but lightweight duffle bag to my feet and stooped down to open it. I unzipped and scrapped together $1.03, enough for two phone calls. I looked up McCartney's number in my mobile, inserted fifty cents and dialed the digits. I held my breath as it rang.

"Hello?" The voice was deep, husky and somewhat masculine and clearly tired. For a moment I thought I must have dialed wrong.

"Maccartney?" I asked.

"Yes, who is this?" A slight femininity confirmed I'd dialed correctly.

"Hey girl, it's Charity," I tried hard to sound casual.

"Charity honey, it's always a pleasure but do you know what time it is?"

"Yes and I'm sorry for disturbing you this early in the morning."

"Well chile, what's wrong? What do you need?"

I carefully peered down the block in each direction. "I was wondering if I could spend the day at your house. It's important."

"Why Charity? I have to work this afternoon."

"I know, I...know. I mean it's cool. I could stay alone."

There was a brief pause. "Honey, are you alright?"

"Yea, I'm fine," I fibbed. "I just can't explain right now. Please. You know I never ask you for anything and you know that I wouldn't ask if I didn't think it was important."

I could hear the wheels of Maccartney's mind clicking and whirring as he contemplated whether or not he should be suspicious of me. "Mmhm...well, that is true. Well come on over here chile, I gotta get up and get ready for work anyway."

"Thanks," I sighed. "I'll grab a cab and be there in a little bit."

"A cab? Chairty!"

I quickly placed the phone into its cradle, cutting him off. I used the last of my change to call Yellow Cab Company.

*

Maccartney opened the door wearing a bright yellow terry cloth bathrobe and coordinated slippers. He had a thin bath towel tied around his head and a plate of eggs and bacon in his hand. It was at that moment I realized that I was hungry. I tried not to stare at the yolk that was running over.

"Chile, you look like you've seen a ghost!" he exclaimed as he leaned in. We air kissed both cheeks. I self consciously held my breath in as more than twenty four hours had passed since I'd brushed my teeth. He stepped aside and allowed me in.

I looked him over in awe at his size. Maccartney was big, slightly larger than Armando who stood at least 6'0" and weighed in at about 230. His facial structure was more masculine than Armando who actually looked very beautiful and feminine in drag. Maccartney had a heavy bone structure with thick, attractive lips. His eyebrows were perfectly arched over his mocha brown eyes. I struggled to recall having ever seen Maccartney both sober and by the light of day. I shrugged and moved to the sofa and collapsed in the cushions.

Maccartney stood shoveling food into his mouth. My stomach churned. "You hungry?"

"Oh no, thank you." Although hunger pangs were beating up my insides, I didn't think I had the capacity to hold any food down.

"Suit yourself," he said through a spoonful of eggs and went about doing his morning rituals calling out to me as he did. "So! What's got your Vicky's in a bunch?"

"Huh? Oh nothing really. It's just…well." I struggled to come up with a quick yet believable fib. "Well, this guy that I was with once, I think he's kinda stalking me. I saw his car out by my house a couple of days so I went to Mando's last night. This morning his car was outside so I snuck out back and called you."

"Did you call the police?"

"Huh?"

He peered around the corner at me, his toothbrush in hand. "Did you call the police?"

"Oh no. I…I didn't think…" my voice trailed off and I picked at my fingernails. I cursed myself for the bad lie I'd told.

"Well maybe you should." He returned to the bathroom and the running water. "Go ahead and use the phone!"

"Oh no, not right now. I'm just tired. I'll deal with it this afternoon."

Mccartney returned to the living area dressed for the day in creased khaki's and a crisp white button down with a cream colored tie. His large, dark curls glistened in the light. His olive skin was clean and freshly shaven. Were it not for his feminine mannerisms and speech, I'd surely believe that Mccartney was all man. I suppose I was staring because he asked in a semi masculine tone. "Surprised to see me like this huh?"

"Oh sorry," I giggled. "You look good like that. Really good."

"Thank you pudding. That's just what my Mexican mama tells me but it ain't gone move no mountains over here. I am gonna be strictly dickly 'til the day I'm buried and gone." He snapped and laughed at his own comment. "Anyway, girlfriend, I have got to hit the pavement running. These uppity rich white folk ain't gone seat themselves, that's for damn sure. Make yourself at home. If you get hungry eat, thirsty drink. There are fresh towels in the linen closet." He paused, placing a contemplative finger on his chin. "Oh, and don't forget to call the police. We can't have anything happening to you, now can we?"

"I'll call. Thanks darling."

"Mmhm." Maccartney headed out the front door but quickly leaned back inside. "I almost forgot, if you decide to leave, there's a spare key in the top drawer of my bureau in the bedroom. Just give it back to me at the club." He blew a kiss and left, locking the door behind him.

I stood and walked to the center of the room trying to determine what my next move would be. I stood…alone, my arms embracing myself...seeking comfort. The quiet became agonizing but I was afraid to move, afraid to make a sound. The chime of my cell was worse than walking up behind a little old lady in a dark alley and yelling "HEMROID!" I jumped and began to shake violently.

I inhaled deeply. "Ima, Ima, Ima, you've got to pull yourself together," I scolded myself. "You didn't do anything wrong."

I took another deep breath and slowly placed my arms at my sides. I closed my eyes tight and exhaled heavily. The ringing ceased. I listened to the ticking of a clock in the distance. The occasional drip of water from the kitchen faucet and engines revving in their driveways. The phone rang again.

My heart leapt into my throat but I managed to move from my position slowly but steadily, nonetheless. Nervously I edged toward my duffle bag and took my phone from inside. I looked at the caller ID, it was Garcelle.

"Hello? Hello?" I answered frantically.

"Ima! My God girl, I've been so worried. Where are you?"

I hesitated. "They're looking for me aren't they?"

"Have you seen the television today?" her voice was far away and I was, once again, panic stricken.

"Hold on." I dropped the phone from my ear and moved swiftly across the room in the direction of the large screen television encased in the entertainment center. The remote control was sitting on top. I took it and powered the television on. Cartoons flooded the airways. For a brief moment I was far removed from my problems and slightly amused at the image of a large homosexual queen eating a bowl of Lucky Charms and watching Cartoon Network.

I shook it off and tuned into the morning news. I walked backwards to the sofa and placed the phone to my ear. The story of yet another car submerged in a canal was being relayed.

"Garcelle, you're still there?"

"I'm here sweetie."

We waited in silence…

"Continuing coverage on the Miami Massacres, for those of you just tuning in, it seems that Miami Dade police finally have a lead on a suspect. We turn it over to our reporter in the field, Rosh Lowe…"

I held my breath for so long, I was certain I'd turned blue. I watched as the reporter, standing beside my Lex parked in front of Armando's neat little home on his (previous to this incident) quiet little street, exposed everything he knew. "…police are looking for this woman, twenty-nine year old Ima Anne Phelps, for further questioning…"

"Twenty eight!" I yelled at the screen. "I'm twenty eight you dumb f'k and I didn't do anything!"

My call waiting signaled…

"Ima, calm down!" Garcelle snapped. "Shut up before someone hears you! Now just where are you?" I didn't answer. "Ima, why don't you turn yourself in?"

"What? Are you insane? I didn't do anything! I'm not going to jail for some crap I didn't do! I screwed those guys, yes but I didn't kill anybody!"

"I know that and you know that but they don't. And your running makes you look guilty!"

"Guilty…they already decided that didn't they, when they plastered that god-awful picture of me on TV! Where did they get that picture anyway? And why are you pushing me to turn myself in, why don't you turn yourself in? You were there…with Rell. Why isn't your picture posted?" I paused and cringed. Too many years of watching cop shows kicked in. "Did you plea bargain or something? What did you do? You trying to sell me out?"

"What the hell are you talking about? Ima I didn't-"

"Are you with the police right now? Is this call taped?" I jumped from my seat in hysterics. I rushed to the window and peered out to the streets from behind the blinds. All was quiet and still, with the exception of an occasional person heading to their car for work.

"No I am not with the police and I *have* been questioned and I don't doubt they will come back again but I'm not hiding! Armando is dealing with the police but he can't cover forever and you can't run forever. Now tell me where you are and I'll come and get you and we can go in together and get this over with."

"No! No, no, no, no, no," I answered hysterically.

"No what?"

"No, I'm not telling you where I am, you can forget about that."

"So now you don't trust me?"

"Right now Garcelle, forgive me but I don't trust anybody."

I closed my phone and powered it off. I turned to face the television. In utter aggravation, I threw the phone with all my force, crashing it into a nearby lamp.

The dam finally broke. A wail escaped from within me. Indescribable, something like the sound of a wounded animal. I pulled myself into a ball in the corner and cried...

8 Last Chance Part I

"Bitch, get up! Wake yo' ass up!"

I blinked my eyes, adjusting to the light. My body ached, I felt as if I'd run a triathlon. I massaged the crook in my neck. Maccartney was hovering above me with one hand on his hip. It all came flooding back and if Maccartney knew, everyone knew.

I opened my mouth to explain but was cut off. "This is the gratitude I get for being a friend, huh. Thought I could trust you alone in my crib."

Tears gushed forth. "Look Maccartney, I am so very sorry...so sorry I lied, but I... I just needed a chance to think things through and –"

"Oh, whoa, whoa. What are you talking about little girl? Lied about what?"

I sniffed hard and smeared my assuredly red eyes with the backs of my palms. "Why I came here. What are you talking about?"

"Heifer, I was talking about my busted up lamp but now I'm quite interested in this lie you told."

Shit, the lamp! I jumped to my feet quickly and brushed past Maccartney and reached for my bag. I stuffed everything inside and scanned the room for any evidence that I'd once been there.

The last thing I needed to do was implicate someone else. I spotted my scuffed phone and grabbed it.

A look of nervous fear washed over Maccartney's face. For the first time since I'd known him he seemed to identify with me as an actual human being with problems and not just a fun loving, party girl. He grabbed my shoulders and looked into my eyes. "Baby, what's going on?"

I opened my mouth to say the words, confess the truth but no sound would come out. I shook my head and tried again but all I could utter was, "I'm very sorry about the lamp. I promise I will replace it. Thank you...for being here for me."

I kissed his cheek and rushed out of the door and down the street.

*

I decided that Garcelle was right; I would turn myself in to the authorities. I was shaking like a leaf in an earthquake as I made my made way home. I wanted to shower and change in my own home before having to do it in government facilities.

The house was dark and empty when I arrived. I paused in my foyer inhaling its scent, trying to commit it to memory. I walked into my living room and dropped my bag to the floor and turned on a lamp.

"Oh my God!" I jumped and covered my heart with my hand. When I regained my composure, I was angrier than frightened. "What the hell is wrong with you, you insane son of a bitch!"

"Sorry Ms. Phelps. Did I startle you?"

"You asshole."

"Where have you been? We've been looking all over for you." My response was rolling my eyes. "Oh come now. You can't tell me that you honestly believed you were just going to return home like nothing happened and no one would be waiting for you."

I glared at the ceiling and tapped my foot against the hardwood. The beautiful chocolate Detective Crane stood and guided me to the sofa. I sat averting my eyes while feeling his on me. For a time neither of us spoke. He watched me and I watched the wall.

Finally he said, "I asked you if you were guilty."

"And I told you I was not."

"Then why run?"

"I didn't run. I…left."

He chuckled heartily and flicked nothing from the corner of his eye. "I have a arrest warrant. The boys'll be here in any second. You want to tell me something."

I sighed. Tired. Defeated. Sweaty and dirty. "I didn't do it."

As if on cue my door was flung open and it felt to me as though the entire Miami PD was charging through my home. Detective Crane blew air from his lungs, placed his large palms on his large thighs and pushed his strong frame up. With no further words and without looking in my direction, he left my home and me to the mercy of the Miami Police Department.

"Ima Phelps?"

I instinctively refocused my attention at the sound of my name and directed it at a young blonde officer who appeared to be fresh out of the Academy. I sighed and groaned all at once.

"Yes."

He reached down and pulled me to my feet. "You have the right to remain silent. Anything you say can and will be used against you in a court of law…"

I dropped my head, tuning out his warning as he placed the cold steel upon my wrists.

*

Mommy was beyond livid and I was ashamed. She stood stock still with folded arms and a look of pure disgust upon her face. I was at home, released on a hefty bail thanks to an excellent attorney.

"Mommy, you can have a seat while you wait," I whispered hoarsely as I flicked away a tear. She merely scoffed.

I listened to the sounds of Natasha in the room that once belonged to her, gathering her belongings as swiftly as possible. The only other sound was the ticking of the clock that Peta Gaye had tried to hit me upside my head with that dreadful day.

"Mommy-" I began.

"Ima Anne how could you? How could you embarrass your family in this way? How could you shame yourself?"

I whispered, "I didn't kill anybody."

"I know you didn't kill anyone but how dare you defile your body with these...these men! If you were not out here being such a whore this may not have happened! And a girlfriend?! You've been sleeping around with women?! Who knows what other despicable activities you've been exposing your little sister to!"

"Mommy, I would never-"

"Never what? Never do anything to harm your sister? Is that what you're going to say? *Never what?* You just shut up! Shut your mouth right now!" My mothers face became contorted, her nostrils flared and her complexion changed at least two shades of red. A freshly manicured finger was pointed at me. "Thank God in Heaven that your father is already dead because if he were not, this would surely kill him."

I looked away slow and silent.

I turned at the sound of Natasha stumbling through the room with her luggage in tow. Our eyes met. The contempt I'd expected to see was non-existent. I chewed gently on my bottom lip and watched her walk to our mother. Mommy placed a hand on Natasha's back, rushing her forward. She followed behind leaving me alone with my thoughts.

"Mommy..." I started.

My mother paused and turned to face me. "I am so ashamed to know that I released a person like you into this world," she hissed her final words and turned and stalked out, slamming the door.

*

My job wasn't waiting for me. I was not surprised. I couldn't imagine myself going back there anyway. All the prying and pathetic souls with no real life or excitement of their own, fascinated by what they deemed a real life soap opera. Ugh. I did take my chances going into the vicinity, on the property to meet up with Garcelle (who wasn't arrested but advised not to leave town) to gather my belongings.

Her expression was strained. Her name was not mentioned publicly in conjunction with the murders. My little disappearing act assured that I'd overshadow any perceived involvement by her as far as the media was concerned. But I was certain without asking, that she was feeling the brunt of my ordeal in her everyday life regardless. I felt a need to apologize for something I had neither done nor caused to occur.

I avoided eye contact and our conversation was choppy at best. What her demeanor betrayed her words did not. She insisted that I stay in the car while she loaded my things in the trunk. She walked to the driver's side and leaned in to kiss my cheek. She promised that she and Armando would visit with me later and I thanked her.

As she walked away to return to yet another tumultuous workday, glancing around nervously at those that may be most likely to recognize my vehicle and her contact with me, I started up my engine in preparation to drive away.

"Ms. Phelps, fancy meeting you here."

I sighed and leaned back into the leather. For a fleeting moment I considered speeding off and leaving Detective Crane choking on my exhaust. He leaned into my window chewing casually on his gum. The delicate scent of his personal pleasure wafted to my senses, altering my own sense of pleasure. I reminded myself that no matter how sexy and fragrant he was, it was his goal to see me locked away for a lifetime for crimes that I had not committed.

"Cleaning out your space, huh?"

"Yep."

"Any special plans now that you're a free woman again?" He smirked that infamous, devilish grin and my nipples hardened. I cursed myself silently.

"If you're asking if I plan on skipping town, I sure as hell would not tell you if I were."

He raised an eyebrow and paused mid chew. He chuckled and removed the used gum from his mouth as he stood upright. "Point taken. Well pretty lady, have a good day. I'll see you around."

"Yea, I bet you will," I shifted gears and stepped on the gas.

*

My cheeks were flushed in hot anger. I slammed my fist against the steering wheel and cursed. I leaned my head back against the headrest, staring at the phone in my hand. I whisked away the tear that tried to fall. I'd dealt with the torture of being locked up in jail only to come home and find Peta Gaye's belongings had been cleared out and now I had to suffer through the nearly equal torture of finding out they'd been transported to Teddy's home.

I'd begged and pleaded for her forgiveness, let her know how sorry I was and how badly I needed her but to no avail. She was angry and had been betrayed and would not hear me.

My eyes became slits. I sat up and turned the key in the ignition. I had to see her. I needed for her to hear me out. I pulled out of my driveway and headed north toward Deerfield.

The gaslight put a hindrance in my plans and I pulled into the nearest service station to fill up.

I got out of my car and placed the nozzle inside and locked the trigger in place. I ran my nails across my scalp, deep in thought until the click of the trigger unlocking snapped me back to reality. I replaced the nozzle and went inside the shop. I grabbed myself a juice and headed to the counter to settle up.

"Any gas, ma'am?"

"Yes, pump five."

I twisted the top off of my juice and took a swallow as the petite West Indian man totaled my purchases.

"This too."

I glanced down to the counter at the pack of gum that had been placed there and the deep brown hand holding it in place.

"What the hell!" I blurted, startling the clerk. I glared and contemplated hitting him across the face with my full bottle but didn't think that would help my case. He responded only by flashing his killer smile and dazzling white teeth.

"Ma'am?"

"Hell naw!" I answered not taking my eyes off the detective.

I paid for my purchases and rushed out and toward my car, soon feeling the cop's presence. I stopped abruptly and turned to face him. "What? What do you want? Everywhere I turn, you're there. *Why?*" He only smiled which angered me more. I rushed to him. "Maybe it's you. Maybe you're the one that killed those people and now you want to torture me before you kill me too."

He laughed. "Are you always this dramatic, Ms. Phelps?"

I let out an exasperated groan and headed to my car with the detective on my heels.

"I know where you're headed and I wouldn't go there if I were you." He was so close I could feel his winter fresh breath on my neck.

"Why not?" I asked without looking back. "I love her, why shouldn't I go?"

"And I do not doubt it but don't you think you're in enough trouble without having a domestic dispute on your plate?"

"See you later Detective," I responded. "And I'm sure I will."

I revved up and pulled away leaving the detective behind. This scene was becoming all too familiar…

8.5 Last Chance Part II

I parked my car across the street from Teddy's dingy little two-bedroom house. On cue Peta-Gaye stepped from the home. My eyes roamed the length of her brown body. I was used to her being scantily clad but seeing my woman in a beater and no bra and stop sign red pom-pom shorts while in the company of another made my stomach turn.

She was pretty on that day. She'd had her beautiful dreads weaved into thick cornrows that hung to the center of her back adorned with little cog shells placed about. Her eyebrows were perfectly arched and her brown slanted eyes glistened in the sunlight.

I swallowed my pride, feeling it digest as I made my way across the limited traffic while she sauntered toward Teddy's dated Explorer, for the moment oblivious to my presence. She reached for the handle and did a double take when she spotted me on the approach.

"What ya doing here?" she scolded as she rushed in my direction.

"Get your things Peta, we're going home," I stated calmly as though I still had some pull with her…I hoped that I had.

"Who da hell do ya think you're talking to?"

I ignored her and continued, "We've been together for much too long for you to let this break us apart and you know it. So come on now, let's go."

"Ima."

"Peta."

We stood unflinching, eyes locked on one another. She was waiting for me to leave and I was waiting for her to leave with me. I swallowed my tears whole and watched as time froze. The tension was thick yet patient until we were interrupted.

"Ima, what are you doing here? Peta get inside, away from this psycho bitch. Ima get off my property right this instant."

I moved my gaze to Teddy's massive frame. It wasn't my wish to engage in any sort of physical altercation with a woman of her girth but if it came to it, I would not back down. Peta moved away and headed toward the house. My world rocked and my heart plummeted. My eyes became pools of rejection behind my Versace lenses.

"Since when are you obeying this bitch, Peta?" I blurted out. "Since when? I said I'm sorry! Will you listen to me, please..."

I moved toward her but Teddy jumped between. Instinctively I shoved but not surprisingly, did not move her very far.

"Put your hands on me again and watch how fast I beat your narrow ass into a puddle on the asphalt."

"You do what you gotta do but I ain't leaving her without her."

"Ima, why are you doing this?" Peta cried out from the archway.

"Because I need you! Because I can't breathe without you let alone survive this without you!"

"Get away from here!" Teddy growled locking her powerful fist around my throat, nearly crushing larynx. "Can you breathe now? Huh? Breath now, bitch!"

"Teddy, stop it! Put her down now!"

I clawed at her hands and kicked while struggling to breathe. I began to feel lightheaded as my supply of oxygen was being cut. Just as suddenly as the torture began, it ended. I dropped to a stoop, wheezing and massaging my neck. For several moments I was deafened and oblivious to what was happening around me. A strong hand pulled me to my feet. I was being guided away. I turned to, for the umpteenth time come face to face with Detective Crane.

I snatched my arm away. "What are you doing here?"

"You need to leave here right now, Ms. Phelps."

"Why can't you all get it? I've loved that woman for longer than I can remember. I am not leaving her here with this…this…"

"Yea you are. One way or another and I really don't think you want it to be in a patrol car. You're in a shyt load of trouble right now. You may be innocent of one crime but you're on the verge of committing another which is only going to hinder your defense, do you understand me?"

Did he believe me? Was that what he was telling me? Defeated, I relaxed my tensed muscles and allowed myself to be led away. Detective Crane opened the passenger's door of his car and helped me inside. I kept my eyes glued to Peta-Gaye. Her eyes were wet with tears as were mine. She mouthed the words, 'I am so sorry'. I lowered my eyes as the detective drove away into the sunset.

*

The sun hid from sight and darkness enveloped the coast. I continued to stare blankly ahead, silent as the car rolled forward down a secluded path. The gravel crunched beneath the tires of the Oldsmobile. I tugged at the back of my hair…disappointed. The car rolled slowly to a stop and the engine was turned off. We sat in silence, me looking out into the distant dark Atlantic waters, him looking at me.

"Where are we?" I asked in a hoarse voice without altering in the least my line of vision.

"Just a little quiet spot in Boca I like to come to when I need to think."

We were quiet yet again. This time he broke the code.

"So you really love Ms. Sinclair," he stated more than asked. I nodded. "And you were going to fight that big broad for her?"

I nodded with a chuckle.

"You know she could have killed you."

I laughed just louder than I'd intended and looked his way. I studied the structure of his face, his wide nose and full lips. His hair was cut into a Caesar and there was a spark in his ebony eyes as he watched me. I blushed and looked away.

"May I ask you a personal question, Ms. Phelps?"

"For as much time as we've spent together, against my will I might add, I think it'd be okay if you just call me Ima."

He chuckled. "Ima. Well Ima, call me David. But Ima, you haven't answered my question."

"Yes, you may."

He bit gently on his bottom lip and leaned back into the seat. "Why do you do it? Sleep around with so many men. What makes you do it?"

I felt as though I'd been backhanded directly across my cheek. My eyes became slits and a look of disdain took up residence upon my face. "Why is it your business?"

"Because my mother always taught me, if you want to know the answer to something then you'd better ask the question. Otherwise you're only making an assumption and well, uh...we know what is said about those who assume." He casually pulled a strip of gum seemingly from thin air and eased it into his mouth.

"Well that isn't any of your business."

"Ima, there's no need for you to get so hostile."

"Ms. Phelps."

He laughed. I did not.

"Listen to me. I only asked a question. There was neither judgment nor malicious intent behind it. I'm a cop assigned to an investigation. Yours. I ask questions, you give answers. I piece the puzzle together. That's all."

"You brought me all the way out here to ask me that." He didn't answer, only chewed his gum. I sighed. "Look, I don't know why I do it. I'm not from Florida, I was born in this small town outside of Alexandria, VA. My mommy and daddy were having problems when I was like…I don't know, fourteen or fifteen. Mommy had an uhh…reputation, I guess. They pretended but people talked.

"So when I was 17, getting ready to go into my senior year, daddy up and moved my family to Miramar. I was pretty upset about the sudden move at such a crucial time in my life but things got better with my family so I adjusted. I graduated and went away to college."

I paused and tilted my head back preventing water from escaping. It was pretty amazing to me just how much recalling these memories was bothering me. I'd lived my life and not stopped to analyze any aspect of it. I popped the lock and eased from the car. I leaned against the hood and stared above at the quarter moon, glowing in the sky. I sucked in my breath and reflected as Detect – David, exited the car.

"Year one my parents were great and I lost my virginity while away. By the middle of year two, I'd loved my first woman and an unspecified number of men. My parents were still doing fine. I spent a wonderful Christmas with mom and dad and my baby sister Tasha. By spring break, daddy was gone and Tasha stopped speaking to me.

"Apparently my father wanted my mom to see someone…a specialist or something, a shrink or whatever. She pretends it never happened… suppresses it I guess. She never did see anyone to get help and neither have I." I turned to face him. "So to answer your question in short, I don't know why. Hereditary I suppose."

Our eyes locked. David stepped closer to me, sliding an arm around my waist and pulled my body against him. Our eyes locked and it was as though we were competing to see who'd blink first.

His voice was thick when he spoke, "I'm going to ask you one last time. Did you do it?"

Without flinching nor breaking our penetrating gaze I answered, "No I did not."

His lips pressed to mine soft and delicious. His kiss was engaging…strong. His minty juices slowly filled my mouth. He tenderly bit into my tongue, pulling it to him and sucked it like it was the last of his favorite orange Popsicle. His hand pulled my body firmly to his. I could feel him awakening against me.

The alarms went off inside of my head. This was a detective…*the* detective. The one assigned to seal the deal on my potential conviction, so why was he here kissing me like a long lost lover returned? Better question – why was I not stopping him?

Our kiss became deeper and more than passionate. My body relaxed in his strong grasp, my problems and the accusations forgotten. His hands moved down and grasped firmly my rear as he lifted my body placing me on the warm hood of the car. His mouth moved from mine and kisses were planting a trail along my neck. I grazed my nails across his scalp, through the short hairs that sprouted on top and sighed, reveling in the prelude to pleasure he was granting me. My chestnut brown nipples were hard inside of my bra and an intense shiver of pleasure electrified my body when a hand swept lightly across.

Another hand found its way to my love below and I squeezed with a firmness that confirmed my desire and intent. He backed away slowly and looked into my eyes with pure lust evident. A hand craftily shimmied my skirt up my legs and thighs, his long fingers gliding across clearly attracted to the warmth and wetness I was emitting. His gaze remained locked on mine as he pushed aside the annoying bit of material that was serving as a barricade between his desire and my creamy center. One thick, finger slipped inside of me and I gasped, my moans caught in my throat.

My head fell back and my muscles tensed and relaxed in spasms as he probed and pleasured me. His warm breath closed in on my neck, the eventual suckling increasing my pulse and the sensations he was already creating within me.

His hand shifted and he was pulling my pink lace panties from my body. I breathed heavily caught up in a rapture of sorts. I tuned out all sounds around me; continuing to feel the ghost of pleasure those fingers incited within my walls.

"Yes," I whispered and soon my undergarment was at my ankle, then the earth below us, surely to be left as a symbol of our appreciation of each other on this night...buried in the sands. I didn't know when he pulled his manhood forth from his jeans. I had no idea at what point he'd embraced it with the convenient protective covering. I was only aware of the very moment his immense stiffness plunged deep inside. He lifted my body and supported my weight as I balanced on his shaft. He slowly guided me back and forward, forward and back.

My arms wound tightly around his neck and I buried my face into his shoulder. I could feel him deep inside of me, touching more than my sexual core. I moved my body against his, for the first time not feeling as though I had to wear a disguise...had to be in control. For the first time I could allow myself to make love. For the first time...I allowed myself to be vulnerable...

9 According To Plan

I awoke before the sun rose above the Ocean waters. Sleep was difficult to obtain and harder and harder to maintain. The nearer I came to the court date, the more difficult it became for me to concentrate and live some semblance of a normal life. I stared into the darkness that cloaked my bedroom. In that moment I was relieved that Jonathan believed and trusted in me enough to continue to help me with my finances. I tried hard to focus my mind while trying to focus my eyes. I vaguely recalled something important about the night prior. There was movement beneath my sheets.

"Peta?" I whispered.

There was no response. I turned to my left and reached out to stroke the silhouette. My fingers grazed hard flesh. I moved my palm up and gripped a strong bicep. It all came flooding back to me and I smiled despite the disappointment of the realization that Peta was still wrapped in the manish arms of Teddy.

I spoke quietly to myself, "Detective David Crane."

I moved my body against his and began planting soft kisses along the upper part of his spine. His flesh was warm. I pressed my breasts firmly against his back. He stirred and shifted a bit before reaching back and taking my arm and wrapping it tightly around his waist.

"Good morning, Sunshine," I whispered into his ear.

"Good morning, Lovely," his voice was deep and coarse when he spoke.

We laid quietly for moments more, the cop and the crook. I thought about moving my hand down his waist and stroking that pretty piece of man between his thighs and starting up an early morning game of dirty Cops and Robbers, but I surprisingly found myself enjoying the peace in his embrace. And well, it isn't hard to conclude that during these trying days in my life, peace was hard to find.

Detective Crane turned over onto his back and pulled me into his chest, his fingers moving through my hair and massaging my scalp. "What's on your mind?"

"I don't know...nothing...everything. I don't even know why we're here like this. I've been charged with crimes I didn't commit and you're responsible for having me convicted. You don't think this is just a little weird?" I chuckled lightly and looked up at him. "And with my court date on the horizon... I just don't know."

He sighed. "I hear you but don't worry about it, something will come up. Try to rest."

He kissed my forehead and I snuggled deeper into his body. I rested there peacefully until my lids dipped low and I drifted back into sleep.

*

"Are you sure about this?" I asked, my eyes wide with hope.

The scent of navel oranges wafted from the flavored gum he chewed, filling my senses when he opened his mouth to speak, "What do you mean, am I sure? Ima c'mon, I'm not a novice."

"I know that but -"

"No buts. Okay. I've been a cop for twelve years; I know

what I'm doing. My part is easy. You on the other hand have to be strong enough to handle this. You have to be able to relax, to be natural. If we're going to do this I need to know that you can move through this smoothly and quietly, as if none of this has ever happened. As if your life is completely normal."

"But it isn't normal." I stood from the bed and paced the room. What Detective Crane – I mean David, was asking me to do was…well, nerve wrecking to say the least. A sting operation. He wanted me, a civilian who is soon to be a convict, to help him with a sting operation. What if I got someone else killed? Could I live with that? Would it tack onto my potential sentence?

I sat again and massaged my temples with the tips of my fingers. Soon to be a convict…soon to be a convict…the words played over in my mind. I couldn't let that happen, not without a fight no matter what the consequence. I turned to face the Detective. My, how beautiful he was. He stared back with his rich ebony eyes.

"Okay, what do I do?"

David smiled. "Ima, don't worry about this. I'm going to take care of you, okay? I promise you." He placed a strong hand on the side of my face and stroked my cheek. I shuddered as a chill ran up and then down my spine. "Can you trust me?"

I leaned forward and kissed his lips. "Yes. I trust you."

＊

The Whole was packed. It'd been ages since I'd been inside. I was nervous yet excited at the same moment. By this point it was public knowledge that I was "dangerous". I'd only been let out on bail because the case against me was purely circumstantial and my mother, though angered, bitter, and embarrassed, dipped into her substantial savings and vouched for me financially. But to outsiders, circumstantial or not, I knew in their eyes, I was a killer if for no other reason than a television news anchor said so. I was either that – or the most unlucky woman walking the face of the Earth.

I didn't know what type of reception I'd receive once we arrived. Garcelle and Armando both agreed that I was insane for even the thought of going into the vicinity of the Devil's playground where I'd in the past spent so many hours of recess. At the same time it was this insane and fearless side of me they both admired and envied. So when I made the suggestion that we go, seeing as I could soon be locked away for a very long time relatively soon, neither could turn me down.

I took a deep breath, straightened my back, held my head high and led my little crew past the crowd and right up to Warren. He was the gate keeper. Warren alone, though he did not know it, was the holder of the key to my salvation. It was imperative to David's plan that I gain entrance to the club as it was equally important to not tell anyone about the plan and to perform as I normally would so not to arouse any suspicions and hopefully lure the real killer out of the dark.

There were stares and whispers as the three of us passed by. Warren's eyes were large as saucers when he spotted me. For a moment I was embarrassed and afraid to proceed. For a second I wanted to about face but then I recalled those all too important words – soon to be a convict.

I licked my glossy lips and kept forward. I thought that I must be hearing things. It was slow and sporadic at the start but soon people were clapping and cheering. Warren's arms opened wide and he held me in a tight embrace and for a moment Charity was over, history. Wasn't fooling anyone anymore anyway. My face had been seen on the news, two-and-two connected, they all knew who I really was and many of them believed that I was innocent – and it felt good.

"Go on in baby girl, we'll get your regular table ready," Warren told me as the three of us went inside.

I felt as though I'd entered the Twilight Zone or some sort

of time warp once we were behind those doors; it was as though nothing had happened. The vast majority of The Whole's patrons were much too inebriated to care about what I'd been accused of. Bottles were brought to the table and little tin foil packages appeared from nowhere, all for my pleasure and indulgence. As flattering and tempting as it was, I was there on a mission.

"They're treating you like you're some sort of got-damned celebrity," Garcelle uttered.

I turned toward her in confusion. "You sound upset about it."

"Are you aware of what you're accused of?"

"I know what I'm accused of, I also know that I didn't do it," I said defensively.

"I know you didn't do it but..."

"But? There's a but? But what Garcelle?"

"It's just odd, that's all I'm saying."

I didn't respond to her, just stared as she leaned back and deeply inhaled the mary jane. She handed it to me, I took a small puff and passed it down the line to 'Sasha' who happily took responsibility for it. This night wasn't about partying and I had to keep my indulgence in moderation so that I could remain focused and alert. I felt Garcelle's hand slide inappropriately high on my thigh. I turned to face her. Her eyes were soft when she looked at me.

"I just want to enjoy myself," I informed her.

"I know," she said. "It's just...these people...it could be anyone."

"I know."

She didn't look away, she was so close to me I could pick up the scent of the mangoes in her hair. I didn't know what to think or to say.

"Look you crazy bitches," Sasha interrupted, "We didn't come all the way out here for a pity party. Okay. Y'all two about to blow my high and I ain't even hardly got started yet."

"Fine, pour me a drink," I laughed as I discreetly moved Garcelle's hand from my leg.

I avoided every other rolled up or ground down drug that crossed my path. I claimed a need to use the ladies room. I had to get away, I was in this psychotic environment sober and Garcelle was being weird. She'd been behaving oddly ever since I was released and became apparent that Peta was leaving me for good. Besides that, I was supposed to meet a man.

I had a vague sense of what he looked like so I had to have a clear mind. He would approach me at some point in the night and make mention of a pitcher for the St. Louis Cardinals and his love for Louis Armstrong and Beagles. That would be my cue. I'd been approached several times but none showed any interest in baseball, jazz music, nor implied any regard for animals.

From where I stood on the opposite side of the club I could see Maccartney standing near our table, chatting it up with a glass in her hand and a hydro filled Black in her mouth. I started in that direction to greet her when I felt a hand gently touching my wrist.

"Excuse me, I couldn't help but notice you standing here alone. You're absolutely stunning," the stranger said to me.

I smiled politely. "Thank you."

I was poised to continue on my path when he said, "Do you come here often? This is new to me; I'm more of a jazz club, Louis Armstrong type of guy."

I paused and tried to breathe. My heart moved quickly to my throat. I swallowed hard. "Y-yea? Me too. You don't happen to be an animal lover, do you?"

"As a matter of fact yes. I have a Beagle named Kyle. It's kinda corny but I named him after Kyle Lohse. I'm a big St. Louis Cardinals fan."

I exhaled in relief. I smiled at him. "So you wanna get out of here? Go someplace quiet?"

"Sure," he answered.

"Okay. Well, I came with friends. I just have to let them know I'm leaving."

"Sure thing, I'll wait by the door."

I nervously adjusted my dress. I tried to focus on behaving normal. But what was normal? I wondered if everyone around could tell that I was up to something. That wasn't normal. I ran my fingers through my hair as I approached the table.

"Well look who had the balls to show her face. If it isn't Madame Scandal herself." Maccartney leaned in, air-kissing both of my cheeks. "If you ain't the baddest bitch chile I don't know who is."

I tried to respond sincerely but my thoughts were elsewhere. I shrugged and said the only thing I could think to say, "Can't hide forever. Hey beautiful, I have to speak to Sash and Garcelle about something. Would you mind?"

Maccartney looked down on me in feigned disgust. "Oh y'all got secrets."

"It's not…well, it's just…"

"Whatever. I got business to tend to anyway. Look, you see that charming little Brunette over there?"

I followed her line of vision through the crowd. "Who is that?"

"Business, okay?"

"Go on and do your thing," I laughed. When Maccartney was gone, I slid into the booth beside Sasha.

"Ima is everything okay? What's going on?" she asked concerned.

"It's nothing, just a dilemma. Over there…at the door."

"Mm, now that's a scrumptious little chocolate munch. You plan on leaving with him?"

"I want to."

"No!" Garcelle abruptly protested. "You can't do that."

"Just listen-"

"No! Are you completely insane? Have you f'king lost your mind? Have you forgotten what kind of shyt you're in?"

"Of course I didn't forget."

"Well maybe you just forgot how you got into it."

"Garcelle, would you just listen."

"Don't be stupid."

"Stupid?"

"Enough!" Sasha commanded placing her large hands in between Garcelle and me who were coming close enough that one wrong word and we could come to blows. "Now Ima, honey, do you think this is a good idea? I know you got to be horny as a monk at a porn convention but think about what you're doing."

I looked at Garcelle when I replied, "I know what I'm doing but – he knows what I'm facing and he doesn't care. He'll be on guard. Those other guys, they didn't know what they were getting into but he does. I think it'll be fine."

"You're sure."

"Yes, I'm sure."

"Well, I have to go on the record saying that I disagree," Garcelle added.

I let out a frustrated sigh. "I understand your point but damn, I can't take much more of this self gratifying bullshyt! I just need this one night; it could very well be my last opportunity!"

"Don't you think you're being just a tad bit melodramatic? You don't have to self gratify, Ima. If you would just…"

I shook my head knowingly. "Garcelle, I can't do that again."

Sasha raised an eyebrow. "Uhh, why do I feel like I'm not being included in something here?"

I refocused my attention. "It's nothing. I'll be at Brucie's, it'll be okay." I looked back to Garcelle. "Alright?"

She turned away and slid from the bench. "You do whatever you want, just don't forget that I tried to warn you."

Sasha shrugged and turned up another glass. I kissed her cheek and left. When this was over, if it went according to plan, Garcelle would understand. Until then, I had a task to complete and that task was to guarantee that I'd never become a convict…

10 Unusual Suspect

I was breathless and fighting off my edgy emotions as Kendall Mathers and I made our way to the hotel. There were no words shared between him and me during the short drive in my car. He was a sexy man and under different circumstances I would definitely screw his brains out once we arrived but these were highly unusual conditions that brought us together and besides, he was a cop and a good friend of my Detective David Crane.

I pulled up and then backed into a spot near the hotel. I turned the engine off and took a deep breath before I reached for the door handle. Kendall placed a hand against my forearm and moved me back against my seat. I turned to face him and was discomforted by the scowl on his face and apparent anger in his eyes.

"I just want you to know that I'm not doing this for you. Quiet as kept I really do not want to do this but Dave is my boy and has been for ten years. He believes you, I do not." He finally turned to face me. "You better got-damned not be lying about this. It's enough that you're carrying on like a f'kin slut but if it turns out that you are in fact a murderer too I will make sure you never see the light of day again."

He was gone from the car before I could digest his promise to me. I didn't know this man from Steve let alone Adam and couldn't appreciate his marked disdain for me but I didn't know how I should respond. I'd been caught off guard.

My eyes were slits as I snatched the key from the ignition and jumped from my vehicle. I jogged in my heels to catch up to him, stopping when I was in front of him. I spoke low and fought to keep my expression free of my true emotions in case we were being watched.

"Let me get something straight. We don't know each other so let's keep our uneducated opinions about one another to ourselves. Thank you anyway for agreeing to this but no matter what you think about me personally, I didn't do this and no matter how I choose to live my life, I do not deserve this."

He looked as though he wanted to respond but thought better of it. Instead he leaned in close enough that from a distance it would appear as though we were kissing. He spoke through gritted teeth, "If you're telling the truth get back into character now before you blow this."

Inside I was fuming but instead of giving in to my instincts, I slid my arm around his waist and entered the hotel in Detective Mathers' embrace. I laughed as though he'd shared the most tickling tale as we approached the counter for a room. I made casual small talk with the manager as he set us up with an available suite.

It was all very typical behavior, nothing should have triggered suspicion. I was proud of my acting abilities. Detective Mathers ushered me into the elevator. He placed a quick call once we were inside, simply stating our room number, then closed the phone abruptly and placed it in his pocket. Our brief love affair had ended as swiftly and awkwardly as it'd begun.

We moved fast once we were at our floor. We didn't know who the killer (or killers) were, how they operated, their m.o., nothing. So our entire operation was risky at best and based on chance. I smiled and relaxed when I spotted David lurking by the room Mathers and I rented. Quickly and quietly the two officers of the law exchanged room keys and Mathers was gone. David rushed me inside. He wrapped his arms around me and held me close. I was relieved that this next phase of the plan removed me from the judgmental glare of his policeman friend. For as much as I appreciated his loyalty, I didn't like him for obvious reasons.

David smiled down at me in the scarcely lit suite. He chewed the gum with his back teeth while flashing me his pearly whites. His hands moved softly up and down my back.

"So what happens next?" he asked.

"What do you mean?"

"You know, in following your normal routine. What happens next?"

I raised an eyebrow. "Do we have time for that?"

"Your killer strikes after you've had sex with and left these guys, right? He expects it. Actually he requires it, for you to have your pleasure before he strikes. As I see it, it's a crucial point in the plot." He licked his lips slowly as he gazed at me.

"Maybe you're right. You're the professional, who am I to question your tactics?" I reached to grab his shirt but he stopped me.

"Oh no, no, no my pretty. I'm the detective and this is my case. I'm the one in charge here."

David swept me into his arms and carried me to the Cali King sized bed. He laid me softly on top, so delicately it was as though he thought I may break. He slowly eased the spaghetti straps from each shoulder, planting kisses along the way. I gasped and my body writhed beneath his touch. Carefully, David turned me onto my stomach.

"Just relax," he whispered.

I felt the coolness of the conditioned air make contact with my skin as my zipper slowly came undone. David's lips explored every square inch of flesh. He moved his hands managing to hike my dress up to my waist and remove my lacy panties at the same time. He kissed my tush, nibbling sweetly at unscheduled intervals. I moaned and my eyes closed. A tear escaped one and slipped into the other when I felt his fingers tease my opening.

No one had ever before attended to my needs in such a way. I'd always been responsible for my own pleasure and it seemed no matter how many positions I created, how many ways and times my body was explored, the epitome of my pleasure was always just out of reach. But this experience was like no other. My body reacted to the feel of David's fingers stroking my slippery wetness and his mouth massaging my flesh.

I shook and vibrated and sighed and cried until I climaxed. I was out of breath, panting and wondering how he'd done this to me without even penetrating me. My body was limp as he removed my dress and tossed it to the floor. He pulled me up on uncertain legs.

"Undress me," he commanded to which I obliged, planting kisses of my own and licking exposed skin as I obeyed.

We stood naked before one another in the semi-darkness. I glanced down between his legs and licked my lips instinctively. He was thick, hard, long, and slightly angled. His thighs were firm and bulging. My eyes traveled up past his six-pack abs and solid chest to the sinister smile he wore on his face.

"How do you want me?" he asked.

I walked up to him, once again confident in my sexuality. "How ever you'll have me."

He grabbed me, lifting me high to land on his shoulders. He moved until I felt the wall supporting my back. His tongue danced around my pussy, teasing and taunting before landing firmly against my clit causing shivers to run through me. He sucked me into his mouth and flexed his jaws firmly commanding that I vocalize my appreciation.

And I did. I screamed and flailed my hair from side to side. I held tightly the sides of his head, force feeding him my juices knowing that he loved every second of it.

"Oh my goodness…oh my…goodness," I hoarsely shouted as my body filled with anticipation.

I squealed and squirmed, even laughed aloud as his thick tongue flicked back and forth and counter-clockwise. I couldn't take much more, I could hardly breathe. I let out a high pitched wail as I gushed, filling his mouth with my sweetness. I fully expected an end but he was greedy and commanded more to which I obliged.

He growled as he finally dropped me onto my back on the bed, his body hovering high above mine, arms still wrapped around me. He rolled onto his back bringing me with him. He raised my body and eased me onto him, his hand firmly grasped my ass as his tongue tasted the perspiration between my breasts. My hips gyrated back and forth as my body moved up and down on him. I was riding him and enjoying the depths in which he was touching me on the inside. Holding me tight, he led me back onto the bed once again commanding that I surrender control. My body vibrated and my breasts bounced with each thrust deeper within.

I'd heard others talk about it but I'd never cried during sex before now. I was amazed at the intensity of his loving. My nails dug reminders and left evidence that I'd been there. His hand wrapped firmly around my neck as he f'ked me harder and moments later his mouth wrapped around my shoulder as he made slow love to me.

There was no fear, no nervous energy, no thoughts to anything other than the pleasure I was experiencing as the two of us meshed into one.

*

I didn't want to accept the reality that I'd been thrust back into. I had to leave now – alone. Just as I would have had I picked this man up at The Whole, I had to leave ahead of him. He would wait and we'd both cross our fingers and hope the killer would show equipped with his tools for castration and murder.

"Ima, I want you to go straight home. I'll call you when we have the person in custody. If he doesn't show by morning I'll call and let you know," he was serious again, all business. It was as though we'd never shared such an intimate time together.

"Be careful," I said for lack of anything better. I glanced at my watch; it was well past two in the morning. David took my face in his palms and kissed me deep and passionately causing me to wish that we could nix this plan for the night and jump back into the bed. Instead he stepped back into the shadows and I rushed into the hall and to the elevator.

I tried my very best to be calm and natural as I crossed the lobby. I bid the night clerk farewell as I rushed out into the warm night air and to my car. I started the motor and pulled away but I couldn't bring myself to go home as instructed. I needed to know, I needed to be there when Detective Crane exited the hotel with a cuffed criminal in his grasp. I had to be around when cop cars illuminated the night sky outside of the hotel as they'd done only a few months ago outside of Brucie's.

I turned back and parked in the shadows kitty corner from the hotel, and turned off the car. I was nervous and antsy as I waited. I hated that I had no one to talk me through this. I wanted to call Garcelle or Armando, just to chat and keep me company while I waited but David insisted that I couldn't tell anyone a thing. I tried to relax. I thought to play some music but I was too fearful of being spotted to make any sounds.

It was getting later and later and my eyelids were heavy. The more time that passed the least likely I believed that the killer would surface. I jumped each time I heard sirens in the distance but every time was the same, the sounds would fade away never making it onto this street. I thought maybe I should give up and go home. I swallowed the lump that had formed in my throat and sat up in my seat, reaching for my keys.

I inhaled sharply when I saw the figure moving hurriedly out the side door. I was sure from the distance and being that I was so tired that I wasn't seeing clearly. But as the figure moved quickly through the street light and to a parked car, I clearly recognized who it was.

"Maccartney!" I gasped. "Oh no."

I reached toward my phone then moved my hands back to the steering wheel. I was shaking wildly and confused, I didn't know which to do first. I peeled away moments after Maccartney and made my way to the expressway.

"Shit! Shit!" I screamed. I struggled to pick up my phone and dial David's cell phone number. There was no answer. I closed my eyes tight, warding off tears then opened them. I tried his number again and once more, each time being greeted by his voicemail.

"Dammit!" I pounded my hand hard against the steering wheel. This couldn't be happening. And if Maccartney recognized the Detective she'd know it was a set up, she'd come after me! I sped home as cautiously as possible, praying that I weren't stopped.

I screeched into my driveway and jumped from the car. I ran to my door trying the Detective's number yet again. There was still no answer. My keys dropped from my grasp to the concrete as I struggled to unlock the door. I couldn't stop shaking. I managed to pick the keys up and open the door.

I didn't know what I should do. David could have very well been dead and Maccartney – he could have been on his way to finish me off or worse, leave me to take the fall for a cops death ensuring that not only would my bail be immediately revoked but I'd be guaranteed a conviction and likely sentenced to death!

Tears were streaming down my cheeks and I was frantic. I needed time to come up with a new plan. I collapsed on my sofa and called Jonathan. I didn't know if he would answer this time of morning, I didn't even know if he were alone or home in bed with his wife but I couldn't stop to care. It seemed that the line rang forever. I was just about to give up when Jon's voice came through.

"Ima, are you okay?" he asked in a concerned whisper.

I fought back tears. "No. I can't explain right now I just...think I need to hide out for a few days. I saw the killer."

"Oh my goodness. Where...how? Did something else happen?"

"I'm not exactly sure." My voice was thick with my emotion. "I can't explain it now. I just have to get out of here 'til I can figure out my next move."

"Of course, meet me at the house. Leave now."

"Jonathan, what about your wife?" I cursed myself for even asking.

"That's nothing for you to concern yourself with, just go. Now."

"I'm on my way, thanks."

"I love you Ima, I'd do anything to protect you."

His line disconnected. Under regular conditions I'd have been shaken by his words but now, I only hoped he could deliver what he promised. Immediately, I tried David's number again but there was no answer. This time I left a voicemail saying that I'd seen Maccartney leaving the hotel and I was going to my friend Jonathan's.

I left the address to the home in West Palm Beach in case he was okay. I closed my phone and sat it beside me on the couch. I sat wringing my hands and trying hard to pull myself together. I decided I needed to pack a small bag. My land line rang interrupting my plan. I paused and glanced at the clock. My heart and breathing was frozen until I read the name Garcelle Washington on the Caller ID display.

"Hey what's up?"

"Hey mama," Garcelle said through a yawn. "You're home. Mando just called waking me up, asking me if I'd heard from you yet. Did things go…y'know?"

I could detect the apprehension in her tone. I had to work hard to not betray my own emotions. "Fine, it went fine. Hey, I gotta go."

"Wait! Geez, are you okay? Ima, did something go wrong?"

"Nothing to worry about. I just have to go. I'll call you later."

"Don't tell me nothing!" her voiced was raised now and she suddenly sounded wide awake. "Something happened tonight didn't it? I told you not to go!"

I wondered whether or not I should say something to her about Maccartney, about the detective and the operation. Was Garcelle in trouble too? I quickly dismissed that notion; there wasn't enough evidence to support that.

"Listen to me, everything's fine but I'm going to disappear for a few days. I'm going to stay with Jonathan. If anyone asks, you know nothing okay? I'll call you when I have things figured out."

"Have what figured out? Why do you need to stay with Jonathan? Where is that, in West Palm?"

"Yes. Garcelle listen, don't worry okay? There's nothing to worry about, I promise."

She paused for a moment as though she were considering this. "Fine, I'll be cool for now. Hey real quick, did you happen to see Maccartney tonight before you went home?"

I snapped to attention. "Why are you asking me about Maccartney?"

"She left something seemingly valuable behind and I want to get it back to her. Do you have her number?"

My voice was raised and uncontrolled when I spoke, "I don't know anything about Maccartney!"

"Fine. What's with you? It's no big deal, I'll ask Armando.

I'm worried about you Ima, will you be safe at Jonathan's?"

I was suspicious. "What is that supposed to mean?"

"What? What is what – just give me Jonathan's address. I'm becoming really worried and I want to know where you are."

"I'm not giving you got-damned thing!" My eyes were wide and I was on my feet now. "Why are you asking me these things?"

"What do you mean…Ima? Ima!"

A soft thud startled me. Slowly I crept toward the end of the couch and leaned toward a mirror on my wall. "Oh my goodness, I have to go."

"Ima!"

I ended the call. Slowly and quietly I crept past the sofa just a bit further and looked again at the reflection in the large mirror. My eyes widened and I gasped quietly. The cordless phone slipped from my hand and landed on the carpet as I turned and ran from the house, jumped in my car and peeled away.

11 Salvation

I couldn't believe that I'd left my cell phone behind. But in my haste, I didn't have time to pause and get my thoughts together. From where I stood I could only partially see the reflection but I am sure it belonged to Maccartney and I had to get out of the house before she saw me watching her.

I was a wreck. Maccartney was indeed after me and I didn't know how long he'd been there, how much he'd heard. I could no longer trust Garcelle and didn't know if she somehow played a part in all of this. She'd "warned" me not to go and asked about whether or not I'd seen Maccartney. Why? And David, I didn't know if was dead or alive but I was certain that if he were dead, Detective Mathers would soon have the cavalry hot on my trail.

I deduced that it wouldn't be safe for me at Jonathan's for very long but I didn't have enough money to flee very far. I'd go and have Jon fill up my purse and then I'd disappear. I'd figure out the rest later.

I pulled into the driveway and parked beside Jonathan's Jag. I'd get him to open the garage door and move my car inside. I jumped from my car and rushed to the door. The sun was preparing to rise over the coast, I had to move fast. I knocked on the door and waited. My leg shook violently and I chewed my thumbnail. When there was no response I knocked again, this time harder. Still no answer.

I jiggled the doorknob. It turned and I pushed the door open and stepped inside. I stopped immediately and looked around the large room. Something didn't feel right but what? Maybe I was being paranoid. Garcelle didn't know Jonathan's exact address and Maccartney was still at the house when I left. There was no way possible he could have beat me here assuming he'd heard where I was going.

Perspiration pooled beneath my armpits as I stepped deeper inside the home. I tried hard to steady my breathing. I could hear running water in the distance, it was coming from the bathroom in the master bedroom just off the front room of the house. He hadn't heard me. I couldn't believe how I'd lost control. I dropped my head and shook it side to side as I quietly laughed at myself.

"Jonny!" I called to him as I removed my heels and sat them against the wall. "Jon!"

I entered the bedroom and my head swam. My eyes filled with water and my lip trembled. I repeated a quiet call to the Lord above over and over as I stepped carefully toward the bed. I didn't know why, I should have run but I seemed to be drawn closer. It was as though I had a need to confirm that it was really him lying there. My knees buckled and I collapsed backward into the bedside table.

Jonathan was lying on the bed naked and covered in his own blood, he'd been castrated. I was woozy as I looked around the room, this couldn't be real. This made no sense. And then I saw it. Jonathan's bloody organ had been carelessly tossed to the floor.

I couldn't stop it from coming up. All the contents of my stomach spilled forward onto the soiled carpet. I continued to gag and heave even though there could be nothing left inside.

When it finally ended, I leaned my head back against the table allowing my eyes to ease close. It was over. As long as I was free, no one near me would be safe. I may as well call and have myself picked up. It was only a matter of time anyway. There was nowhere else to run, no place to hide.

My head jerked up and my eyes scanned the room from my position on the floor. All was quiet, too quiet. The running water had stopped but I hadn't noticed when. The game was hardly over. I scrambled to my feet.

"Holy shit, it can't be you."

Armando, still dressed as Sasha, was walking toward me slowly. He was watching my every move. In his hand he carried the largest knife I'd ever seen, he was wiping the blade over and over with a bloodied hand towel.

"You look surprised to see me."

"No. No, no, no. Armando you couldn't have done this."

"Sasha! My name is Sasha!" he screamed as he charged at me. I was too fearful to move. He was on me, the tip of the blade applying pressure against my larynx. I tried to swallow as carefully as possible. He grabbed a handful of my hair and yanked me low, staring into my eyes. "You think you're better than me don't you bitch? You think you're smarter than me? Do you still think you're smarter? Huh? Answer me got-dammit!"

My voice was a hoarse whisper when I responded, "N-no. I don't know what you're talking about. I don't think-"

"Shut up you dumb bitch!" he screamed throwing me across the room and slamming into a dresser.

The force of the blow winded me momentarily. I leaned forward coughing hard and trying to regain my oxygen. I cried softly, "Why?"

"You think you're so much better than everyone else!" His eyes were bulging and spittle foamed around his mouth. "I hate bitches like you! So self absorbed you have no clue what's going on around you. How many people had to die, Ima? How many before you noticed? How many before you even considered that maybe it was you?

"Peta loved you and look how you disrespected her? You treated her like she was dispensable but you cry when she finds someone to love and appreciate her the way she wanted you to! What about Garcelle? She did everything she could to show you how much she loved you and you only played with her emotions. Fk'd her and blamed her for your fk'n up your relationship with Peta."

My head was pounding. Armando – I mean Sasha, was pacing the room and waving the knife carelessly, telling me how I deserved everything I got because I treated others as though they were beneath me. I didn't notice him coming my way until his palm was firmly wrapped around my neck and I was being lifted from the floor. I scratched and clawed for dear life.

"And then you try and set me up? Nice try bitch," he spat the words as I was released and allowed to drop back to the floor.

I caught my breath. "Did you... kill... him?" I asked desperately between breaths.

"Oh no, you'd think so wouldn't you. I could have. I considered but no sweetheart, he'll have one helluva headache but he'll be front and center when your ass is hauled off to the lethal injection chambers for the five murders you committed!"

My hand landed on a small hand-weight that was beside me, I used it to steady myself. Sound traveled from the front of the house and to the bedroom distracting Sasha. From where I'd landed on the floor near the bedroom door I couldn't see outside to the other room.

"What took you so long?" Sasha yelled.

"What took me so long? How about your directions sucked."

I cringed at the sound of her voice.

"You're going to get us caught. She's already been here for like fifteen minutes. I want to get this over with and get the hell outta here."

"Did you take care of the cop?"

"I let him go."

"You what?"

Sasha pointed the knife in her direction as she spoke, "I know what I'm doing. I didn't expect you to take so f'king long! We have to finish this and get out of here, not much time left to enjoy now is there?"

"I thought you were going to kill that got-damned cop. What if he catches us?"

"He didn't see you and he didn't recognize me. It's much better this way anyway. I told you, I know what I'm doing. I've done this before."

"You're treating me like a rookie. This part of the plan was my idea, remember? Did I not call you and tell you she was coming here?"

"Your point."

She made a strained sound before stepping into the room where I could see her. "Where is she?"

Sasha's words echoed in my head. Get what over with? Wasn't it enough that they'd made me responsible for the horrible deaths of five innocent men and they'd make it look to David as though I'd lied to him the entire time? What else could they have been planning to do to me? I gripped the small hand-weight tighter. Consumed by fear and led by adrenaline I moved quickly to my feet. I saw Sasha point my way but didn't hear what was said. Maccartney turned to face me. I swung the seven-and-a-half pound weight with all of my might.

The force of it all pulled me forward, leaning toward the floor. I cursed myself for having tried something so stupid. I felt my body being yanked backward and the weight snatched away.

"I can't say I'm not impressed," Sasha spoke in my ear.

I looked over and saw Maccartney laid out cold on the floor, a trail of blood trickling out of his ear and down the side of his face.

"I'll deal with you myself you crazy bitch."

"Freeze! Drop the weapon."

Sasha and I looked up at the same time. David was alive! Alive and well and standing in Jonathan's doorway with a shiny black gun aimed, his finger on the trigger. But my relief was short lived, I was far from safe. Armando's fingers pressed hard into my cheeks holding my head high, the blade was pressed firmly against my throat. Hot tears spilled from my eyes as Armando's weapon slowly seared my flesh.

"Well if it ain't Captain Save-a-Ho himself. I will slice this bitches throat, don't f'k with me!"

"Armando put the knife down!" David commanded.

"My name is Sasha!"

"Your last chance, drop it or I swear I will blow your got-damn brains out!"

"Then her blood will be on your hands!"

"Say goodnight you crazy transgendered bitch."

*

The sound was deafening…then all went silent. I didn't know if I was dead or alive. My body landed on the floor beside Maccartney. When I felt pain in every inch of my frame, I knew that I'd survived.

My body was limp. I felt a strong hand grip my arm, guiding me from the floor. I staggered out as unrecognizable faces and figures rushed past. The reality of it all hit me as soon as I stepped outdoors into the early morning sunshine. I'd survived but at least one of my very best friends had betrayed me in the most unimaginable way.

My walk ended at an ambulance. I looked up to see my savior, Detective David Crane. He turned me over to the caring hands of the paramedic's whose job it was to check me out and patch me up. I looked around as they did what they were trained to do. My eyes connected with those of Detective Kendall

Mathers, he nodded. I quietly accepted. I noticed Clunky in the midst of the action, likely avoiding acknowledging my lack of conscious involvement.

"Are you going to be alright?" David asked.

I looked at him and smiled. "Yea, I'll be just fine. But how'd you-"

"You left me a message remember." He leaned in and kissed my forehead. "I gotta get back in there okay."

"Okay. David?"

He turned back to face me.

"Thank you…for everything."

He took my hand to his lips. "I love you, Ms. Phelps."

He didn't wait for me to respond. I watched as this man that I too had fallen in love with headed, off to clean up the mess I'd unwittingly created.

Epilogue

It was over. My life would never be the same again. My careless actions had led to the deaths of six people:

Andor Johnson – father of three; engaged to marry the mother of his youngest child.

John Daniel – second year law student who took care of his mother and two younger sisters.

Kadir Watson – local music producer and husband.

Aurelius Carter – College student and star basketball player.

Jonathan Cooper – Husband of twenty years, father of two.

And Armando Rivera – Schizophrenic with bi-polar disorder, stalker, and murderer.

I hadn't known that David was a sharpshooter. Had he not have been I may have been added to the list of the deceased. Maccartney survived. I was grateful. My mother couldn't understand why, she'd hoped the head trauma would have ultimately killed him. It didn't though. Tash understood, we both agreed that someone had to pay the price for all of the blood shed. After all, I'd forever pay the price for all those broken families.

David wanted to leave South Florida, escape all of my pain and shame. Seattle sounded nice. About as far as we could go without actually leaving the U.S. We could start a new life there; pretend none of this ever happened. I couldn't do that. That path was all too familiar. I'd already been down that road (though one dare not speak of it in the presence of Mommy), I wouldn't repeat that pattern. Besides, those destroyed families couldn't runaway...they couldn't pretend nothing happened. Why should I be so lucky? Its okay, we'll figure it out. The first step was counseling and I was more than ready to take it.

Peta has since forgiven me. Can't say we're friends but far from enemies. Seems as though Teddy makes her happy after all; I guess that means I'm happy for her. Teddy is still a dyke bitch not worthy of respect – in my opinion

Garcelle moved away. She said it was all too much and as it turned out, she'd fallen in love with me. I hadn't paid attention. I guess in some ways...Armando was right about me. She told me that she couldn't handle my engagement to David. It hurt to see her go but I knew our relationship needed to end for me to be able to move on. I needed to sever all ties with my past life in order to move forward, that's what my counselor said. I couldn't hold on to any of it...only the hope that Detective David Crane brought to my future. He and I side by side...I'm sure we'll be just fine.

About the Miki Starr Storybook

The Miki Starr Storybook – How to Write a Love Story is a collection of short stories written between 2002 and 2004 as a way of giving me more exposure and marketing myself as a writer.

In 2002, after publishing my very first novel, *Well Runs Dry*, I was asked by a co-worker to write a story using them as a character. From there I had the idea to create a 12-week online series titled *Mikaela's Story*, where all the characters were based on the personality traits of my colleagues. Lots of fun to do though a dangerous idea given that some took the plights of their parallel egos a little too personally. Despite a small amount of backlash, the series was closely followed and was a success.

Following that series was *Charitable Taboo – An Erotic Murder Mystery*. At that time, I'd read a very popular "erotica" novel...one that though it received very high praise (and still does), I thought was poorly written. This 12-week series was my way of illustrating that one can appeal to a market that craves very sexually explicit tales, and still have an in-depth storyline and thoroughly developed characters.

In 2004, after an ugly break-up I wrote *Fantasy of Love* as a means of dealing with my emotions and true feelings behind the break-up. Though the characters and situation is fictitious, the feelings were real which, in my opinion, is what brought that story to life.

The Miki Starr Storybook brings together the greatest variety and most well written short stories that I have created to date. After going back and forth with the idea of immortalizing these tales…these representations of my past, I chose to do so for me. Because they are mine and because I am proud of them.

But…should anyone other than me take the time to enter into these worlds, I do hope they enjoy themselves and take the stories for exactly what they are – stories.

Love always,

Miki Starr